A Fatal Booking

Also available by Victoria Gilbert

A Fatal Booking

A BOOKLOVER'S B&B MYSTERY

Victoria Gilbert

CROOKED LANE

NEW YORK

Copyright © 2022 by Vicki L. Weavil

Published in the United States by Crooked Lane Books, an imprint of The Quick Brown Fox & Company LLC.

Crooked Lane Books and its logo are trademarks of The Quick Brown Fox & Company LLC.

Library of Congress Catalog-in-Publication data available upon request.

ISBN (hardcover): 978-1-64385-914-9
ISBN (ebook): 978-1-64385-915-6

Cover design by Ben Perini

Printed in the United States.

www.crookedlanebooks.com

Crooked Lane Books
34 West 27th St., 10th Floor
New York, NY 10001

First Edition: June 2022

10 9 8 7 6 5 4 3 2 1

For all my friends, old and new

There is nothing on this earth more to be prized than true friendship.

—Thomas Aquinas

Chapter One

The only thing constant in life is change. That's one lesson I'd learned the hard way.

Staring out over the Morehead City, North Carolina, harbor, I considered the changes that had taken place in my life over the last few years. I'd not only left my teaching career, I'd also taken over Chapters, the literary-themed B and B I'd inherited from my great-aunt Isabella Harrington.

A new beginning, I reminded myself.

But now the past was intruding on my new life—in the form of one of my guests.

Shading my eyes with one hand, I reframed my thoughts and focused on watching a captain skillfully guide his charter fishing boat into dock. Several people were draped over the boat's upper deck rail, their skin flushed with too much sun and their expressions conveying exhaustion. I shook my head. I'd never been interested in fishing but knew day trips were popular with visitors to this coastal town.

A beep from my smart watch pulled me from my reverie. It was time to head inside the restaurant, one of Morehead City's more popular eateries. I was meeting Lora Kane, an artist who'd once been an instructor at the same high school where I'd taught English. She'd invited me to dinner to discuss the events scheduled for her book club's upcoming visit to Chapters. The rest of the group would check in on Friday, but Lora had arrived a day early to iron out a few last-minute details.

I didn't mind the extra meeting, especially since Lora had insisted on planning the week. Typically, groups left it up to me to arrange the special events, but Lora apparently had very specific ideas in mind. She'd sent me some information so I could stock our pantry and provide recipes for my cook and housekeeper, Alicia Simpson, as well as our part-time chef, Damian Carr. But I still felt a bit at sea. Being an organized person, I preferred to know all the details ahead of time.

But you must always respect the wishes of the guests, I reminded myself as I adjusted the scooped neckline of my blue-and-white-striped top before I strolled into the restaurant lobby.

"Charlotte Reed," I told the hostess. "I'm here to meet with Ms. Kane."

"Your party's already seated," the young woman said, leading me to a small alcove covered in maritime memorabilia.

Although I hadn't seen Lora in over eighteen years, I immediately recognized her. Slender and of medium height, she had luminous dark eyes and walnut-brown hair cut in a sleek bob that just skimmed her jawline. With her porcelain skin and vivid ruby-tinted lips, she could've easily played the vamp in a silent movie.

"Hello," I said, as Lora rose to greet me.

"Charlotte, so nice to see you again." She leaned in to give me a quick hug before stepping back. "You look great. You've hardly aged at all."

"Thank you, but I think you're exaggerating." I patted my feathery cap of brown hair. "I've quite a few silver strands now, and then there's the wrinkles." I tapped my forefinger at the corner of my eye.

"Not that many. I mean, we're both forty-four, right? One has to accept a few crow's-feet." Lora inspected me closely before sitting back down. "There's a sadness in your expression that wasn't there before, but I suppose that's to be expected." She offered me a sympathetic glance over the top of her menu. "I was so very sorry to hear about Brent."

"Thanks." I sat down across the table from her. "It's been five years." I took a deep breath. *Five years and a lot of changes.* "I have adjusted, although of course I still miss him."

Lora looked up at me again, her inquisitive expression tempered by a kind smile. "I guess leaving your teaching career and becoming an innkeeper was a way to make a new start after Brent's death?"

"Yes, I felt I needed a major change. My great-aunt Isabella thought so too, which is probably why she left Chapters to me in her will."

"Do you miss it? The teaching, I mean."

"Sometimes." I swallowed back any further expression of my feelings on that topic. I did miss teaching, more than I liked to admit. "You quit long before I did. Do your ever regret that decision?"

"Heavens, no." Lora rolled her eyes. "I was never really cut out for the job, to be honest. Not like you. I always considered you a born teacher, while I only chose to do it because twenty-something me thought being a freelance artist was too scary."

"But then you took off for parts unknown." I fiddled with my fork. "After you left that last day of school, none of us knew where you'd gone."

Lora swept one slender hand through the air. "It wasn't meant to be a big mystery. I just headed to England." She flashed a bright smile. "I lived in London for a few years as a child, in the early eighties. My dad, who was a lawyer for a shipping company, got posted there." Her expression sobered. "Dad died about seven years ago."

"I'm sorry to hear that," I said. Although I'd met the man only once, at Lora's lavish wedding, I recalled Lora often talking about her dad during the short time we'd taught together. "I know you two were very close."

Lora managed a faint smile. "Yes, we were. Only child, you know. Anyway, I always remembered London as one of the best times in my life, so when I quit teaching, I decided to see if I could go back and recapture the magic."

"And did you?" I asked, with a lift of my eyebrows.

"Somewhat. Of course, I didn't have much money, so it wasn't quite as glamourous as I remembered. But I did stumble into an apprenticeship with a jewelry designer, which turned out to be a very happy accident."

"You've done quite well since then, though, especially with your illustrations." I examined her calm face with interest. "I've seen your work in several of the books my friend Julie stocks in her bookstore."

Lora settled back in her chair. "I have a decent number of commissions every year, but it's really the jewelry that makes me a living." She lifted one hand to brush back her dark hair, revealing a pair of exquisite earrings. They were a unique design—a peacock in a circle, its tail delicately worked in a filagree of gold and brilliant enamel.

"Those are gorgeous," I said. "Your creation, I assume?"

"One of my more popular items." Lora lifted her water glass and took a sip. "But we're not here to talk about me. We're here to discuss the upcoming week of events. First of all, let me say I appreciate you taking the time to meet with me before my group arrives at the B and B."

"No problem at all," I said, glad the conversation had finally focused on the reason for our meeting. I glanced over my own menu briefly, just to make sure the item I wanted was available.

"Still, for you to allow us to book a week at Chapters at the last minute was very kind." Lora laid down her menu and settled back into her chair. "When you told me you might not be able to fit us in, my book club was so disappointed."

"It was fortunate I had that cancellation." I snapped my menu shut and placed it across my plate. "Well, not so fortunate at first, but when it turned out I could accommodate your group, I was glad it had happened. The first reservation had nothing to do with Chapters' literary offerings."

"While that was the real draw for us," Lora said. "What could be better for a book club retreat than a literary-themed B and B with a splendid private library?"

"It is the perfect combination."

Lora nodded. "I hope you don't mind that I've done all the planning for this week's events. I know from your website and brochure that you usually handle such things, but my book club is pretty decisive about what we want to do each year." She smiled brightly as the waiter approached the table. "I'll try the soft-shell crab sandwich," she told him. "I understand that's a specialty of the house."

I gave the waiter my own order, a tuna melt sandwich I'd enjoyed before. "If I understand correctly from the notes you sent, the focus of your event is classic children's literature."

"Hans Christian Andersen fairy tales, in particular," Lora replied. "Which, I admit, is rather self-serving of me. I just illustrated a new edition of Andersen's tales, so we'll be talking about that during our discussions, among other things."

"And you're obviously also celebrating Lewis Carroll, since you requested a Mad Hatter's tea party," I said, with a lift of my eyebrows. Alicia had vehemently complained about that particular request. Fortunately, I'd already engaged Damian to help out with the more complicated food offerings, which had mollified Alicia to some extent. "I thought we should hold the tea party on the back patio, near the garden, so I suggest we schedule it for Saturday afternoon. The weather's supposed to be good this weekend. Unfortunately, since it's late May, I can't promise it will hold throughout the week."

"Sounds perfect." Lora's eyes sparkled with good humor. "Just don't be shocked when you see what we're wearing. We're going to be dressed as some of the *Alice* characters. It's a tradition to have one costumed event at our annual get-togethers."

"You sound like a very dedicated bunch. How long has your book club been meeting?" I asked, before taking a drink of water.

"About five years now. We actually met at another book club, one set up by an independent bookstore in Cary, where most of us live. When that club folded, some of us decided to form a group of our own." Lora brushed back her hair, displaying the lovely earrings again. "We came together as readers, first and foremost, since we have little else in common. Although, full disclosure, our oldest member, Arnold Dean, and I have known each other for years. He and my father were both lawyers, and great friends. Arnie's actually my godfather. He's the one who invited me to the bookstore club in the first place."

I swirled the water in my tumbler. "That's nice. A little cross-generation bonding over books."

"Something like that," Lora said. "The rest of our group is an equally eclectic bunch. There's every age group—from Linnea Ruskin, who's in her late twenties, to Arnie, who's seventy-five." Lora tugged gently on one of her earrings. "Linnea's an art teacher, by the way. Reminds me of myself at that age, although she seems to enjoy teaching more than I ever did. Anyway, I'm actually training her how to make jewelry. Sort of an apprentice, I guess you could say."

I examined Lora's perfectly composed face, curious why she'd felt compelled to share that tidbit. *Wanting to let me know she hasn't totally abandoned teaching, perhaps?* "You said there were five of you. Which is ideal, given the number of suites at Chapters. No one has to share."

"And, as I mentioned in one of our phone calls, there won't be any children or spouses tagging along. We only allow actual book club members to attend our retreats. It's meant to be an escape from everyday life."

"Always a good idea, every now and then," I said, my attention diverted by the waiter approaching our table. "Here's our food. Why don't we save any more business talk until after we enjoy these lovely meals?"

After Lora polished off her crab sandwich and sweet potato fries, she took a moment to rave about how delicious they were before sliding a piece of paper from her purse. "I thought you might want to double-check the names of all the guests," she said, passing the paper to me.

As my gaze flitted over the page, I noted a discrepancy. "I see six names here. I thought the plan was for no one to share a room?"

Lora set down her glass of iced tea. "Sorry. I didn't mean to confuse you. There are only five guests staying at Chapters. The sixth person lives in New Bern and is planning to drive over for the events."

"Really? It's a good forty minutes each way, and that's without traffic."

"I don't think Stacy minds the drive. She wanted to participate but couldn't leave her business for an entire week." Lora waited until I'd folded the list and tucked it into my shoulder bag before adding, "She owns a jewelry store in New Bern. She used to live in Cary, which is how she originally became a member of our group, but closed her shop there and moved her entire business to New Bern. Even though she can't come to our monthly meetings now, she likes to be involved with any retreats and such." Lora shrugged. "She carries a lot of my designs, so I do like to accommodate her if I can."

"It's fine. I just like to be sure of the numbers when it comes to parties and dinners. We never want to run short of food or drink."

"Of course not. That's a criminal offense in the South, isn't it?" Lora grinned. "Stacy won't be around for breakfasts, of course, even though she does plan to attend all the other events." Giving me a conspiratorial glance, Lora added, "I'm a little surprised she decided to join us this week, because she's embroiled in a running feud with at least one of the guests and on the outs with a couple others."

"Oh dear, I hope that won't cause any unpleasantness for you," I said. "Who's she feuding with?"

"Vonnie Allen. I don't know all the details, just that it's connected to Vonnie's son. Something to do with him being accused of something Vonnie swears he didn't do." Lora shook her head. "I hope to get to the bottom of it one of these days, if only to make peace in the group, but neither woman is willing to talk to me about the situation."

"I'll try to stay out of that quarrel, trust me."

"Just as well." Lora's voice rose as a busboy cleared a nearby table. "Actually, a word to the wise—in general it's best to be careful what you say around Stacy Wilkin. She's not a bad person, but she's a terrible busybody. She'll pester you for all the details if she thinks you're harboring a secret."

A crash resounded through the alcove. Lora and I turned to stare at an adjacent table, where a weathered-looking middle-aged man had leapt to his feet and knocked his chair back onto the floor.

The man strode over to our table. "Did I hear you say something about Stacy Wilkin?" he demanded, his hazel eyes blazing with fury. "You know her?"

"Excuse me, sir, but I don't think that's any of your business," I replied, fixing him with the stare I'd been told could silence even the most belligerent teenager.

Lora, clutching her purse against her chest, opened and shut her mouth without saying a word, although a little squeak escaped her lips.

"It's definitely my business." As the man crossed his arms over his chest, I noticed he had the ropy muscles of someone who did physical labor. "It's all about my business, in fact."

And the permanent tan of someone who works on the water, I thought, examining his lined face. Based on his sturdy build, straight back, and chestnut-brown hair, I suspected he was in his late fifties, even though he had the wrinkles of an older man. "And what is your business, Mr. . . . ?" I allowed my words to trail off but kept my gaze locked on his face.

"Captain Sam Joiner," he said, meeting my stare with a defiant lift of his square chin. "I own a few charter fishing boats. And if this Stacy Wilkin is the same person, she and her worthless boyfriend ripped me off a few years ago."

Lora's eyes widened. "Did they skip out without paying you? That doesn't sound like Stacy."

Sam Joiner snorted. "Worse than that. They rented one of my smaller boats, claiming they knew what they were doing. The boyfriend even flashed something that looked like a boating license." His eyes narrowed. "But when they took the boat out, they ended up beaching it on a sandbar. Tore up the bottom so bad, I had to have the blasted thing rebuilt. Then they skipped out of town. They never paid me the second part of their rental fee or anything for the repairs."

"You didn't take them to court?" An unconscious reflex made me curl my fingers around my knife. I lifted my fingers when I realized what I'd done.

"I did, but they claimed it was my fault. Said I hadn't kept the boat in proper condition." The fire flashing in Sam Joiner's eyes told me this was the worst offense. "Their fancy lawyer trashed my reputation, and I ended up paying all the court fees on top of everything else."

"I'm sorry to hear that," I said mildly. "It certainly doesn't sound fair."

"But that wouldn't have been Stacy's fault," Lora blurted out. "That man she was dating was a total loser. She dumped him as soon as she realized his true colors."

Sam Joiner turned his piercing gaze on her. "Not surprised, but that doesn't excuse everything. You don't know . . ." He rubbed his fist under his right eye. "Never mind," he said, in a calmer tone. "I shouldn't have gone off like that. It was just— hearing that name brought up a lot of bad memories."

Lora eyed him with distrust. "I hope you aren't looking to make trouble, Captain Joiner."

"Not if your friend stays out of my sight." The captain's anger had evaporated, only to be replaced with something more concerning.

I examined him, my eyes narrowed. *I'm not convinced he's telling the absolute truth. Or at least, he's not sharing the whole story.* "I think perhaps the better option would be for you to stay away from Ms. Wilkin. If it is the same person, which I doubt."

"Staying at that fancy bed-and-breakfast in Beaufort, is she?" Sam Joiner narrowed his eyes. "I recognize you, Ms. Reed, even if you don't know me. Heard you took over Isabella Harrington's old place." He tapped his temple with one finger. "Overheard you all talking about guests, and I have to assume they're staying at Chapters."

I didn't bother to ask how he knew Isabella. I'd learned almost everyone in the region over a certain age knew of her, even if they'd never met. She'd spent years cultivating her social butterfly cover, and once she'd turned her home into a B and B, she'd also extensively promoted its charms throughout the area.

"Now listen, Captain Joiner, we don't want any trouble," Lora said. "My friends and I are looking forward to a pleasant week at Chapters. I'd thank you to steer clear." She squared her slender shoulders. "I'm willing to go to the police if necessary."

Sam Joiner flicked one hand through the air. "No need for that. But maybe you should tell your friend to stay out of Morehead if she doesn't want to run into me." His chapped lips twisted into an ugly grin. "And trust me, she doesn't."

I stood up, thankful I was tall enough to look him in the eye. "I think it's time for you to take your leave. Or do I need to inform the waiter to call security?"

By this point, we'd drawn the unabashed interest of all the diners at the surrounding tables, as well as several members of the waitstaff and someone who looked like a manager. Sam Joiner glanced around the area. "No need. I'm going. Already paid my bill," he told the manager as he strode past her.

"Goodness, I hope he doesn't decide to show up at Chapters," Lora said as I sat down. "I'd hate to see Stacy harassed for something that loser boyfriend of hers did."

Something she never resolved and easily could have, if it went as far as the courts, I thought, picking up my dropped napkin. But

I just straightened in my chair and offered Lora a comforting smile. "I'm sure it's all just bluster. No need to worry."

But I made a mental note to inform a member of the Beaufort police force, Detective Amber Johnson, about Samuel Joiner's veiled threats as soon as I returned to the privacy of my car. I'd learned too many hard lessons about being safe instead of sorry to let this go. "Now—shall we ask about dessert? I think a little something sweet would be perfect after that display of bitterness."

Chapter Two

I always loved spending time in my kitchen. With its beadboard paneled ceiling, white cabinets, dark soapstone counters, and tall windows, it was bright and modern yet didn't clash with the historic style of the rest of the house. Isabella had overseen its renovation a few years before her death. After trying to run the B and B with an outdated kitchen for far too long, she'd finally installed high-grade appliances and other modern features.

"The guests seem to be enjoying the first-night cocktail party," I told Alicia as I set down the basket of empty wine bottles I'd carried in from the outdoor bar.

Alicia narrowed her dark-brown eyes as she stared at the full basket. "A little too much, I'd say." She nodded toward the French doors that led to a walk-in pantry housing metal shelving and a standing freezer as well as an oversized washer and dryer. "Just set that inside the pantry. I can dump it in the recycling bin later. And honestly, Charlotte, why don't you let Damian take care of that? It's part of what he's paid for," she added, tugging her bejeweled hairnet down over her springy black-and-silver curls.

"It's fine." I straightened, emphasizing my height. I'd always been taller than the average woman, which had admittedly bothered me in my youth. But I'd gotten over that insecurity in college. Now I was glad I could easily stand on tiptoe to access the top shelves in the kitchen and pantry. "Damian's pretty busy filling drink orders right now. It's a thirsty bunch."

Alicia sniffed. "Like most of our so-called intellectual guests, they drink like the Fifth Fleet. What's the world coming to?"

"They're on vacation. That tends to make people indulge," I said with a smile.

Alicia looked up from the hors d'oeuvres she was arranging on a large metal plate. "If you really want to help, maybe you can carry this out to the bar. I'd do it, but I don't want to get waylaid by any of the guests asking questions." She cast me a side-eyed glance. "I may be done with this evening's fare, but I still need to prep some stuff for tomorrow's breakfast."

"Of course. Glad to help." I crossed over to the kitchen island and picked up the plate. "I should mingle with the guests anyway. That's one of my primary duties as hostess."

"And you're welcome to it." Alicia dabbed at the sweat beaded above her lip with a tissue. "I don't mind cooking and cleaning and even dealing with check-ins and that sort of thing, but I draw the line at chitchatting with the guests. Not something I enjoy, or am good at, if I'm honest."

I swallowed a comment confirming her statement. Alicia was a gem when it came to managing the house and the cooking, but she wasn't exactly *the hostess with the mostess*. Which had worked fine in the past, as that had always been Isabella's strength.

And it works now too, since I believe I've grown into that role, I thought as I bumped open the door to the back porch with one foot. *Although it doesn't come as naturally to me as it did my great-aunt, who was a social butterfly extraordinaire.*

Balancing the plate against the crook of my elbow, I made my way out the back door and down the few steps to the backyard and crossed the gravel driveway that separated the house from the patio and garden. I carried the hors d'oeuvres over to the bar set up under a wooden pergola at one end of the flagstone patio, nodding at some of the guests but not stopping to talk.

"Reinforcements," I told the tall, lanky young man behind the bar, whose skin glistened with a sheen of perspiration. "Hope you're not getting overheated in that outfit."

"It's fine." Damian Carr tugged down his black button-up vest. "I'm used to working in the heat and humidity. Comes with the territory around here, especially in the summer."

"True. Even though it's not quite summer yet, it's already pretty warm." I fanned my face with my hand as I eyed his pale-yellow dress shirt. "I don't think anyone would mind if you rolled up those sleeves."

As he shook his head, his dreadlocks, which he'd pulled into a low ponytail, fell over his shoulder. He flipped the hair back with one hand. "Not a professional look. I should've worn a short-sleeve shirt, but I didn't think it was supposed to be quite so muggy this evening."

"Late May in coastal North Carolina? Where have you been all these years, Damian?" I asked with a lift of my eyebrows.

He flashed me a grin. "Yeah, yeah, I know. Not my best move. But I'll be fine. I've worked in kitchens a lot hotter than this. Now"—he held up an empty tumbler—"what can I get you? I'm sure you'll want a little fortification before mingling with the guests."

"Just a white wine spritzer," I said. "I need to keep my faculties intact."

"As if that would ever be a problem for you." Damian gave me a wink.

I grabbed the drink and thanked Damian before turning to survey the guests. They were clustered in two groups. In one, an older man with white hair and a brown-haired man in a peacock-blue silk shirt and white tennis shorts stared out toward the garden, while a middle-aged woman wearing a tight fuchsia-and-purple-print dress talked with them. *Or at them*, I realized, noting both men's silence and tensed shoulders. *Some bad feelings there.* This thought was confirmed when the woman barked something unintelligible, threw up her hands, and marched away, heading for the bar.

I frowned. That wasn't a promising start to the event. I'd already informed Detective Johnson about Captain Joiner's reaction to hearing Stacy Wilkin's name. Now I had to hope I wouldn't have to tell her about any other conflicts involving my guests.

The second group included Lora Kane and two other women. "Hello there," I said as I approached. "Nice to see you again, Lora. I know I wasn't around when everyone checked in, so please introduce me."

Lora shared my name and motioned toward a petite woman with close-cropped black hair. "This is Evonne Allen, but she goes by Vonnie. She's an accountant, but don't let that fool you—she also knows her literature. And this tall drink of water is Linnea

Ruskin. She teaches art in a private high school and is the baby of the book club."

"I'm not that young," said Linnea, a willowy strawberry blonde whose ivory skin was highlighted by a splash of freckles. She was taller than me, and dwarfed Vonnie and Lora by several inches.

Lora rolled her eyes. "To those of us who are middle-aged, you are. Right, Vonnie?"

"Hold on now, I'm only forty-four, same as you, Lora." Vonnie flashed me a grin. "Not really middle-aged these days, is it?"

"Since that's my age too, I'd say no," I replied.

Linnea, ignoring this banter, curved her pink-tinted lips into a smile. "Hello, Ms. Reed. Thank you for allowing us to spend the week here. It's a beautiful place."

"I was happy to do it, especially since Lora and I used to be teaching colleagues. And it's really your book club doing me the favor. My original guests backed out, so Chapters would've sat empty this week if you hadn't decided to hold your retreat here." I tipped my head and studied the three women in front of me. They all seemed pleasant enough, but I detected an air of tension enveloping them. It was evident in Lora's taut lips, the fingers Vonnie had clenched around the stem of her wineglass, and the wariness in Linnea's blue eyes.

"We're delighted to be here," Vonnie said. "I confess to doing a little research and uncovering the fascinating history of the house. The original portion is quite old, isn't it?"

I nodded. "Eighteenth century. Of course it's been renovated over the years and, like most older homes, has seen several additions."

"In my research on the Web, I ran across digitized photos of the amazing parties held here in the past, featuring numerous famous guests. There were politicians and statesmen as well as New York socialites and Hollywood stars. It must've been quite the scene." Vonnie's dark eyes sparkled with interest.

"That was before my great-aunt turned Chapters into a B and B," I said, amused by Vonnie's obvious fascination with the social history of the home. Not that I blamed her—perusing some of Isabella's photo albums had often made me a little starstruck. "But it's true that Isabella Harrington was quite a celebrated hostess in her younger years."

"That she was. She was absolutely stunning as well as charming," said a man's voice behind me.

I turned, sloshing my drink, and faced off with the older man from the other cluster of guests. He was a few inches shorter than me, but his burly build filled the space in a way that negated any physical advantage on my part.

"Hello, you must be Arnold Dean," I said, meeting his bright smile with one of my own.

"In the flesh. But please, call me Arnie. Everyone does." The older man's thick white hair, bushy eyebrows, and rosy cheeks made him look like a trimmed-down Santa Claus. But his eyes, though light, weren't the traditional Saint Nicholas blue. They were as gray-green as the sea.

"You talk like you knew Isabella Harrington," I said. "Lora didn't tell me you had any connection to my great-aunt."

"Because I didn't know if he'd approve of me disclosing that fact." Lora's eyes were narrowed in a way that made me wonder if she was peeved at Arnie. "My godfather doesn't always like me to share information from his past."

Arnie chuckled. "Come now, Lora, you must remember me mentioning to our book club that I had visited Chapters. Of course, my visits happened before the house had that name."

"Before it was a B and B, then?" I asked, intrigued by this information.

Arnie turned to me, his smile widening. "Yes, back in the seventies, when it was still a private home. My father was in politics at the time and moved in some elevated social circles, at least in the South. He was invited to several of Isabella Harrington's parties and brought me along a few times. I was a young fellow, still in law school, when I first met Isabella. I suppose she was in her late forties or early fifties then, but I must admit I fell madly in love with her despite the age difference."

Lora cleared her throat. "I'm not sure Charlotte wants to hear about your youthful infatuations, Arnie."

"Is that why you wanted to stay here so badly?" The dark-haired man I'd noticed earlier walked up behind Arnie. He arched his eyebrows above the glasses framing his brown eyes. I looked him over, judging him to be in his mid to late thirties. He had the lean but toned physique of a runner, angular features, and a nose with a distinctive hook.

Rather like a hawk, I thought, flushing under his intense scrutiny. "Hello, I'm your hostess, Charlotte Reed. I assume you're Zachery Bell?"

"Yes, but it's Zach," the man said, before bumping Arnie's arm with his elbow. "That explains a lot. You were pretty keen on

Lora snagging a reservation at this B and B. A little walk down memory lane, huh?"

"Something like that," Arnie said, a trace of irritation coloring his tone.

Zach kept his gaze locked on me. "I just thought it was odd that ol' Arnie here would want to pay for a room when he has a pretty spiffy boat he could've docked in the harbor. A small yacht, really. Probably fancier than the rooms here." Zach spread wide his hands. "No offense."

"None taken," I said mildly.

The woman in the fuchsia-and-purple dress, returning from her trip to the bar with a full tumbler, joined us. "What's this—am I missing a juicy discussion?" she asked, her hazel eyes widening.

I narrowed my eyes in response. She had to be the only other guest—Stacy Wilkin. The busybody Lora had warned me about. *And the woman whose mere mention made Captain Sam Joiner so irate*, I reminded myself, examining her with renewed interest. Short and curvaceous, she was attractive in an extravagant sort of way. Her figure, while slightly plump, was stunning. Her flowing cinnamon-brown hair and carefully made-up face made it difficult to guess her age, although I suspected she was in her early fifties.

"Apparently Arnie's been holding out on us. He says he visited Chapters before, in his wild youth," Zach said. "Which is, I suspect, why he was so adamant about Lora choosing this place for our retreat."

Stacy fluttered her heavily mascaraed lashes. "Really? How interesting. Perhaps Ms. Reed has some photos from that time she can share with us. I'd love to see what Arnie looked like back in the day."

"My great-aunt did leave behind photo albums, but there are so many pictures, I doubt I could zero in on any featuring Mr. Dean," I said, hoping to nip this request in the bud. I didn't mind sharing Chapters with guests, but opening up my family's memories to their scrutiny seemed a step too far.

"Surely we can persuade you to try?" Stacy Wilkin looked me up and down like a dog show judge appraising a questionable entrant.

I caught the thunderous look Vonnie leveled at Stacy. *There's definitely a story there*, I thought as I twitched my lips into a smile. "Hello, Ms. Wilkin. Welcome to Chapters."

"It's just Stacy," she replied with a toss of her wavy mane.

Linnea tapped her sandal-clad foot against the patio flagstones. "I did think it was a shame when you decided to park your boat at the New Bern docks, Arnie, rather than here in Beaufort. I was hoping you could take us all out for a little sightseeing trip or something."

"One doesn't say *park*, my dear. Not with a boat." Arnie cast Linnea an indulgent, if sarcastic, smile. "Anyway, I have a semi-permanent slip at New Bern. I always keep my boat there in season. It's close enough to Cary for weekend trips and far enough inland to avoid the worst of any hurricane winds. Usually," he added, when Stacy cast him a questioning look. "I know New Bern sometimes takes a major hit."

I waved my hands, hoping to catch everyone's attention. "Anyway, I just wanted to meet you all and let you know I'm available to answer any of your questions about the area or facilitate any of your activities and events during the week."

"Good to know," Lora said, flashing me a warm smile. "Okay, everyone, just a reminder—we don't have anything scheduled for tomorrow morning, so you're free to tour Beaufort or whatever else interests you. However, the Mad Hatter tea party will start precisely at four o'clock, so please make sure you're back in time to get into costume."

"Where's it going to be held?" Vonnie asked. "Inside or out?"

Lora swept her silky hair behind her ears. "Since it seems the weather will cooperate, right here on the patio. I plan to work through the morning to arrange the table and decorations."

"If you need extra hands, just let me know," Arnie said.

"Thanks, but I think Charlotte and Ms. Simpson are assisting with the setup." Lora glanced at me with a question in her eyes.

"Absolutely. And Damian has volunteered to help as well. On top of filling the roles of chef and bartender," I said, raising my glass in the direction of the bar.

"Thank you," Lora called out, earning a thumbs-up gesture from Damian. Turning to the other guests, she said, "Now, if you'd all go mingle elsewhere, I have a few things I'd like to discuss with Charlotte. In private," she added, when Stacy opened her mouth as if to protest this turn of events.

The other guests drifted away, leaving me alone with Lora. "Would you like to walk into the garden?" I asked, sotto voce. Motioning toward Stacy, who was hovering nearby, I added, "It might be the best place for a more private discussion."

Lora nodded and followed me to the picket fence that separated Chapters' garden from the patio. We entered through the open gate and walked into the center of the garden before Lora spoke again.

"I guess you noticed the tension between some of our members. As I mentioned at the restaurant, Vonnie has some sort of serious issue with Stacy, and then there are the others . . ." Lora laid a hand on my arm. "I just wanted to apologize in advance. I'd hoped things wouldn't be quite so acrimonious, but I'm afraid we must brace ourselves for a few outbursts."

The drooping limbs of a spirea bush tickled my bare forearm. Brushing the branches aside, I cast Lora a speculative glance. "I'm guessing Captain Joiner isn't her only enemy."

Lora sighed. "I don't know if I would go so far as to label them enemies, but Stacy has ticked off several people in the group. Everyone, really, except me and Arnie." She looked up at me from under her black lashes. "Anyway, if there is any unpleasantness, I don't want you to think it has anything to do with you or the Chapters staff."

"I appreciate that," I said, making a mental note to observe the guests carefully. If I could discern any reasons for the rifts between Stacy and the others, I might be able to stave off future problems.

"Snuck away, I see." Arnie's voice sailed up from behind us. As we turned, I caught the sharp glance he leveled at Lora. "Sharing some of our group's dirty laundry before Charlotte gets slapped in the face with it?"

Lora tossed her head. "Just finalizing the schedule for the week. We switched the Andersen book discussion from Tuesday to Monday, you know."

"Right." Arnie didn't appear to be fooled by this distraction. *He's obviously aware of all the tensions in the group*, I thought, fixing my gaze on his pleasant face. *Probably knows all the details, too.*

Lora looked from Arnie to me. "I should get back to the others." She tapped my arm with her scarlet-polished fingernails. "Thanks for everything, Charlotte. Talk to you later."

After Lora left the garden, Arnie strolled over to the fence that separated Chapters' garden from the neighbor's. "Nice roses. I bet they've been here for a while, as thick as these vines are."

"Don't you remember them from when you visited here before?" I asked, curious to hear his response. It intrigued me that he'd met my great-aunt when she was young. *Before I ever knew her*, I thought. *Before I was even born.*

Arnie fiddled with the collar of his white polo shirt. "I didn't actually wander out into the garden during those visits. It was late fall or winter the few times I was here."

"I hope you don't think I'm being intrusive, but I'd love to talk to you about Isabella at some point. Your impressions of her, I mean." I offered him a smile. "Since my grandmother was her sister, she did visit with our family quite often throughout my life. But she was older then, and had pretty much given up her busy social life to run the B and B. I've always been curious to know more about what she was like in her prime, when she was throwing all those glamorous parties I keep hearing about."

Arnie, his attention apparently caught by some movement in the adjoining backyard, didn't look at me as he responded. "I'd be delighted to do that. As I said, I was quite enamored of your great-aunt. Now"—he motioned toward the neighboring house—"excuse me for changing the subject, but who lives next door?"

I followed his gaze, noticing that my seventy-seven-year-old neighbor had opened her back door to call her Yorkshire terrier, Shandy, back into the house. Her tall, sturdy figure, clad in one of her characteristic bright ensembles, was outlined by the early evening light, which also created a nimbus around her short white hair. Her distinctive profile was handsome rather than pretty, but all the more striking for it. "Oh, that's Ellen Montgomery. You might want to chat with her too, since she was one of Isabella's closest friends." *And her handler when Isabella was in the spy game,* I thought, but of course I didn't express that out loud.

"Who could imagine such a thing?" Arnie said, making me wonder if he'd somehow read my mind.

But when I stared at him, I noticed the faraway look in his eyes and realized he was talking to himself. "I'm sorry?"

Arnie shook his head before turning to me with a smile. "Never mind, my dear. Just the ramblings of an old man." He patted my arm. "Your neighbor reminded me of someone I knew many years ago, that's all. A friend," he added, as Shandy and Ellen disappeared back into her house. "She was an Ellen too. But her last name wasn't Montgomery. Unless, of course, your neighbor is, or has been, married?"

"Not that I'm aware of," I said, realizing I didn't know much about that aspect of Ellen's life. She'd never mentioned a husband, but then, she'd never discussed any man in any context other than friendship.

"Well, plenty of time to ask." Arnie flashed me another disarming smile. "I'm sure we'll see your neighbor again."

"You will. She's likely to drop by Chapters for the discussion of Lora's work on the Andersen book, since Lora invited our local book club to join that event."

"How delightful. I always enjoy meeting other book lovers," Arnie said, his tone as bright as his eyes. "Shall we rejoin the others? Or rather, why don't I go back and mingle with my fellow guests." He gestured toward the garden gate. "I'll even venture to distract them so you can slip into the house and enjoy a few minutes of peace."

"Thanks, I appreciate that," I said with a smile. "Sometimes one needs a few moments of solitude to recharge."

Arnie gave me a wink. "A greater truth was never spoken."

Chapter Three

The next morning I woke early so I could take a walk before I needed to help Alicia prepare breakfast for our guests.

Strolling just a few blocks brought me to the waterfront, where I could reach the boardwalk that separated the docks from a row of shops and restaurants. I paused in front of Julie Rivera's bookstore, Bookwaves. Of course, it was closed at this hour, but I took a moment to admire the Memorial Day display Julie had placed in the picture window that fronted the shop. American flags and bunting surrounded a wide selection of books about world history, the military, and similar topics.

Crossing the boardwalk, I stared out over the water. The dock slips were filled with boats of all shapes and sizes, from small motor craft to tall-masted sailboats and impressive yachts. I rested my arms on the top rail and allowed my thoughts to wander. The previous summer, I'd met a man who lived on his vintage cabin cruiser. *Gavin, where are you now?* I wondered, knowing it could be anywhere. Like my neighbor Ellen, Gavin Howard worked as an agent for a U.S. intelligence agency, although he was still active whereas she was now retired.

Gavin and I had stayed in touch since his departure from Beaufort, frequently texting as well as video chatting and talking over the phone. But since he was involved in some top-secret operations, there were times when he had to go dark. He'd given me a code word to alert me to that. When he dropped the word *shellfish* into one of our conversations, I knew I might not hear from him for a while—and definitely should not contact him. We were in the middle of one of those incommunicado periods, which always put me slightly on edge. I was aware he could be embroiled in a dangerous operation, but since I had no knowledge of where he was or what he was doing, there was nothing I could do but wait to hear from him again.

"Charlotte," said a familiar voice behind me. "Good morning on this fine day."

I turned to face Ellen. "Hi. Out walking the pup, I see. Hello, Shandy." I bent down to pat the Yorkie's head as he strained at his leash. "I'm afraid I don't have any treats for you this morning."

Shandy's black eyes shone bright as polished buttons under a thick fall of fur "That's okay. He's getting a little too chunky anyway." Ellen gave Shandy's harness a little tug, and he stared up at her in reproach. "I noticed your latest guests arrived yesterday evening. I'm glad you were able to fill in with this group after that sudden cancellation."

"It was great I had that option, although I don't expect this to be the easiest week." I straightened and stared back out over the harbor. "They have very definite ideas about all their special events and activities." I shot Ellen a rueful smile. "Today's the Mad Hatter tea party. Complete with costumes, if you can believe that."

"How . . . immersive," Ellen said, her blue eyes sparkling with amusement. "I hope you didn't have to supply those."

"Fortunately not, especially considering my sewing skills. The guests have created their own. We didn't actually have to come up with the decorations either. Lora Kane, who's in charge of the group, brought them with her. Alicia and Damian and I just have to help her pull everything together later."

"That's good." Ellen glanced over at the boats. "Heard from our friend lately?"

I shook my head. "It's one of those times when we can't communicate. You know how it is."

Shandy erupted in furious barking as a flock of seagulls dive-bombed the boardwalk.

Ellen leaned down to pick up the dog. Holding him close to her chest, she cast me a sympathetic smile. "I see. Well, I'm sure he'll get in touch when he can."

"He always does." I tapped the rough surface of the railing with my fingernails. "Changing the subject, I observed something interesting yesterday evening. When you appeared outside, waiting for Shandy to come in, one of the guests, an older man named Arnold Dean, went on high alert. Like he knew you or something. Is that possible?"

Ellen dipped her head until the wide brim of her sun hat blocked my view of her eyes. "Perhaps," she said, as she gently lowered Shandy back to the ground. "Does he go by Arnie?"

"He does, and he's medium height but stocky, with white hair and a closely trimmed beard. He has eyes about the color of this water." I motioned toward the harbor. "A greenish gray that's changeable. Ruddy complexion, with full cheeks. Honestly, he looks like a trim Santa. Out of costume, of course."

Ellen straightened slowly. "Arnie Dean," she said, her voice as wispy as the clouds drifting overhead. "Now there's a coincidence."

"He told me he attended a few parties at Chapters when Isabella was alive. Is that how you two met?"

Ellen shot me a sharp glance. "No, I was never here when Isabella was throwing her famous parties. As I told you when we first met, I didn't move to Beaufort until the early eighties, after Chapters was already converted into the B and B. Isabella wasn't playing her high-society hostess role at that point."

"Oh, right, I remember." Frowning, I stepped back from the railing and turned to look directly at Ellen. "So how do you know Mr. Dean? He seemed extremely interested in you. To the point where it made me a little nervous."

Ellen, her eyes hooded beneath her pale lashes, absently coiled Shandy's leash around her hand. "I'm surprised he recognized me. It was a long time ago." Shaking her head as if to clear her thoughts, she met my gaze with a wan smile. "Nothing to worry about. Arnie and I met in college. He was a few years younger than me, but we were in the same Russian language classes."

"Russian? No wonder you were recruited into intelligence work."

"That really wasn't on my mind at the time. I just enjoyed learning languages, and Russian seemed like an interesting challenge. Anyway, Arnie and I bonded over our mutual love of exploring other cultures. We both hoped to travel the world one day. Which I did, of course. Not sure about Arnie."

"You were good friends?"

"We were very close, at least at that time. We spent hours watching foreign films and even joined a campus cultural exchange group. Not to mention dining at every ethnic restaurant in our little college town."

Ellen's expression was uncharacteristically dreamy, as if she was recalling beloved memories. I sucked in a quick breath, wondering if she and Arnie had been romantically involved. It seemed likely, given her comments about how close they'd been. I opened my mouth to ask if Arnie was an old boyfriend but pressed my lips together when another thought crossed my mind. *Obviously it didn't last.*

Ellen, as if sensing my interest, shot me a wry glance. "He's not a former lover, if that's what you're thinking." She pushed her straw hat away from her forehead. "To be honest, that was the problem. He wanted that. I didn't."

"You don't have to explain," I said, feeling heat rise up the back of my neck. Although Ellen and I were friends, I'd never discussed such a personal topic with her before.

"It's all right. I used to be embarrassed to talk about such things. I'm not anymore." She loosened her grip as Shandy, distracted by a splash from the water, yipped and danced on the end of his leash. "You see, I discovered something about myself many years ago, although I've only recently put a name to it." She shrugged. "To be fair, there's only recently been an accepted name for it."

I studied her for a moment, putting the clues together. Her current statements, and the lack of any mention of certain things in the past . . . "You've never been romantically interested in anyone?"

Ellen's lips quirked. "Exactly. Honestly, it was a plus rather than a minus in my former career. I couldn't be swayed by things that often compromised other agents."

"I can see how that might be useful," I said in a thoughtful tone.

Ellen shrugged. "But it wasn't so easy when I was young, For years I thought there was something wrong with me; that I was defective in some way. Or, as Arnie told me before he disappeared from my life, that I was cold and unfeeling." She grimaced. "*Frigid* was the exact word, as I recall."

I bit back a swear word. "No wonder you went your separate ways."

"It was for the best, although it was still painful. He was my closest friend at the time. I felt we could share anything. But then it all blew up into this horrible fight where he stormed out of my apartment." Ellen's chest rose and fell with her deep sigh. "I never saw him again after that night."

"And now he's staying next door to your house." I frowned. "Do you want me to try to keep him away from you? I mean, I can be diplomatic, but firm."

"That isn't necessary." Ellen tugged her hat down on her brow and gazed toward the water. "We're both so much older now and have lived full lives. All the pain has dissipated, at least for me. Perhaps we can even be friends again."

"That would be nice." Studying her profile, I realized I couldn't read anything in her calm demeanor. "Anyway, not to rush off, but I probably should get back. I need to give Alicia a hand with breakfast and then help with the tea party preparations."

"We'll walk with you." Ellen gave Shandy's leash a little tug. "Come along, you rascal."

With Shandy trotting in front of us, we made our way back to our homes. Sensing that Ellen didn't want to discuss anything more from her past, I didn't ask any questions, happy to keep the conversation centered on innocuous subjects like gardening,

*   *   *

"Thought all that effort would be appreciated, but seems we still have complaints," Alicia said as she entered the kitchen from the back porch. "That woman in the strange rabbit getup—the gray one, I mean, not the white—was demanding jam for the scones." She plunked an empty pewter tray on the counter near the sink. "Wasn't told to include any jam or jelly."

"That's Stacy Wilkin, who seems to complain about everything, so I wouldn't worry. At any rate, there's no jam because Lora Kane didn't want any provided." I placed a ceramic teapot on a silver-plated tray. "It's all part of the Lewis Carroll theme."

Alicia shot me a questioning look. "What's jam got to do with anything?"

"In *Alice Through the Looking Glass*, the White Queen tells Alice, 'The rule is, jam to-morrow and jam yesterday—but never jam to-day.'" I used both hands to lift the tray, balancing it so the teapot didn't slosh. "It's actually not in the scene they're reenacting, but I guess it's still an inside joke."

Alicia rolled her eyes. "Not a very funny one. Anyway, if you could tell that rabbit woman we had nothing to do with the lack of jam, I'd appreciate it."

She's actually the March Hare, I thought, but decided against mentioning that detail. "Grab the doors for me, and I'll carry this out to the party."

"Better you than me." Alicia eyed my grip on the tray as she met me at the door to the back porch. "We should've asked Damian to stay. He could've helped with the service along with the prep."

"I can manage. Better than paying Damian's fee for an extra hour or two," I replied, before offering her a smile. "Thanks for the assist."

Holding open the outside door, Alicia wrinkled her nose at me. "It's clear you're related to Isabella. Same sort of stubborn."

I flashed another smile and carefully maneuvered my way down the steps to reach the ground. *I think I may have inherited a few other traits as well,* I mused as I crossed the driveway. *A certain craving for excitement and danger. Which I never knew I possessed until I moved to Chapters.*

Approaching the setup on the patio, I had to admire Lora's dedication to detail. She'd asked me to provide a folding banquet table that could seat at least ten and had covered it with a white linen tablecloth—decoratively rumpled to represent the messiness of the tea party described in *Alice in Wonderland*. Then she'd instructed Alicia, Damian, and me to pile extra plates, cutlery, and cups at one end of table, while the other end held place settings for the six guests. Although our additional tableware was clean, it was meant to evoke Carroll's tea party scene, where the Mad Hatter, March Hare, and Dormouse simply shifted from seat to seat to use new plates, cups, and utensils rather than washing the dirty dishes.

"More tea," I called out as I approached the table. I eyed the group, impressed with the effort they'd put into their costumes. Lora, wearing a white tuxedo, had attached a large pocket watch on a gold chain to her multicolor brocade vest. She also sported a pair of white rabbit ears attached to a black plastic headband.

The ears wobbled as she leapt to her feet. "Here, let me help with that," she said, taking the tray from my hands. Setting it on one of the few clear spaces on the table, she turned to Zach Bell, who was dressed as the Mad Hatter. "Would you pass the teapot around, please?"

Zach tugged on his oversized polka-dot bow tie. True to the popular Tenniel illustrations, he'd also donned a white shirt whose large starched collar framed his face, and a tight waistcoat. *And the giant top hat, of course*, I thought, my lips curving in amusement. *He wouldn't be the Mad Hatter without a hat.*

Stacy Wilkin, who was portraying the March Hare, also wore a waistcoat and tie, but her outfit was constructed of a softer material that gave the impression of short fur. Like Lora, she wore a pair of rabbit ears, but like the rest of her outfit, they were a shade of gray. She lifted one hand, which was covered by a mouse hand puppet. "Still peeved about the lack of jam, so at least pass me that tea, please," she said in a squeaky voice.

Of course, the Dormouse, I realized, admitting it was a clever way to include that character in the scene. "You all look quite splendid."

Vonnie Allen, dressed in a crimson gown decorated with images of playing cards, adjusted the crown perched on her head. "We did have to add some extra characters to the scene. It should only be the Mad Hatter, March Hare, Dormouse, and Alice, but that didn't work with a group our size."

"Well, the White Rabbit and the Queen of Hearts do figure prominently in the book." I turned my gaze on Arnie. "And the Cheshire Cat, of course. Very clever."

Dressed in black like a theater stagehand, Arnie's costume focused all attention on his grinning cat mask. "Unfortunately, it's difficult to eat and drink while wearing this thing." Arnie pushed the mask up until it rested on the black hood he'd pulled over his white hair.

I looked around the table. "But where's Alice?"

"Right here," said Linnea Ruskin, walking past me to reach the table. "Sorry, I had to take a call. Pulling out my cell phone at the table somehow didn't seem in character." She tossed her silky hair—held away from her face by a velvet headband—behind her shoulders. Attired in a simple puff-sleeved blue dress and white pinafore, white tights, and black Mary Jane shoes, she made the perfect Alice. *She even has the dark hair of the Liddell girls who inspired Carroll's story. I think that's really more appropriate than the blonde Alice presented by Tenniel and Disney.*

Linnea plopped down in a chair next to Arnie. "This guy chose the perfect costume, though. I sometimes think he's just as enigmatic as the Cheshire Cat," she added, tapping his arm.

"Nonsense, I'm an open book," Arnie replied, meeting my questioning gaze with a wink.

I ignored this, focusing instead on the other guests. "I should head back inside and allow you to enjoy your event without any intrusion. But of course, if you need anything, please let me or Alicia know."

"What I need"—Stacy lifted her teacup above her head—"is that handsome bartender you had last night. To add some liquor to this tepid tea, I mean."

I met her saucy grin with a tight smile. "I'm afraid Damian had another gig today. He did help us set up and prepared some of the delicious tea cakes, though, so I hope you'll thank him when he returns for other events this week."

Zach leaned back in his chair and fixed Stacy with a glare. "Really, can you not?"

"Such a spoilsport." Stacy set her teacup on the saucer so roughly that it rattled. "No wonder your mother sold off all her heirlooms rather than bequeath them to you."

The color in Zach's face faded like an old Polaroid photo. "How dare you?" he said, his tone razor edged. "Have you been hitting the bottle already this morning?"

Stacy sat up in her chair, her eyes blazing. "I'd thank you not to imply I'm some sort of alcoholic, Zach Bell."

"I'm not implying it," Zach said, his eyes shadowed behind the lenses of his tortoiseshell glasses. "I'm stating it."

Stacy jerked her head back, dislodging her rabbit-ear headpiece. It flew off her wavy, cinnamon-tinted hair and landed on a plate of tea pastries. "Liar," she spat out, before grabbing the ears. She shook them at Zach before dropping them back onto the table.

"Now, children, let's behave," Arnie said in an indulgent tone. "We don't want Charlotte to think we're feuding."

Zach's eyebrows rose above the rims of his glasses. "Even if we are?"

I looked over the group, observing both the angry glares shared by Stacy and Zach and the concern drawing Lora's lips into a thin line.

"Forgive us, Ms. Reed," Linnea said, shooting Stacy a sharp look. "Some people like to stir the pot, and not just for tea."

So she doesn't like Stacy either. One more enemy, I realized, as I caught the nod of approval Vonnie gave Linnea. *It seems no one does. There must be a reason for all this animosity, but I'm honestly not sure I want to know the details. At least Stacy isn't staying at Chapters, so she won't be around as much.*

"I say we get back to our discussion of the *Alice* books," Lora said, "That's the point of this tea party, after all."

"Exactly right, my dear." Arnie cast Lora an approving smile. "I read a new article last week that I found quite fascinating. It discusses all the ways Carroll incorporated mathematics into the stories."

This segue seemed to divert the participants, especially after Zach leapt into a lively debate with Arnie about the emphasis on logic versus the importance of dreams and fantasy in Carroll's writing. Leaving the group to their bookish conversation, I made my way back into the kitchen.

I took a seat at the small kitchen table while Alicia washed up some pots at the sink. We'd had a good chat about her recent family reunion before I realized something had slipped my mind.

"Darn it," I said, when Alicia mentioned the jam issue again. "I was distracted and forgot to explain that to Ms. Wilkin."

"Oh, never mind. Appears she's forgotten all about that now. And the entire purpose of their event, it seems." Alicia gestured toward the window that overlooked the backyard. "But she's not the only one. They've all been jumping up and down and moving around rather than sitting down to enjoy their tea."

I crossed to the sink and peered out the window. Alicia was right—some of the guests had disappeared from the table. I caught a glimpse of Lora and Vonnie huddled at the other end of the patio, near the bar. Vonnie was gesticulating wildly, while Lora was pressing the air with her hands as if to calm Vonnie down. Arnie lingered at the table with Zach and Linnea. Stacy was nowhere to be seen.

"They've been bouncing up and down like that for a while." Alicia moved closer to my side. "Lots of coming and going in different directions. It's like one of those French farces Isabella used to watch on her DVDs."

"I wonder where Stacy Wilkin is," I said, stepping away from the sink. "Maybe I should go check on her. I'd hate to think she just walked off and abandoned the party. There was a good deal of tension simmering between her and the others, but surely she wouldn't just disappear."

"Good riddance." Alicia wrinkled her nose as if smelling sour milk. "She's a royal pain, if you ask me."

"Maybe, but we can't really ignore any of the guests. I'll be less than thrilled if one of them gives the B and B a bad review because we didn't ensure they were taken care of properly."

Alicia sniffed and draped the kitchen towel she was twisting between her fingers over the clean pots. "If a guest wants to stalk off because they're not getting along with their so-called friends, I don't feel that's any of our business."

I looked her up and down, wondering what Stacy Wilkin had done or said to engender so much disdain. My eyes narrowing, I considered the possibility that, on top of her other flaws, Stacy was one to make racist remarks.

Alicia would never tell me that. She was too proud to admit being slighted in such a way. But if that was the case, perhaps I could find out from prodding Stacy a little. If she revealed her prejudice, I wouldn't hesitate to give her a talking-to, guest or not. "I suppose it isn't, exactly. But I'd like to stave off any further unpleasantness if I can." I strode into the hallway, planning to see whether Stacy might be on the front porch before I headed around to the back patio.

She was there, but not alone.

"What are you doing here?" I asked Captain Sam Joiner as the screen door slammed behind me.

Chapter Four

I cast a swift glance at Stacy, whose face had paled under her makeup, causing her rouge to stand out like the red circles on a clown's face. "Are you all right?" I asked her.

She bobbed her head without replying.

"No problem here. Just old friends catching up, right, Stacy?" Sam Joiner tugged the brim of his well-worn sailor's hat before turning and clattering down the porch steps.

The ceiling fans, spinning slowly overhead, cooled the sweat that had beaded up on the back of my neck. "Come back and I will notify the police," I called after him.

He simply jerked his arm back over his shoulder, as if sweeping my words away, and kept walking.

"Not a friend," Stacy managed to spit out. She reached out for the china teacup she'd set on the tall wrought-iron serving table placed under one of the front windows.

"I know." I cast her a sympathetic glance. "Seriously, Ms. Wilkin, if he so much as shows his face here again, call 911. I'll back you up."

"It's okay," Stacy replied, although the trembling of her fingers as she lifted the cup told me otherwise. "I don't think he'll be back."

I wasn't so sure, but I nodded, hoping to put her at ease. "I understand he has some sort of issue with you." When Stacy shot me a questioning look, I added, "I ran into him when Lora and I were having dinner in Morehead City Thursday night. He overheard us mention your name and reacted rather badly."

"He blames me for something an old boyfriend did. It wasn't my fault, but apparently Sam . . . Captain Joiner still feels I should pay for another person's mistake." Stacy pressed the cup to her breast. "Men can be so childish, can't they?"

Color and vitality had bloomed again in her face, even though her smile appeared brittle. "I'm not sure we should single out one gender for that," I said, keeping my tone mild. "It seems to me that we can all act a little foolishly sometimes."

"Yes, of course," Stacy said with a toss of her lush hair. "It's just that when men are hurt, they tend to nurse a grudge longer, don't you think?"

I looked her over, wondering exactly how she had hurt Sam Joiner. *Perhaps it was more than tearing up his boat*, I thought, considering his anger and her overtly flirtatious personality. "I can't say that's been my experience, but you may be right in terms of the good captain. He does appear to hold a grudge."

"Well, I'm not going to allow his bad behavior to ruin my day," Stacy said. "I believe I will rejoin my companions. I wouldn't mind another little nosh. And I definitely need more to drink." She held up the cup. "Still has some dregs of sugar and tea, but I think I'm due for a refill."

Not sure if she meant tea or something else, I simply nodded. "There should still be plenty on the table, but if it's gotten cold . . ."

"Oh, I don't mind cold tea." Stacy swished her free hand through the air. "Just add sugar and it's perfect. Sugar, and maybe a little something extra," she added, giving me a wink as she patted her hip.

The outline of a small flask bulged through the pocket of her soft gray leggings. "Whatever you prefer," I said.

After Stacy sauntered off the porch and around the side of the house, I surveyed the sidewalk and street. I wanted to make sure there was no sign of Captain Joiner before I walked back inside, locking the front door behind me.

I grabbed an open bottle of wine from the fridge and carried it over to the small kitchen table. "Reinforcement," I told Alicia, who brought me a clean wineglass without comment. "Found that guest, by the way," I added, after taking a swallow. "As well as an unwelcome visitor." I provided Alicia with a description of Sam Joiner, warning her to alert the authorities if he showed up again.

"A fishing boat captain, you say?" Alicia's expression grew thoughtful. "That name rings a bell. I need to ask some of my relatives about him, see if they know anything."

"That would be helpful, but don't confront him on your own."

Alicia wrinkled her nose. "You think I can't hold my own with some old guy?"

"I'm sure you can." I replied with a smile. "But let's not test out that theory."

After a few minutes, I rose to my feet and told Alicia I was going back out to the patio. "Better check on the guests. Make sure they don't need anything," I said as I headed for the back door.

When I reached the patio, I noticed that the group had shifted once more. Now Lora was hovering near the table, Zach at her elbow, and Vonnie and Linnea were seated again. Arnie stood a little apart, leaning against the front of the bar. He seemed to be intently studying the others.

With a few glances toward Ellen's house, I thought as I approached him. "Is the party already over?"

"Pretty much," he said. "We managed to discuss Carroll's writing for about thirty minutes before all the personal feuds erupted again."

I raised my eyebrows. "Are there feuds among the guests?" Of course, Lora had already warned me about this, but I thought it wouldn't hurt to get another opinion.

"Oh yes, several. Surely you noticed. Honestly, I'm not sure why Lora thought this retreat was a good idea, especially after Stacy agreed to participate. She seems to have made enemies of most of the other book club members, although I confess I don't know all the particulars." He shrugged. "Nor do I want to."

"Speaking of Ms. Wilkin"—I shaded my eyes to survey the entire patio—"did she decide to take a walk or something? Last time I saw her, she was headed this way."

"I have no idea," Arnie replied, as Lora joined us.

"I think she's in the garden. I saw her stumble off in that direction, anyway. After stopping by the table to pour a little tea in her cup and offer a few more pointed comments," Lora said with an embarrassed smile.

"I'd better go and see if she's all right." I noted Arnie's questioning expression and added, "Of course she has the right to wander the garden whenever she wishes, but I'd hate to think she's unhappy with the retreat already."

Arnie's lips quirked into a smile. "You mean you're worried that her unhappiness might reflect poorly on your business. Especially if she decides to take her anger out in a review, fair or not."

"Exactly." I strode off, headed for the open garden gate. I was actually more concerned about the possibility of Captain Joiner somehow climbing into the garden from the back alley but didn't want to share that fear with the other guests.

I stopped in the middle of the main garden path, gazing over the beds with a frown. Chapters' garden was lush but not overgrown. There was a clear view of the central section, where well-worn paths and low boxwoods enclosed beds of herbs and flowers. If someone wasn't deliberately hiding behind one of the lilacs or other larger shrubs or the trees lining the fence, they should be visible from the gate.

As I surveyed the area, I noticed movement at the back of the adjacent garden and strolled over to the fence. "Ellen, is that you?"

"Just checking on my vegetable patch," she said, dusting her hands on her apron as she joined me at the fence. "Anything wrong?"

"I'm not sure. One of the guests supposedly wandered in here, but I don't see her. Which makes me afraid she fell or something." I pointed toward the back corner of the garden. "She's wearing a gray costume and has light-auburn hair. Could you peer through the lilac and see if you spy her while I check the other corner? I'm just worried because she did seem a bit tipsy earlier."

I made my way to the opposite side of the garden but turned and ran back when Ellen called my name. Brushing past a few overhanging lilac branches, I stared into the small clearing in the corner, where a bench had been placed under a pin oak tree.

Stacy Wilkin was lying on the ground. Her visible skin was flushed pink as the blossoms of an almond tree, and that fragrance, faint but unmistakable, wafted through the air. Near her outstretched fingers lay the remnants of a shattered teacup.

I stepped forward but stopped when Ellen barked at me to halt.

"Don't touch the body," she said.

I cast her a swift, panicked glance. "We don't know for sure that she's dead."

Ellen's voice was as firm as mine was shaky. "I do, and I also know what killed her."

I stared at the woman lying lifeless in my garden. Fixated on the rose-tinted foam bubbling from Stacy's bluish lips, I managed to squeak out, "Something you've been trained to identify?"

"Unfortunately, yes," Ellen said. "I'm afraid, my dear, it's cyanide."

Chapter Five

E llen pulled a cell phone from her pocket. "We shouldn't disrupt the scene. I'm going to call 911. Perhaps you should exit the garden and then keep anyone else away from the gate."

"Good idea." My mind raced with thoughts of how I should handle informing the guests about Stacy's death as I walked back through the garden. Leaving the gate open, I waved at Lora, who was fortunately standing apart from the other guests clustered around the table.

"Something you need to tell me?" she asked as she approached.

"Yes, and I want you to prepare yourself for the news." I pointed toward another bench, this one placed under a tree at the garden fence edge of the patio. "Please, sit down."

"I don't see why that's necessary," Lora said, although she complied with my request. "What can be so shocking? Did someone trample your flowers?"

I crossed to her, keeping an eye on the garden gate. "Stacy Wilkin is dead."

"What?" Lora leapt to her feet. "How did that happen? Did she have a heart attack or something?"

I stretched out an arm to block her from dashing toward the garden. "Please, relax." I laid a hand on her shoulder, gently pressing until she slumped onto the bench. "My neighbor, Ellen Montgomery, has already called the police. They should be here shortly. For now, we need to leave the scene undisturbed." I glanced over at the table. "That includes everything on the patio."

Lora's eyes widened. "Come to think of it, Stacy was acting a little odd before she disappeared into the garden. Her hands were visibly shaking." Lora's own hands were trembling. She noticed my concerned gaze and clasped them together. "I thought it was the effects from too much drinking. Or even just anger, because she'd had yet another argument with Zach."

"I saw them sparring earlier. What was that all about?" I kept my tone mild. Questioning witnesses wasn't exactly my business, but I wanted to gather a few facts. I'd aided police investigations before; perhaps I could help them again—and clear Chapters' reputation.

"It's some personal feud. Or was," Lora said, staring down at her clenched hands. "Zach claims Stacy cheated his mother." When Lora looked back up at me, her face was pale as beach sand. "I don't know all the details, but it seems that right before she died, Zach's mom sold some estate jewelry to Stacy, and Zach thought Stacy grossly underpaid her. She 'took advantage of a slightly befuddled older lady,' is what I've heard him say, more than once."

"I guess that could cause some hard feelings."

"And from what I hear, Zach's mom was forced to sell the jewelry due to medical bills." Lora sighed. "She didn't go to Zach for help, even though he has a very good job in the Research Triangle. He's a chemist with some R&D firm and probably had the money, but apparently his mom was proud and independent and wanted to handle things herself."

"So he's a scientist." I pursed my lips. *Someone who might be able to get his hands on cyanide, or at least know where to obtain it, legally or not.*

"They were family heirlooms too, and Zach has kids from his soon-to-be-dissolved marriage, so I think he was also angry that Stacy didn't try to talk his mom out of selling the jewelry, or at least give him a heads-up about the situation." Lora shrugged. "Anyway, when I overheard them arguing earlier today, Zach again accused Stacy of taking unfair advantage, and she shot back that maybe if he'd paid more attention to his mom, he would've known she needed the money and could've provided some help."

"That's a pretty low blow." I mulled over the implications of this. *Maybe enough to fire up someone's anger—and even drive them to murder?*

Siren wails cut my musings short. As the police cruisers pulled into the driveway, the other guests leapt up from the table. I motioned for Lora to remain seated and hurried over to them.

"Please, don't panic," I said. "There's been an unfortunate occurrence, and the authorities are here to deal with it." I looked at Vonnie, Linnea, and Zach in turn, trying to glean anything from their expressions and body language. "I'm afraid Stacy Wilkin is dead."

Linnea's freckles stood out in sharp relief as all other color fled her face. "Dead? What do you mean?"

"I mean she is deceased," I replied calmly. "My neighbor and I found her lying on the ground in the garden. That's why the police have been called."

Zach crossed his arms over his chest. He'd risen to his feet, taking a pugilist's stance—his legs spread wide and his fists clenched. "Heart attack, I assume? Or perhaps a stroke? I doubt her underlying health was good, what with the lifestyle she led."

"Really, Zach." Linnea shot him a sharp look. "Someone has died. Whether we liked her or not, we should be respectful."

Zach snorted. "Right. Like you didn't have a reason to wish her harm."

"Knowing Stacy, I'm sure more than one person did," Vonnie muttered.

I help up my hand in a *stop* gesture. "I think the best option is to simply keep your own counsel until the police can individually question you," I said, noting the approach of a tall, lean woman in a tailored business suit. "Hello, Detective Johnson."

"Charlotte, happy to see you, as always, but sorry about the circumstances," Amber Johnson said.

I clasped my hands at my waist. "It isn't how I wanted to meet up, for sure."

"Okay, we'll take over from here." Detective Johnson instructed her officers to separate the guests and take them inside Chapters for questioning before turning back to me. "Were these all the people present today?"

"Yes, except for Alicia Simpson, but she was inside most of the time." I frowned, realizing my error. "Damian Carr was here earlier, but he left before the party began, which was around four PM." I took a deep breath. "And then there was Samuel Joiner. I was going to call you about him later. He showed up uninvited to talk to Ms. Wilkin today. Well, it was more like verbally accost her. As I told you before, it seems he has, sorry, *had* some sort of vendetta against her."

Amber Johnson tapped her pen against her small notepad. "We can talk to Damian Carr later. As for Captain Joiner"— she grimaced as if that name was far too familiar, and not in a good way—"I'll send someone to locate and question him immediately. But right now I have to focus on your other guests." She fixed me with an intent gaze. "You didn't call this in, did you?"

"No, that was Ellen Montgomery, who was with me when I discovered the body. She wasn't in my garden, though. She was next door at the time but was able to see everything over the fence. She seems to think . . ." I swallowed back the rest of the sentence as the detective's stare intensified. "I guess I should let her express her thoughts on the cause of death," I finally said. Although I didn't doubt Ellen's expertise in the matter, it was probably best for her to communicate her theory about cyanide directly to the police.

The detective's expression turned grim. "If this truly is a case of murder, everyone here must be considered a suspect. You know that better than anyone."

"I doubt it could be anything else," I blurted out. Noticing Amber Johnson's surprise, I added, "I suppose it could be a suicide, but the woman gave no indication that she was contemplating such a thing, and I don't think . . . well, the method would not be a likely choice, especially from what Ellen told me."

Detective Johnson stared at me for a moment before ordering her team to set up a perimeter around the garden. "And talk to Ms. Simpson, who's inside Chapters, as well as Ms. Montgomery, who lives next door," she said. "We need statements from them as well as the others."

"And me, I suppose." I shifted my weight from one foot to the other.

Detective Johnson nodded. "Yes, but we don't need to do that out here. Perhaps you could walk over and wait on your neighbor's front porch? I can have an officer take statements from you and Ms. Montgomery at her house." She offered me a tight smile. "Better use of space. My team will likely need all of Chapters' public rooms to question your guests, and we must cordon off the patio, since it could be part of the crime scene."

"Sure, no problem." I cast a quick glance toward Chapters' back door. I'd have preferred to alert Alicia before she was blindsided by the police, but that wouldn't be possible.

Amber Johnson provided further instructions to a few officers about processing the patio as well as the garden before turning back to me. "If you like, I can have one of the officers walk you over to Ms. Montgomery's house, where they can take your statement. I'm sure you want to get that over with but suspect you may feel a little shaky right now. We don't want you to pass out or anything."

"Thanks. I mean, I'm fine, but I appreciate the concern," I said, my words belied by the quaver in my voice.

Detective Johnson looked me over, her expression composed but sympathetic. "I'll speak with you again later to let you know how long we'll keep a patrol on the area and that sort of thing. For now, please follow Officer Dennison"—she motioned for a uniformed man to join us—"and give him your full statement. Include your encounters with Samuel Joiner as well as what Ellen

Montgomery said about the body and why she instantly assumed it was murder."

I lifted my hands. "That's no mystery. I imagine she's seen something like it before."

Amber Johnson didn't reply. She simply drew in a deep breath, turned on her heel, and marched off into the garden.

I followed Officer Dennison over to Ellen's front yard. "Do you want to sit outside?" I asked as we climbed the steps to the covered porch.

Before he could answer, Ellen opened the front door. "Come in, come in. I can wait in the kitchen while you speak with Ms. Reed in the parlor."

Officer Dennison stepped into the front hall, using some fancy footwork to evade being tripped by Shandy. *But he must be a dog lover*, I thought, noticing that the Yorkie wasn't nipping at him. *Shandy can always tell.*

"Sorry, let me take this little pest to the kitchen," Ellen said as she scooped up the excited dog. "Charlotte, you know the way to the parlor. Just come find me when you're done."

As she disappeared through a door off the back of the hall, I led Officer Dennison into the parlor. "Here you go. A quiet place to talk."

"Suits me." Dennison glanced around the room. "Your neighbor a world traveler or something?"

"She was a film and TV location scout," I said, not mentioning the truth—that her occupation had been a cover for clandestine activities. As the officer took his seat, I allowed my own gaze to sweep over the room. Ellen had kept many of the Victorian features of her home, including the hardwood floors, rich brown wainscoting, and wide moldings, but she'd furnished the space in muted tones accented by pale wood. That palette set off the colorful paintings and other works of art she'd accumulated during her travels.

And they aren't simply mementoes of her travels, I thought with a sad smile. Ellen had once told me that every piece—Asian ceramics, Indian wall hangings, and German cuckoo clocks among them—reminded her of a specific place. I eyed a silver-plated Russian samovar. *And operation*, I thought as I settled into a suede-upholstered armchair facing the policeman.

I knew Ellen had actually kept a few of the items primarily to evoke the memory of certain assignments—and people. A sort of penance in some cases. *The times where everything went wrong*, I thought, remembering a late-night conversation where, spurred to confidences over a bottle of wine, Ellen had confessed that people had died under her watch. She'd also told me she never wanted to forget that fact, or them; that they deserved at least that much from her.

Officer Dennison pulled out a small notepad and pen. "All right, Ms. Reed, can you please tell me what you saw and heard today, before and after you discovered the body?"

I walked him through all my movements, making sure to mention the run-in with Samuel Joiner as well as the spans of time when I wasn't outside and thus unable to closely observe the guests. "I did see some of their comings and goings through the kitchen window, but I can't claim consistent surveillance."

"Thanks for your very thorough information, Ms. Reed." Dennison pocketed the notepad and pen. Running his hand through his curly auburn hair, he studied me for a moment before rising to his feet. "If I didn't know better, I'd suspect you of having a background in law enforcement."

"Definitely not." I straightened in my chair. "I was a high school teacher before I took over Chapters."

"I think that job sometimes requires similar skills." Dennison flashed me a smile as he tucked the notepad and pen into his jacket pocket. "It's just a pity you weren't on the patio the entire time. Your observations might've more concretely established the exact movements of the guests."

"I'm sure you and your colleagues will sort it all out. Your department is quite capable, in my experience. And of course I'm always available to answer any additional questions," I said, standing. "No need to get up. I'll go and let Ms. Montgomery know you're ready to take her statement. That way I can stay in the kitchen with the dog. He might start fussing otherwise, and for a little guy, he's got a pretty ear-piercing bark."

Officer Dennison nodded and wished me a good day. I headed back to the kitchen and told Ellen he was ready to talk to her.

"I'll stay with Shandy if you want. That might keep him calmer. With a stranger in the house, he's likely to bark his head off if he's left alone."

"Good idea." Ellen gave me a little nod before leaving the room.

Shandy whined once after she disappeared but then ran over to the back door and pawed at it. "Oh, you need to go out, huh?" I opened the door, quickly stepping aside to allow the dog to dash past me.

Unfortunately, after taking care of his business, the terrier began barking, excited by all the activity next door. I called for him to come back inside, but he refused to comply. As the coroner's van pulled away—carrying, I assumed, Stacy Wilkin's body—I thought of a new tactic and yelled, "Treat!"

That word caught the dog's attention. He gave one last yip before bounding up the steps and dashing inside. "Did you have fun barking at everyone?" I asked as he danced around my ankles.

Shandy followed me across the kitchen to a cabinet and hutch where I knew Ellen kept a ceramic jar filled with dog biscuits. "Now the question is, who among Chapters' guests is a killer?" I absently tossed Shandy a biscuit. "It seems several of them had a quarrel with the victim. Certainly Zach did, and I suspect Stacy was embroiled in conflicts with both Vonnie and Linnea as well." I drummed my fingers against the wooden cabinet. "Then there's Captain Joiner. He may have been able to spike her tea while they were on the porch. I mean, I don't know how fast acting cyanide is, but I think we should still include him. What do you think, boy? Who should top the list?"

Shandy, munching loudly, didn't reply.

Chapter Six

After Officer Dennison finished taking Ellen's statement, she and I shared a glass of wine and talked about everything but the murder. By the time I walked back to Chapters, most of the police had departed, leaving behind only one officer to guard the perimeters established around the patio and garden.

"The guests are staying put, as least for now," I told Alicia as she stretched plastic wrap over a plate of cinnamon rolls. "Detective Johnson told me they've been asked to remain in town until the investigation is further along."

"I heard." Alicia slid the platter of breakfast pastries to the back of one of the soapstone counters. "Which is why I thought I'd better make up some breakfast options for tomorrow morning. Not sure how much anyone will feel like eating, but I wanted to have a few things prepared."

I glanced around the empty kitchen. It was seven o'clock in the evening, a time when guests often popped in for a snack or drink. But not only were Alicia and I alone in the kitchen, there was no indication that anyone else was on the ground floor. I looked up as footsteps creaked the floorboards overhead. "Are they all holed up in their rooms?"

"I think so." Alicia crossed to the sink. "After the authorities questioned everyone, they all vanished. I haven't caught a glimpse of any of them since the two men grabbed a couple of bottles of wine and some glasses." She motioned toward the window overlooking the backyard. "Said they didn't want any sandwiches, but later I spied a pizza delivery to the carriage house, where that Zach guy is staying. I guess they didn't lose their appetites quite as much as the ladies did."

"I'm surprised the women didn't at least ask for a snack," I said, meeting Alicia's wary gaze with a faint smile. "Or a bottle of wine."

"I did offer, but they weren't interested. Suits me. I'm dead on my feet, to tell you the truth."

"You should just call it a day. If the guests refused your kind offer of food and drink, they can fend for themselves." I lifted my hands. "I suppose that isn't the most hospitable attitude, but we've experienced the same trauma they have. In my humble opinion, they had their chance, and now we should be allowed to retire to our rooms as well."

Alicia yanked off her hairnet and shook out her short, tight curls. "I believe I will. By the way," she added, shooting me an approving glance, "I think you did a great job handling everything today."

"Thanks." I grabbed a clean glass from an upper cabinet and strolled over to the refrigerator. "You know, it's weird, amid all the chaos, but seeing Lora, my former colleague, has made me think about teaching and how much I miss it."

Alicia leaned back against the edge of the sink. She looked me over, her eyes narrowed. "You mean you'd like to go back to it?"

"Sometimes." I turned away to fill my glass with ice and water from the refrigerator. "I do enjoy running Chapters now, much more than I did when I started, but . . ."

"It isn't your first love. I get that. And I know why you wanted the change, but I guess you've moved past most of your grief now. It's pretty natural that you'd start to question if this is what you really want."

I turned to face her. "Not that I would ever sell the place or ask you to leave. You don't have to worry about that."

Alicia sniffed. "I'm not worried. I could get a job anywhere, you know. An experienced cook and housekeeper in a tourist area? Not a problem."

"But you love Chapters." I examined Alicia, noting her stoic expression. She'd never admit being concerned, but I was well aware of her disappointment over Isabella having left the B and B to me. *She felt it should've been hers, after all the years she'd put in helping Isabella set up and run the place. And maybe she's right. Maybe it should have been.*

"It's a place. I like it and enjoy the job, but as for love"— Alicia shrugged—"I love my family, and they love me. That's something which isn't going away, whatever happens."

"You aren't going to lose your job, or Chapters, either," I said firmly. "I'll never sell the place. Maybe someday I'll hire someone to cover my duties here. Which isn't nearly as much as what you do," I added with a smile.

"Good to hear. But it's totally your call." Alicia straightened and stepped away from the counter. "I know you've been communicating with that Gavin Howard fellow a lot over the past year. Not poking into your business, but you've been pretty obvious with all your video chatting and talking on the phone. So I figured maybe that was another thing making you consider a change."

I took a sip of my water before replying. "We're friends, that's all."

Alicia rolled her eyes. "Sure, whatever," she said tartly. But her expression immediately softened. "I don't begrudge you finding someone new, Charlotte, especially at your age. Truth is, I was never much interested in anything serious. Oh, I dated quite a bit when I was young and enjoyed male company just fine, but I never wanted to get married. Seemed like a lot of trouble for little return. But I know other people feel differently."

Remembering Ellen's recent confession, I offered Alicia a smile. "I think whatever makes a person happy is what they should do. But honestly, Gavin and I haven't seen each other in person in a year. It's a little premature to say there's anything serious going on."

Alicia arched her dark brows. "You don't think people can really get to know each other through talking as much as you two have done this past year? I'm surprised. Thought you'd believe in that sort of thing, what with your reading and studying classic literature and all."

I met her amused gaze with a lift of my glass. "Guess you know me a little better than I thought," I said, before taking a swallow of water.

"Fancy that. Even without all the book smarts, I do know a thing or two."

"Or three," I said. "Anyway, you needn't ever worry about losing your place at Chapters. I'd be foolish not to keep you on.

Even if I hired someone else to act as manager, they'd need you here to make the place work."

Alicia lifted her chin. "That's no lie."

"Definitely not. You know more about Chapters than anyone." I grinned. "No one's going to dispute that."

"I should hope not," Alicia said with an answering smile.

*   *   *

Every evening at around eleven o'clock, I walked through the house. I liked knowing all the windows and doors were secured, including the front door. Guests who arrived back at Chapters after eleven had to ring a bell for entry, which was a bit of an inconvenience. Fortunately, few of our visitors stayed out that late. Still, I'd been looking into a key card system for the front door as well as the suites—one where the codes could be changed with each new guest. It was expensive but would allow our patrons to come and go more freely while still providing security. Always a little short of funds for major renovation projects, I'd finally convinced Ellen to allow me to withdraw some cash from the trust she managed—money left for that purpose in my great-aunt's will. But since Ellen had just agreed to this proposal, we hadn't started the project yet. Which meant Alicia and I still had to take turns answering the bell if any of the guests stayed out late.

Thankfully, they were all in their rooms this evening. After checking downstairs, I jogged up to the second floor, which housed all the guest suites except the one in the carriage house. Not that I would enter any of the guest suites or worry that anyone could access the upper-level windows, but we did have a fire escape built against one side of the house. However unlikely, I knew it was possible that an intruder could use those metal stairs to climb to the second floor, even if the final steps were a ladder pulled up so it didn't touch the ground.

After making sure the fire door was secured so that guests could exit but no one could enter from the outside, I noticed something that made me pause in the middle of the hall. The door to the attic stood slightly ajar.

That wasn't right—only Alicia and I had keys, and I knew she had no reason to access the attic, especially at night. I crossed to the door and studied it with a frown. The lock had been installed after I'd discovered a few guests wandering around in the attic during the first literary event I'd held at Chapters. Fearing a lawsuit if anyone was injured tripping over the plethora of stored items, I'd kept the attic door locked ever since.

There was no evidence of damage. If someone had jimmied the door, they must've been skilled at lockpicking. Glancing up into the shadowy stairwell, I slid out my cell phone and clicked on its built-in light before tackling the narrow wooden stairs.

The heat rose with each step. I flicked the light switch at the top of the stairs to turn on the bare bulbs that dangled from the rafters before pulling a tissue from my pocket to wipe beads of sweat from my upper lip and brow.

The attic ran the entire width of the older portion of the house. It included windows on either side, darkened into mirrors at night. Dust motes danced in the spill of light from each of the bulbs, while the far corners of the space were buried in shadow.

I sneezed as the acrid scent of aging paper rose in my nostrils. Sweeping my phone light over the small stretch of bare flooring at the top of the stairs, I spied something that made me mutter an epithet I'd never use in front of my guests.

There were footprints in the fine layer of dust that covered the wooden floorboards. Nothing distinctive enough to determine shoe size or style, though. In fact, it looked like the individual had a shuffling gait.

Or they've deliberately obliterated their steps, I thought, following the prints to a teetering stack of boxes in the farthest corner.

The top box had been opened, its brittle tape pulled back and left dangling. I held up my light and peered inside.

I was looking at a collection of photographs enclosed in cloudy plastic sleeves. I swore again, more over the condition of the materials than the fact that someone had rummaged through the box. *Or has this box always been open and I just never noticed?* I stared at the pile of plastic sleeves filled with photos. I'd thought all of Isabella's pictures were stored in the albums I'd discovered soon after I'd moved to Chapters, but apparently there were more I'd never seen.

Should've checked everything up here before now, I thought as I shoved my phone in my pocket and grabbed a stack of the sleeves. The truth was, the attic was neither heated nor air-conditioned, so there were few times during the year when it was a comfortable environment for exploration. Since those times often corresponded to some of our busier seasons, I hadn't actually investigated every box in the attic. Having opened several only to find moth-eaten linens, old magazines, and other useless objects, I'd focused more on the steamer trunks. They held more interesting items, like bound photo albums and the costumes Isabella had created for special events at Chapters.

Clutching the stack of sleeves, I made my way back to the stairs, pulling out my phone light again when I turned off the overhead bulbs. I could always come back for more of the photos later. In fact, I was sure I'd feel compelled to do so, now that I knew they existed. The attic certainly wasn't the proper storage environment for loose photographs.

I was careful to lock the door to the attic again before heading down the main stairs and into my bedroom, which was located at the back of the first floor. I set the stack of photo sleeves on top of my dresser, fighting the urge to take a look at the pictures. I knew that once I started, I'd feel driven to sort through them all, and I needed sleep.

If I can, I thought as I changed into my nightgown. Staring into the mirror over my bathroom sink, I made a face. *You look like heck*, I told myself, noting the exhaustion tugging down the corners of my lips and the shadows under my eyes.

But that wasn't my biggest concern. I was more worried about the possibility of one of my guests breaking into the attic. The fact that I couldn't imagine why any of them would want to do such a thing didn't reduce my sense of unease.

And betrayal, I thought. *Whoever they are, they seem to have no compunction about acting like a thief, even if there is really nothing in the attic worth stealing. The library, though . . .* I considered some of the rare and valuable volumes held in Chapters' extensive private library and sighed.

As soon as possible, I'd have to check all the shelves, just to be safe. And I'd need to let Amber Johnson know about this latest wrinkle in the case.

If it's even connected, I reminded myself as I crawled into bed, hoping I could get some rest even if sleep eluded me.

Chapter Seven

After helping Alicia serve breakfast on Sunday morning, I decided to do some cleanup of the back patio. The police had completed their investigation of that area and removed the perimeter tape, although they had left the yellow plastic strip blocking the entrance to the garden.

I sighed. *Which means the weeds will take over and I'll have more work to do later.*

Crossing to the area near the table, I picked up a few dropped napkins before the sound of footsteps on pea gravel made me look up. I tossed the napkins into our outside trash bin and focused on the noise. Moving closer to the picket fence, I realized someone was aimlessly wandering through the garden.

Or perhaps not so aimlessly. I narrowed my eyes, recognizing the figure as Zach Bell. His progress through the garden was anything but casual—his head down, he appeared to be intently searching the flower beds and the ground.

"Hello there," I called out. "Looking for something?"

Zach's head snapped up. He straightened and met my inquisitive gaze with a startled expression that instantly turned sly. "Oh, hello. That was a great breakfast this morning, by the way. Please tell Ms. Simpson how much I enjoyed it."

"You can tell her yourself," I said, narrowing my eyes. "You aren't supposed to be in the garden, you know. The police still have it cordoned off."

Zach jogged over to the fence. "Let's just keep this our little secret then, what do you say?" He flashed a charming but obviously practiced smile. "I noticed the cop watching over the site had walked off to deal with gawkers on the sidewalk and decided to take my chances."

"You shouldn't be disturbing the scene." I crossed my arms over my chest.

"I'm not." Zach offered me another smile. "Just looking for something I dropped early yesterday afternoon. I think I may have lost it in the garden. I didn't notice it was gone until later."

"What's so important you'd break a police perimeter?" I looked him over, genuinely intrigued. He might be telling the truth, but my sleuthing instincts told me he could also be removing clues that could tie him to the murder scene.

"Phi Beta Kappa pin." Zach ducked his head as if embarrassed to mention this academic achievement.

I wasn't buying it. The tiny twitch of Zach's left eyelid suggested that he was lying. I pointed a finger at him. "A valuable item, for sure, but if you'd mentioned your loss to the police, I'm sure they would've been glad to return your pin when and if they found it."

Zach widened his eyes. *Pulling the "puppy dog" expression*, I thought, wrinkling my nose. *Trying to use his looks to charm me. Little does he know that I'm not easily swayed by such things.*

"You're right, of course. What an idiot I am. I certainly don't want the authorities to catch me stomping around their crime scene." Zach slapped his forehead in what I felt was a mock display of embarrassment. "Could you lift that tape for me so I can duck out?"

I frowned. "I really don't want to be an accessory to your intrusion on the crime scene. I suggest you walk out of there the same way you got in. By vaulting over the fence."

Zach's smile faded. "If you insist." He turned away but called over his shoulder, "Just keep an eye out for the cops and stall them for me, okay?"

I huffed, not planning to do any such thing. In fact, I hoped the police officer assigned to watch over the crime scene would catch him in the act. Unfortunately, Zach was able to step up onto one of the fence braces and hop over onto the patio before the officer completed her task of shooing off any inquisitive neighbors. As she headed our way, Zach gave me a little salute before dashing across the patio and into the house.

"You might want to question Mr. Bell about his activities this morning," I told the officer when she reached the patio. "I caught him wandering around the garden just now. He said he was looking for some pin he lost in there yesterday, but since he had to cross the crime scene perimeter . . ."

"Thanks, I'll definitely follow up on that." The woman, whose badge identified her as Officer Warren, frowned. "He just moved himself up a notch on our suspect list with that little stunt."

"That's why I wanted to mention it to you. I was afraid he was trying to remove or cover up evidence."

"We'll get to the bottom of it, don't you worry." Officer Warren, who looked to be all of twenty-five, offered me a smile that told me she felt the need to reassure a nervous older woman.

"Thanks." I knew better than to try to correct her assumption. To be honest, I frequently found it useful to be underestimated.

She gave a nod before striding off toward the garden.

"She thinks you're unnerved by the thought of a killer lurking in the bushes," said a man's voice.

I turned my head to see Arnie standing in the driveway between the bed-and-breakfast and Ellen's house. "You're up early," I said.

"Just out for my usual morning walk." Arnie strolled over to meet me. "I can't run anymore because of these blasted knees, but I still like to get in some daily exercise."

"I enjoy morning walks as well," I said, trying to establish a rapport before asking the question at the forefront of my mind. "It seems you may know my neighbor Ellen after all. At least she believes it's possible that you were college classmates."

"I'm sure we were." Arnie looked me over, his eyes twinkling. "I think she may have changed her last name. Perhaps not due to marriage but for other reasons?"

"I wouldn't know anything about that," I said, realizing Ellen could've done so to protect her family when she went into intelligence work. "She said you were good friends, but then you ghosted her."

"Really? Not sure that's what I would've called it. We did drift apart."

Drift? I thought. *From what Ellen said, it was more like a cataclysmic break.* But I thought better of challenging Arnie on this point. "Which happens, of course, especially when people graduate and head off to new places."

Arnie nodded. "I was two years younger than Ellen, so she graduated before I did. Then I was off at law school and too busy to track her down again." He shrugged. "She seemed to have disappeared, to be honest."

"That's right, you're a lawyer." I eyed him with interest, considering how his depiction of their relationship, and its dissolution, was at odds with Ellen's reminiscences.

"Was. I'm retired now. And to be perfectly honest"—Arnie flashed a cheery grin—"I never practiced much. At least not outside my family's interests. My dad, who was a politician as well as a lawyer, amassed a great deal of money investing in real estate and a few other things. I ended up managing the legal and other aspects of the family holdings."

"I'm sure your law degree came in handy, though."

"Definitely. But it wasn't the same as running a firm or being a public defender or anything like that." Arnie tapped his temple with one finger. "It took smarts, and time, but I had more freedom to travel than if I'd gone into practice."

"Then you and Ellen will have a lot to talk about," I said, hoping to gauge his reaction to the idea of speaking with my neighbor again. "She was a film and TV location scout, you know, so she also traveled the world."

"No, I didn't know." Arnie's expression grew thoughtful. "How interesting. Then I'm surprised we didn't run into each other before this."

My lips tightened. From what Ellen had told me, I assumed she would've taken pains to avoid Arnie if she had spotted him during one of her operations. But that was not my information to share. "I'm sure you'll get a chance to catch up, now that you have to stay in Beaufort for at least a few more days."

"I look forward to that. Next time you see her, please tell her I'd love to drop by for a chat."

"Perhaps I should let you take the initiative on that," I said. "Now, if you'll excuse me, I should go help Alicia prepare some snacks for tomorrow night's book discussion. Lora told me at breakfast that she wanted to continue with this week's planned events as much as possible."

Arnie's unexpectedly somber expression morphed into his typical merry one. "That's my goddaughter for you—steaming ahead despite any iceberg warnings."

"Not a bad quality," I replied mildly. "Unless you're on the *Titanic*, of course."

"And aren't we? On some type of sinking ship, anyway, I'm afraid." Arnie gave me a wink before turning and striding down the driveway toward the street. "See you later, Charlotte," he called over his shoulder.

I frowned. Arnold Dean might feel he could be flippant about the current situation at Chapters, but I certainly did not.

* * *

After lunch I decided to drive to Bookwaves. I usually walked to my friend Julie's indie bookstore, but today I needed to pick up several copies of a newly released H. C. Andersen story collection. Lora, who'd illustrated the new edition, had purchased the books as gifts for her book club. Wanting this to be a surprise, she'd asked Julie to acquire the books and hold them for her.

Knowing Bookwaves was closed on Monday, I'd volunteered to pick them up, spurred to this courtesy when I saw how flustered Lora was at breakfast. She didn't seem to be in the right frame of mind to deal with such a thing, and I wanted to reassure her that the books would be available for the following night's event.

Not that my actions were entirely noble—I'd also thought this would offer me a good opportunity to talk to Julie about the murder without any of my guests present.

Bookwaves opened at eleven o'clock on Sundays, but I knew from previous experience that business was typically a little slow until after lunch. Parking on a side street, I walked a block to the waterfront area, hoping to catch Julie alone in the shop.

Fortunately, no one was shopping in the bookstore when I entered. "Hello there," I called out, assuming Julie was in her office behind the sales counter.

"Oh hey, Charlotte. Have you come for those Andersen books?" Julie stepped out of the office and set a box on the counter. "I just finished packing them up. I figured I could take care of that before you arrived. With the bell on the door, I can hear anyone enter, and as you see"—she swept one arm through the air—"there's nobody here right now."

"Which is perfect for my needs, but maybe not so much for yours," I said, stepping forward to face her across the counter.

"You mean you're not just here to pick up books." Julie flipped her long, dark-brown braid over her shoulder. "If I were to place a bet, I'd say you've taken up your sleuthing hobby again and want to discuss what I heard on the news—the death of one of your guests."

Julie's ebony eyes sparkled with good humor. I'd discovered her independent bookstore soon after moving to Beaufort, and we'd become good friends when Julie volunteered to help run the local book club based at Chapters. Though she was seven years younger than me, we'd bonded over our mutual love of books and intelligent conversation.

"Guilty as charged," I said with a smile. "I thought I could use your not-inconsiderable smarts to help me work through some theories."

"Your usual sleuthing partner isn't interested?"

"If you mean Ellen, I'll certainly be discussing the situation with her too. But sometimes it helps to get other viewpoints."

Julie shoved the box of books aside so she could prop her elbows on the counter. "So what do you know at this point? Have the police even labeled it a murder?"

"Not officially, but I think everyone assumes it was foul play." I ran my finger down the packing tape sealing the box of books. "Ellen told me she suspects the cause of death was cyanide poisoning."

Julie's dark eyebrows shot up. "And she knows this how?"

I shrugged. "She said she's seen something like it before. Maybe on one of the film projects? Not a real poisoning, of course, but a scene that replicated such a thing. She was involved with film and television production for many years."

"But I thought she was a location scout." Julie's intelligent gaze focused on me with razor-sharp precision. "Of course, I'm not entirely convinced that story is the whole truth."

I shifted my weight from one foot to the other. "What makes you say that?"

It was Julie's turn to shrug. "Call it intuition."

"Anyway, the victim was not well liked." I filled Julie in on the conflict between Stacy Wilkin and Sam Joiner, Vonnie's issues with the other woman over something related to her son, and Zach Bell's anger over Stacy's treatment of his mother. "And it appears that another guest, Linnea Ruskin, also disliked Stacy for unknown reasons."

"It seems the victim had a number of enemies. That might make for a complicated investigation." Julie straightened and smoothed a loose tendril of hair away from her forehead as the bell on the door jangled. "Welcome to Bookwaves," she called out as a middle-aged couple entered the store.

Dressed in matching khaki shorts and T-shirts emblazoned with a dolphin logo, both visitors offered cherry hellos.

"Pete, Sandy, nice to see you. For some reason we haven't run into each other in a while," I said.

"Not since the last book club meeting." Sandy Nelson, who with her husband owned a popular local café, the Dancing Dolphin, flashed a bright smile. "Of course, we're planning to show up at Chapters tomorrow night for the book club discussion with your guests, but it's nice to see you before then."

"Is that still on?" Pete Nelson was a little shorter than average and more rotund than his petite wife. His round face was flushed, and sweat dampened the silver-streaked brown hair at his temples.

Probably sweating from working in his busy kitchen, I thought. "Yes, it is. Lora, who's in charge of the visiting group, decided to go ahead with as many events as possible."

"What can I do for you guys?" Julie asked. "Is there some emergency?"

"No, of course not." Sandy widened her gray eyes as she plucked her loose T-shirt away from her body. "Why would you think that?"

Julie tapped the face of her Wonder Woman wristwatch. "It's the time of day. I thought this was the height of your Sunday brunch rush."

"Oh, right. Well, usually it is, but things are a bit slow this morning. Our servers seemed to have everything under control, so we thought we'd pop in and see if we could buy at least one copy of the book we're discussing tomorrow night." Pete ran his hand through his short hair. "We did read it," he added, with a swift glance at me. "Borrowed it from the library."

"But it was due before today, you see." Sandy offered me an apologetic smile. "And we thought it might be rude if we showed up without a book. Especially since the illustrator is leading the discussion."

"I'm sure Lora Kane would be fine either way." I pressed my hand against the box of books. "She may even have ordered some extras, I'm not sure."

"No, Lora only told me to provide eight copies, and I think the two extras were for you and me, Charlotte. Of course, I did order a few additional books for the shop and our club." Julie bit her lower lip before adding, "And now that there are only five guests . . ."

"Goodness, hadn't thought of that," Sandy said, blinking rapidly. "It was weird to hear about that death, especially after we saw the victim just yesterday."

"You did?" I glanced at Julie, who simply widened her eyes. "Did she come into the café?"

"Yeah, I remembered her when the TV news put up her picture. Stacy Wilkin, wasn't it?" Sandy sighed. "She seemed the picture of health when I served her coffee late Saturday morning. I guess you just never know."

Pete draped his arm around Sandy's shoulders. "Any updates on what killed the poor woman, Charlotte? I heard rumors of a heart attack or stroke."

I studied my fingernails for a moment. "Nothing official yet. But I don't think it was either one of those things."

"Charlotte thinks the victim was murdered," Julie said, with a toss of her head. "Apparently she was not the most popular person in her book club."

"Really?" Peter shared a glance with his wife. "That might explain a few things."

I snapped my gaze to the side, focusing on his round face. "Such as?"

He lifted his free hand. "It's just that Sandy overheard a heated exchange between Ms. Wilkin and another lady."

"An attractive African American woman," Sandy said. "They didn't come into the café together. Ms. Wilkin was sitting at the counter drinking her coffee when this other lady walked in. I didn't hear what started the argument, but the other woman, who was younger by, I would guess, ten years, did say something about her son being slandered. It sounded like she was blaming Ms. Wilkin for falsely accusing her son of theft."

"Did you hear the younger woman's name?" I was pretty sure I knew who it was but wanted confirmation.

Sandy wrinkled her pert nose. "Bonnie, maybe?"

"Vonnie," I said. "Another member of the book club."

"You mean another guest?" Julie let out a low whistle. "Uh-oh. That puts a new spin on things."

"Yes, it does," I said thoughtfully. Meeting Pete's and Sandy's concerned gazes, I forced a smile. "I think you should probably share this information with Detective Johnson or someone else at the police department. It might be significant."

"Oh dear." Sandy glanced up at Pete. "Looks like we're going to be dragged into another murder case, dear."

"And this woman is still a guest at Chapters, so we'll likely encounter her tomorrow night." Pete shot me a questioning look.

"I expect so." I tapped the top of the book box. "It's probably best if you don't let on that you remember her or her argument with Stacy Wilkin. Just play dumb."

Pete's somber expression morphed into a grin. "Some people would say that comes naturally to me."

"Don't be silly," Julie said. "No one in our book club is anything less than brilliant." Offering Pete and Sandy a smile, she stepped back from the counter. "Let me go grab you a copy of that Andersen book before I forget."

"I'm going to head out, then." I picked up the box, declining when Pete offered to carry it to my car. "I'll be fine. I know you need to head back to the café." I paused, cradling the box to my chest. "You all could help me out, though, if you would."

"How's that?" Sandy asked, tugging on one of her expertly dyed ash-blonde curls.

"Keep your eyes and ears open tomorrow night as well as going forward. See if anything else strikes you as odd or significant about my guests."

"Charlotte is trying to recruit us as her Irregulars, I think," Julie said as she returned from her office. She handed the book to Pete.

"Not mine. I'm Watson, not Sherlock," I replied, heading for the front door.

Pete strode across the shop to open the door for me. "I suppose Ellen is the master detective, then?"

"Indubitably," I said, before calling out, "See you later," and exiting the store.

Chapter Eight

W hen I arrived back at Chapters, I lugged the box of books through the back door and headed directly for the library.

I'd planned to unload the books onto the large wooden desk that dominated one corner of the space, but as I stepped into the room, my attention was diverted by Alicia, who was perched on the rolling library ladder. She was intently checking the shelves, as if searching for a specific book.

That wasn't really so odd. One of the guests had probably requested a volume from the upper shelves. For insurance purposes, I didn't allow anyone but Alicia or me to use the ladder. "Hey there," I said, setting the box on the desk with a thud. "Can I help you find something?"

Alicia turned her head to look at me over her shoulder. "Sure, but it isn't the usual."

"Not a book?" I crossed to the ladder, holding it steady as she descended. "What are you looking for, then?"

"Photographs." Alicia stepped off the ladder and wiped her hands on her apron. "We need to dust in here."

"I know." Looking around the room, whose walls were covered by elegant wood shelving that topped polished walnut cabinets, I had to admit it was difficult to keep the library clean. So many books filled the shelves that dusting was a major chore. "What do you mean—are some of the photographs missing?"

Alicia placed her hands on her hips. "Take a look around. Remember all those small photos in silver frames that Isabella tucked in at the ends of the rows?"

I narrowed my eyes and did a quick sweep of the room. There were definitely empty spots that Isabella's photographs had once filled. I crossed to one of the shelves and ran my fingers over the end of a row, noticing that the dust had been disturbed. "Most are still here, but you're right—a few are missing." I turned my gaze on Alicia. "Do you remember which ones they were?"

Alicia shook her head. "Not exactly. Most of the pictures in here are candid shots from Isabella's parties. They always looked the same to me—crowds of wealthy people clumped together. You know, good-looking women and men arm in arm, holding up champagne glasses. That sort of thing. I didn't recognize most of the people in the photos, other than Isabella, so they all blurred together."

I moved to another set of shelves and picked up one of the framed pictures that hadn't been disturbed. "Bernadette and Ophelia Sandburg are in this one. Goodness, they look different, don't they?"

Alicia strolled over to examine the photo. "You're right, although I never knew them when they were that young. The rest of these, though"—Alicia swept her hand through the air—"I have no idea. Except for Isabella, of course. She's in most of them."

"Wearing amazing clothes and jewels." I gazed at another one of the framed pictures. "I've examined these photos before, but mainly to see what Isabella looked like back when she was younger. I guess I never really cared who the other people in the pictures were."

"Me either, but someone must've had an interest." Alicia looked up at me, her black eyebrows drawn together. "There's at least three missing, by my count, and look at this." She strode over to one of the lower cabinets. One of the doors was ajar, and I spied a jumble of papers on the shelves inside. "I'd never leave things in such a mess. I think someone was rifling through the cabinets too."

"But why?" I clenched my hands at my sides. "I can almost understand the missing photos. Maybe someone wanted a memento. Something that reflected the glamorous history of Chapters and Isabella Harrington." *Maybe Arnie Dean*, I thought, remembering his avowed fascination with my great-aunt. *Or even Vonnie Allen, who expressed such an interest in the home's history.* "But why dig through random papers or other stuff in those cabinets? It's not like we keep anything valuable in them. Just old maps and scrapbooks and that sort of thing."

Alicia pursed her lips. "A thief wouldn't know that."

"No, but why would a thief take photos that would only mean something to Isabella's family and friends?" I surveyed the upper shelves. "There are several very valuable books shelved in here. Surely they would be the target of any thief worth their salt."

"I don't know about that. I just know a few of the framed photographs are missing and nothing else. As far as I can tell, anyway."

"Maybe we should do a more thorough search." Noticing Alicia's frown, I added, "Or I can do that, if you have other chores you'd rather tackle."

Alicia shrugged. "Nothing going on tonight, so I don't have any food to prepare. I'll give you a hand. Two sets of eyes are probably better than one."

"Absolutely," I said, flashing her a smile. "Thanks."

"No problem. I don't like the idea of anyone rummaging through things they have no business getting into." Alicia tugged on the strap of her white apron. "Makes me feel uneasy, you know? Thinking the guests are the sort to pinch things."

"We don't know for sure it was one of the guests," I reminded her. "I know there's usually someone here to keep an eye on things, but we've found strangers wandering around Chapters before. Especially during the day, when the guests are coming and going. You know they sometimes leave the outside doors open."

"True enough. All right, let's take another look." Alicia headed for the opposite side of the room and popped open one of the lower cabinets. "I'll start over here. If you want to take that side, we can meet in the middle."

"Sounds like a plan." I turned to the shelving unit behind me. Looking up at the rows of books, I sighed. This would take some time. *So much for a relaxing Sunday afternoon*, I thought as I bent down to peer into the cabinet beneath this section of shelving.

But it was something that had to be done, if only so we knew what we were dealing with—perhaps a thief, but perhaps simply an extremely nosy guest. *Or a sentimental one*, I thought, wondering if Arnie Dean had borrowed the photos to reminisce about the past. *Or to make copies of the photos so he can keep his memories of Isabella alive?* I wondered, deciding that I wouldn't approach him, or any of the guests, about the missing pictures yet.

Wait a few days and see if the photographs reappear, I told myself. *No need to cause a conflict where none exists.*

A murder was enough drama for one week.

* * *

After searching for most of the afternoon and into early evening, Alicia and I called it a day. We hadn't noticed anything else missing from the library, and after we determined that all the guests were in for the night, we locked up a little early.

The evening news confirmed my suspicions when the police spokesperson formally declared Stacy Wilkin's death a homicide. Not feeling hungry, I ate a few crackers and cheese and headed to my bedroom. The day had exhausted me mentally as well as physically, and I wanted to relax with my copy of the Andersen stories. It had been a while since I'd read any fairy tales, and I was curious how Lora's illustrations complemented the texts. Kicking off my shoes, I settled into the worn but comfortable armchair in my bedroom with my cell phone and a glass of wine on the table beside me.

About thirty minutes later, my cell chimed out the ring tone I'd assigned to one special caller. I set my book on the table and grabbed the phone.

"Hello, Charlotte," said Gavin Howard.

"Hi. Since you're finally able to call me, I assume your assignment is over?"

"Just wrapped it up." Gavin cleared his throat. "I heard some chatter."

"About trouble at Chapters?" I leaned back in my chair, stretching out my legs. "You didn't hear wrong. I'm afraid to say there's been another murder."

"One of the guests?"

"Sadly, yes. And this time back at the B and B again. Well, out in the garden, actually." I took a sip of wine before continuing. "The police have just officially labeled it foul play, which I already knew. Ellen and I saw the body before the authorities arrived, and it was definitely not a natural death."

"Were they shot or stabbed or what?" Gavin's voice, a calm baritone, betrayed no shock over such news.

Of course, I thought, *he probably deals with this sort of stuff all the time.* "No, this was a poisoning. Not sure how, but according to Ellen, it appears the victim died from ingesting or inhaling some type of cyanide."

"That means it should be fairly easy to track down the culprit, based on their method. Unless it was a suicide?"

"Unlikely." I flexed my feet, examining my unpainted toenails. "Let's just say, given the personality of the victim and her behavior before the event, both the authorities and I definitely think this is a case of murder."

"So what's your theory? Pretty sure you must have one." Gavin's voice held a hint of amusement. "I imagine you're already busy investigating."

"You know me too well."

"Well enough to know that you, along with Ellen, won't sit back and allow the police to do all the sleuthing."

"I just like to help out."

"Hmmm . . . all right, let me offer my assistance. At least in terms of narrowing down the suspects. Talk to me about your guests."

I filled him in on my impressions of the five remaining guests and offered a few comments about Captain Joiner as well. "Several of them appear to have harbored some sort of vendetta against the victim, Stacy Wilkin, so there seem to be numerous people with motive. But means is another thing. I wouldn't think it would be that easy to get your hands on cyanide."

There was a moment of silence before Gavin spoke, betraying the fact that he was choosing his words carefully. "It actually doesn't have to be purchased. It can be made from apricot or apple seeds."

"Not easily, though," I said. "Wouldn't it take a decent lab and some skill?"

"You said one of the guests is a chemist. They probably wouldn't have to go to all that trouble, though, as they might be able to acquire it for research purposes. In any case, they undoubtedly have access to a lab."

"True." I gnawed on the inside of my cheek. "That's just one of the suspects on my list, though. Not sure how the others would've gotten their hands on that type of poison."

"Tell me again exactly what the victim looked like," Gavin said.

After I described the deep-pink blush, her blue lips, and the scent of almonds rising from Stacy's body, I added, "Captain Joiner confronted Stacy on the front porch, and she did have her teacup with her then, so I suppose he could've had access to it. After he left, Stacy walked back to the patio, where the other guests were seated around a table, having tea and pastries and that sort of thing. There was a lot of coming and going, so Stacy's tea could've been tampered with amid that confusion, I suppose. Then, according to all accounts, Stacy disappeared into the garden. I have to wonder if someone followed her."

"Unlikely." Gavin tapped his finger against his phone. "I suspect she may have been poisoned before she entered the garden. Probably sodium cyanide salts in her tea. They can pass as sugar, so if the victim noticed something in her cup, she wouldn't have been suspicious."

"But it's fast acting, right?" I slid my finger around the rim of my wineglass. "Someone had to be very clever to slip the poison in her cup right before she wandered into the garden."

"It depends. The concentration of the poison would affect its speed. If it was a deadly dose but not an extreme one, It wouldn't have been impossible for the victim to move around for a little while before collapsing."

"I suppose one of the guests could've slipped the poison into Stacy's cup without anyone noticing." I sighed. "Lora Kane told me that Stacy seemed very shaky before she disappeared. Lora assumed she was drunk, but maybe it was the poison starting to work."

"Probably. Did the victim carry her teacup into the garden?"

"Yes. Ellen and I saw it, broken in pieces, on the ground not far from the body."

"So it's also possible she never drank from it until she was in the garden. Which doesn't rule anyone out, even Samuel Joiner. If he dosed her cup but she didn't drink anything until later, after adding more tea . . ."

I sighed. "I see what you're getting at. In that scenario, it could've been Joiner or any one of the guests."

"It's still puzzling," Gavin said. "It's not the most likely poison for an amateur to employ, but then again, it isn't impossible to source either. It's used in mining, some science applications, and pesticides, among other things. It's not like someone who's determined to acquire it can't obtain it."

"It really points a finger at Zach Bell, the chemist, though, don't you think?"

"Not necessarily, although I would keep him high on the list. But sodium cyanide is a lot easier to obtain than you'd think, which is one reason we keep tabs on any significant purchases."

"Part of the surveillance of terrorist groups or other bad actors, I suppose." I stared up at my whitewashed beadboard ceiling. "There is one thing you might be able to help me with, given your ability to look into certain information as well as consult contacts I can't access."

"Not exactly at work now—or on the grid, since I'm back living on the boat," he replied. "But I suppose I could make some calls. What do you need?"

"I thought maybe you could double-check the backgrounds of my guests, along with the good captain. Just to see if anything turns up in any criminal databases. Do you have something to write on?"

"Hold on, let me grab a pen." I heard a drawer open and close and the rustle of paper before Gavin said, "Okay, go ahead."

I provided the full names of all the guests, including Stacy Wilkin. "I really don't believe it was suicide, but I suppose it wouldn't hurt to cover all the bases."

"I'll see what I can dig up, although I doubt a book club is going to include anyone affiliated with criminals or terrorists," Gavin said.

"You never know." I took another sip of my wine. "Sorry to dump this on you right after you finished one of your mysterious missions. You probably want a break."

"I also want to help you, if only . . ." Gavin cleared his throat again. "I'm hoping this can be wrapped up soon, so you won't have to worry with it for long."

"So I won't be involved in any additional sleuthing, you mean." I straightened in my chair. "That isn't really your call, Gavin."

"I'm aware I don't have any control over your actions," Gavin said, in a mild tone. "I just don't like the thought of you tracking down a killer again, that's all."

"Admit it—you're just as intrigued with solving this murder as I am."

"Perhaps not for the same reasons." Gavin's voice softened. "I worry about you investigating things without backup. It could be dangerous."

"I have Ellen."

"And she is quite skilled in some areas, but—if your suspicions are correct and there's a murderer among your guests, or even simply roaming the local area—digging into this case could put a target on your back."

"I appreciate the concern, but I do keep Detective Johnson and her team in the loop. I'm not going to run headlong into a threatening situation."

"But how can you be sure ahead of time?" There was a moment of silence before Gavin added, "You know I'd be devastated if anything were to happen to you."

Warmth flushed my face. "Says the man whose entire career is built around risky missions."

"I try not to go looking for trouble. And the truth is . . ." Gavin took a deep breath. "Never mind. I'll talk to you about that another time. For now, what do you say we switch to a more pleasant topic."

"Such as?"

"You and I getting together in person. I might be able to arrange that soon."

It was my turn to take a moment to think. Of course I wanted to see Gavin, but it also made me a little nervous. Our long-distance relationship had brought us closer, but it was also safe. *Now who's the one worried about rushing into things?* I thought, with a shake of my head. "That sounds lovely. Let's hope this murder case is put to bed before then, though, so we can actually enjoy our time together."

"Pretty sure I'll enjoy it, no matter what else is going on." Gavin kept his tone light, but I could hear an undercurrent that made me press my fingers to my lips.

I was no inexperienced girl, but sometimes Gavin made me feel like I was sixteen again. The truth was, I'd been married to the same man for years and had never had any inclination to even innocently flirt with anyone else. Dealing with the emotions engendered by a new relationship was a strange sensation.

Unnerving, I thought, pulling myself together enough to reply offhandedly, "I do look forward to actually interacting without the shadow of a murder hanging over everything."

"Better solve that case soon, then," he said.

Which made me wonder just when he planned to show up in Beaufort.

Chapter Nine

In the morning, I realized I hadn't mentioned the disturbances in the attic and the library to Gavin, but I decided that was just as well. He'd only worry unnecessarily. Anyway, I had pretty much convinced myself that our photo thief was Arnie and that he was just looking for pictures to copy so he could relive an old infatuation. As long as the photographs were replaced before he left Chapters, I wasn't going to make a fuss.

I helped Alicia prepare and serve breakfast to the guests, which turned out to be less work than usual, as both Linnea and Vonnie skipped the meal. After the others had finished eating, I carried the dirty dishes into the kitchen.

Before I could head back into the dining room to straighten up the tables and chairs, Alicia told me she had some news to share.

"It's about my cousin, Christopher Freedman," she said as she loaded the dishwasher.

I wiped my hands on a paper towel. "Does he need a job or something? Because you know we can't really afford . . ."

"No, no." Alicia closed up the dishwasher and turned to face me. "This is about the death of our guest. Remember, when I heard you mention Captain Joiner, I thought the name sounded familiar? Well, I asked my mom about it, and she confirmed he was the guy my cousin Christopher Freedman used to work for. Chris now runs his own charter fishing business, but he had to work under other captains for years to save up the money for his boat."

"And Joiner was one of them?"

"Yep. So I thought—maybe Chris knows something more about the guy. Whether he's the type who might murder someone, I mean."

"Not sure there is a type," I said, thinking back on a few other cases I'd been involved in. "But I get your point. Your cousin would know what kind of temper Captain Joiner has, or whether he's ever been violent."

"Just thought you might want to talk to Chris and hear it straight from him. You and Ellen, of course." Alicia looked me over, her eyes glinting with amusement. "I know you two are digging into the background of every possible suspect. Just glad to not be one of them this time."

"I think you're in the clear. Unless you doctored the pastries?" I said with a lift of my eyebrows.

Alicia snapped a kitchen towel at me. "That would've been Damian."

"Oh, right. Well, not to worry, then." I flashed her a smile before heading back into the dining room.

As I wiped down the tables, I heard a raised voice sail through the window that faced out onto the front porch. Looking up, I observed Zach pacing, a cell phone pressed to his ear.

Of course, Zach's call was none of my business, but since he topped my list of suspects . . . I crept closer, near enough that I could hear what he was saying. But I made sure to stand back against the adjacent wall so he wouldn't spy me through the window.

"Let me tell you one more time—I don't give a flip about your stupid Aspen condo," Zach told whoever was on the other end of the line. "I'm not looking for more from you than what we spelled out in our initial agreement. I just want to make sure the kids aren't cheated out of anything that would ultimately benefit them."

Zach's voice was filled with a cold fury that cut to the bone. *He hates whoever he's talking to*, I thought. *And he's filled with a white-hot anger. The kind of anger that could lead to violence . . .*

"No, I will not be driving to New York to discuss this with you in a *reasonable manner*," Zach said, his tone slicing the air like a switchblade. "We have discussed everything to death. Just sign the papers and be done with me like I'm done with you."

Papers and a mention of kids made me assume Zach was arguing with his soon-to-be ex. I slipped away from the window and, after depositing my cleaning supplies in the kitchen, headed for my bedroom to do a little online sleuthing.

Opening my laptop, I searched for all the Zachery Bells in North Carolina, narrowing my search to the Cary area when I had too many hits. That brought up some mentions of Zach's marriage, twelve years ago, to a pharmaceutical company heiress.

I peered at the picture attached to one of the articles. Zach's wife, Heather, was a willowy blonde who exuded the glamour and confidence that only a lifetime of privilege could supply. Glancing at the comments under the article, I noticed quite a few barbed remarks about Zach "marrying up." *Probably a disgruntled girlfriend or two*, I thought. The conversation I'd overheard, along with Lora's mention of the rocky state of Zach's marriage, confirmed my assumption that he and his wife were in the middle of a contentious divorce.

Not that divorce makes him a killer, I thought, *but he definitely seems to have a temper. If he was already in a bad state of mind when he arrived and then had to deal with Stacy Wilkin, who he believes cheated his mother, perhaps that anger boiled over into murder.*

I studied the glamorous wedding day photo one more time before shutting down my laptop. Zach had been a handsome young man and was still good-looking. By my calculations, he was also probably less than fifteen years younger than Stacy Wilkin. Considering Stacy's flirtatious personality and well-preserved appearance, perhaps there had also been some romantic entanglement in their relationship. Which could've made an eventual betrayal, through her treatment of Zach's mom, that much worse.

Of course, this was all just speculation. I left my bedroom and headed out into the backyard, hoping the fresh air would help me think through the implications of my latest discoveries.

The police had removed the yellow warning tape from the garden, finally allowing access, so I wasn't too surprised to see the gate standing open. One or more of the guests must've decided to enjoy the garden this morning.

As soon as I entered, I noticed someone sitting on one of the white-painted wooden benches. The fall of strawberry-blonde hair told me it was Linnea, even though her head was down over the sketchbook covering her lap.

"Hi. I don't mean to disturb you. I just wanted to take a stroll to clear my head," I said as I approached her.

Linnea looked up, her eyes hooded under her pale lashes. "Good morning. And of course, you aren't bothering me. It's your garden, after all."

"It looks like you're busy with your drawing. I suppose that makes sense. Lora told me you're an artist."

"Art teacher," Linnea said, tossing her long hair behind her slender shoulders. "I do continue to dabble, but my aspirations to be a great artist died with my introduction to some of my fellow students at design school."

"I'm sure you're just being modest." I moved closer to the bench. "Besides, I feel being a teacher is one of the most important careers one can have. I'm biased, of course."

"That's right, you were an English teacher before you took over Chapters." Linnea straightened and looked me over with an intent gaze. "Do you miss teaching? I do enjoy it, for all my grumbling. Pretty sure I'd miss it if I left. Not like Lora, who claims she'd rather work in a fast-food joint than take up teaching again."

"I doubt that's true," I said with a smile. Motioning toward the bench, I added," Do you mind?"

"Not at all. Have a seat." Linnea scooted over to allow me to sit down.

"To answer your question, yes, I miss teaching." I heard the wistful note in my voice. No doubt Linnea did too, since she sent me a sympathetic glance. "But my great-aunt Isabella leaving me Chapters in her will coincided with me needing a break from my previous life, so I jumped on the opportunity. Now I enjoy running Chapters almost as much as teaching."

"It's a beautiful place," Linnea said, her gaze sweeping the back of the house. Ducking her head, she shot me a side-eyed glance. "I heard about your late husband. Lora told me he died saving a classroom full of children during a tornado. That was very heroic."

"Yes, it was." I clutched my hands in my lap. Hero or not, it was still hard to contemplate the manner of Brent's death. "But that was the kind of man he was. It was second nature for him to think of others before himself."

"You were lucky to love a man like that." Linnea blinked rapidly, as if fighting back tears. She looked away before adding, "We can't always decide who we love, can we? I mean, in terms of whether they are selfless or selfish or things like that."

"Can't we?" I wondered what types of relationships Linnea had been involved in to make her feel this way. "Well, there's no helping attraction sometimes, but I think we can decide whether to act on it or not."

"I suppose," Linnea said with a sniffle. She laid her hands, palms flat, over her sketch pad. "Anyway, I'm enjoying drawing your beautiful flowers. They're great inspiration for my designs."

I glanced down at her sketch. "Is that a study for a watercolor or oil painting?"

Linnea lifted her hands. "No, this is for a piece of jewelry. It's what I'm really into these days."

"That's right. Lora told me you were learning jewelry making from her. May I?" I pointed at the sketchbook. "I'd love to see more of your designs."

"Sure, but please understand, these are only studies. The finished pieces sometimes turn out differently. It all depends on the materials you're working with." Linnea handed the wire-bound drawing pad to me.

"Of course." I flipped through the pages of the sketchbook, admiring the detailed drawings of flowers, insects, and other subjects from nature. "Amazing work. I'd love to see some of the jewelry you've created from these."

"I'm actually wearing a pair of earrings I made recently." Linnea tucked a lock of her hair behind one ear. "See?"

Delicate filigrees of gold and enamel, the earrings each captured a bee sipping nectar from a flower. "Lovely," I said. "So full of movement. It looks like the bee could fly off at any moment."

"Thanks." Linnea's smile faded as I turned to a page featuring a gorgeous dragonfly design.

"This is one I'd love to buy for myself. Have you created any jewelry off this sketch yet?" I asked.

"No, and I'm afraid I won't. That design"—she grabbed the sketchbook from my hands—"isn't available. I mean, it can't be used."

"What a shame." As I sat back, I couldn't help but notice Linnea's expression had darkened like a stormy summer sky. "Why not? Is it impossible to fabricate?"

Snapping the sketchbook shut, Linnea shook her head. "It isn't that. Sorry, I don't want to get into it. Let's just say I got ripped off by someone I once trusted."

"That's unfortunate," I said, offering her a sympathetic smile as I tried to make sense of her words. I wasn't sure how her drawing was connected to a betrayal, but it was obvious that Linnea wasn't going to say more about the matter. "Anyway, I'm certainly interested in your work. Do you do commissions?"

Linnea shot me a questioning glance. "I haven't, but I'd consider it. Do you have something in mind?"

"I thought perhaps earrings, with a design based on a sand dollar. For my neighbor, Ellen. She loves unique jewelry, and, well, that would have special significance for her in relation to our friendship. A memory," I said, without adding that it would commemorate the first time Ellen and I had worked together as amateur sleuths.

"I could do that. Would she prefer gold or silver?" Linnea dropped her shoulders. It was obvious that this turn in the conversation had relieved her previous anxiety.

"Silver, I think," I said, picturing Ellen's striking white hair and blue eyes.

"Sure. Let me work up some sketches, and then you can decide if you want to proceed." Linnea rose to her feet. "I think I'll head in now. I'm planning to join up with a few of the others for a walking tour of Beaufort this afternoon, and I need to change my shoes." She held out one foot, displaying a worn flip-flop. "I don't think I want to walk too far in these."

"No, a good walking shoe is a better bet, especially since some of the sidewalks are a little uneven." I stood to face her. "Enjoy your tour. Beaufort has a lot of fascinating history, if you enjoy that sort of thing."

"Thanks. I hope you have a good day too. Of course, I'll see you later, since we have the book club discussion tonight," Linnea said.

"Right." I waited until Linnea left before I continued my stroll around the garden. I'd almost forgotten the book club meeting scheduled for later in the day. *Too much focus on sleuthing and not enough on your real job*, I told myself as I examined a flower bed filled with pink and yellow roses. I immediately decided to cut and arrange some flowers for the evening's event. Heading for the storage bins next to the carriage house, where I kept my clippers and other garden tools, I made a silent vow to focus more on being a proper hostess than on playing at being a sleuth.

Chapter Ten

Sticking to my vow, I spent Monday afternoon helping Alicia prepare additional hors d'oeuvres, then dusted in the library and covered the wooden desk with a white tablecloth. I finished preparations for the evening by arranging a circle of chairs on the room's Persian rug.

Not surprisingly, Lora was the first guest to appear. She carried in a large easel that she set up in front of one section of the library's cabinets and shelves.

"I brought some larger-scale versions of the illustrations," she said, holding up a leather portfolio. "I know everyone will have a copy of the book, but I thought it might be easier to point out details."

"Good thinking." I motioned toward another section of shelves, where books were stacked on top of the lower cabinet. "The copies are there. Just picked them up from Bookwaves yesterday."

Lora flashed me a smile. "Thanks for doing that. And please thank your friend again for acquiring so many copies—and the lovely discount."

"You can thank her yourself, since she plans to attend the discussion this evening." I adjusted the placement of one of the wooden chairs I'd carried in from the dining room. "Will this setup work for you?"

"It's perfect." Lora looked around the room, mouthing numbers. "Only ten chairs, though? There's my group of six . . ." She frowned and cleared her throat. "No, five now. But I thought you said seven or eight people typically attend your book club meetings."

"Usually, but two of our members, Bernadette and Ophelia Sandburg, had another commitment tonight, and one person is out of town." I realized my error and added, "That's Scott Kepler, and he actually lives in another part of the state, so he can't always attend our meetings. He's here a lot, though, because he's Julie's boyfriend and also conducts research in this area."

Lora, fiddling with the knobs on the easel, shot me a quick glance. "Scott Kepler? I remember seeing a few of his books in an indie store at home. He writes nonfiction historical stuff, doesn't he?"

"Mostly about pirates. Factual histories, not the made-up stories you usually see on that topic."

"Too bad he couldn't be here. I would've liked to have spoken with him about his books." Lora unfastened the top of her portfolio and pulled out a stack of large drawings mounted on foam core. "Sounds like the kind of books that might need illustrations," she added, placing one of the pieces on the easel.

"Ah, I see. Always looking for more work?"

Lora cast me a rueful smile. "Freelancers must hustle."

"Hi, hope we're not too early," said Pete as he and Sandy strolled into the library.

Since the Dancing Dolphin was closed on Mondays, they weren't wearing their café attire. From May through September, I was so used to seeing them in their logo T-shirts and khaki shorts that anything else gave me a little jolt of surprise. "I like that blouse," I told Sandy. "Peacock blue is one of my favorite colors."

"Mine too," Sandy said, tugging down the short sleeves of her silky top. "I kind of wish we'd chosen that color for the café logo instead of turquoise."

Pete, wearing a plain gray polo over black-and-gray plaid shorts, shook his head. "Turquoise is beachier." He walked up to the easel and examined Lora's drawing, which featured a young woman wearing crimson ballet slippers. She was caught mid dance step in the middle of a cobblestone road. Around her the thatched-roofed buildings of a Scandinavian-style village, pulled like taffy into odd shapes, loomed over the obviously terrified dancer.

"*The Red Shoes*. Nice work," he said. "You perfectly captured her growing horror in realizing her predicament."

Lora beamed. "Thank you. It's a bit of a horror story, you know."

"Most definitely," Sandy said, with a little shudder. "The poor girl in that story, having to dance until she dies."

"And cutting off her own feet to escape the shoes," Pete added, draping his arm over his wife's shoulders. "But a lot of Andersen's stories seem to feature those gruesome details."

"Most fairy tales are pretty dark," I said. "I mean, the original tales, not the Disneyfied versions."

"Oh, absolutely. But that's one reason I jumped on the chance to illustrate this book." As Lora straightened the drawing, her fingers traced the swirls of the character's wild, strawberry-blonde hair. "I like including a touch of the gothic."

Focusing more intently on the illustration, I noticed the character's resemblance to someone I'd recently met. *It's Linnea*, I thought, wondering if she'd posed for Lora or if my former colleague had simply decided to base her drawing on the younger artist. *And what does that mean? Is Linnea, who seems relatively well adjusted, secretly as troubled as the girl cursed to wear the red shoes?*

Pete chose one of the hard-backed dining room chairs closest to the easel. He patted the seat next to him. "Sit here, dear. Unless you prefer one of the armchairs?"

"Let's leave those for the actual guests," Sandy said. She sat down, balancing their copy of the Andersen fairy tales on her knees. "Glad you picked the seats near the front, though. My old eyes aren't what they used to be."

I made a dismissive noise. "You're only a few years older than me."

"Ten years or so, to be exact," Pete said.

"But that's only mid-fifties, so don't act like you're ancient," I replied with a smile.

"Yes, leave that to me," said Ellen as she entered the room.

I widened my eyes, taking in her vivid purple silk tunic top and palazzo pants. The flowing trousers were patterned with green-and-purple palm trees and pink flamingos. I was amused to observe a matching pink streak highlighting her white hair. "I see you've brought a tropical flair to the evening."

"Always like to brighten things up," Ellen said, before acknowledging the Nelsons. "You must be the artist," she told Lora as she stepped forward to examine the illustration on the easel.

Vonnie, Zach, and Linnea walked into the library just as I was introducing Ellen to Lora, so I continued the introductions all around. "Oh, I meant to ask, Zach—did you ever find that pin you were searching for in the garden?"

Zach stared at me, his mouth slightly agape. "Pin?"

His eyes were clouded with confusion, which I found curious. "You know, the Phi Beta Kappa pin you said you lost," I said, more convinced than ever that Zach had been lying about his reason for searching the garden.

"No, uh, I . . ." Zach blinked rapidly.

"Remember, you discovered you'd left it in your suite," Linnea said, tapping his arm with her fingers.

"Oh, right. Yes, I found it later in the carriage house. Guess I dropped it there instead." Zach met my inquisitive gaze with a wry smile. "Too much on my mind these days, I guess."

"That's certainly not surprising," I said, examining Zach and Linnea with interest. *There's something between the two of them,* I thought. *They're covering for one another for some reason.* But I decided it wasn't the time or place to follow up on this suspicion. "Where's Arnie? Isn't he coming?" I asked, as the others sat down.

"I saw him head into the kitchen," Zach said, the tension draining from his face. He was obviously pleased with this change in the conversation. Another thing that piqued my interest. "He said something about helping carry in the drinks."

"That should be my job." I crossed the room but had to step aside when Alicia bustled in, hauling a wire basket filled with wine and water bottles and canned soft drinks. Following right behind her, Arnie carried an ice bucket and tongs.

"I have the glasses, Charlotte, so no need for you to grab anything." Julie's cheery voice rang out from the hallway.

Slightly embarrassed by my failure as a hostess, I instructed Arnie and Julie to deposit their items on the linen-covered desk, where Alicia was already setting up the drinks. "Thank you. And please, forgive me for being so lax in my duties."

Alicia waved this off. "No problem. They wanted to help," she said before leaving the room.

Arnie strolled over to one of the two armchairs. "Looks like I get one of the premier seats," he said, directing his words toward Ellen, who was still standing by the easel. "The perks of being one of the oldest here, I guess."

I'd already noticed Ellen's intense scrutiny of her former friend. She narrowed her eyes until they glinted like sapphire shards. "Well, well. Fancy meeting you here, Arnie Dean."

"I suspect you already knew I was one of the guests." Arnie settled back against the buttery leather of his chair.

"Of course," Ellen said.

Arnie's broad smile tightened. "But you didn't bother to drop by to say hello."

"Sorry, the time was never right, what with the police conducting an investigation and all," Ellen replied sweetly.

"You two know each other?" Sandy asked, looking from Ellen to Arnie and back again.

"From college. Long, long ago." Arnie shrugged. "What's it been, Ellie? Fifty-five years?"

"Not quite that long. Close, though." Ellen crossed to one of the hard-backed chairs, Julie on her heels.

"You should take the other armchair," Julie told her. "I'm fine with this."

There was a sparkle in Julie's eyes that told me she'd sensed some sort of connection between Ellen and Arnie and was now engaged in one of her favorite activities—matchmaking. I shot her a warning glance, which she countered with a lift of her feathery eyebrows.

"If everyone is ready, I'd like to start the discussion. But first, anyone who doesn't have a book, you can grab one from the stack over there," Lora said, gesturing toward the appropriate shelf.

Julie bounced back up out of her chair. "You guys stay seated. I'll hand them out."

While she passed around the copies, I surveyed the group, noticing Arnie studying Ellen's profile as she resolutely refused to meet his gaze. Meanwhile, Vonnie drummed her fingers against one of her knees, and Linnea and Zach focused on the books that lay open in their laps.

They all seem a bit on edge, I thought, taking a seat in the remaining wooden chair, which was situated next to Julie's. *Not that it's surprising, what with a murderer in their midst. But I do wonder if it's also due to guilt, at least for one of them.*

Lora launched into a description of her designs, sharing information on the specific stories and how each had influenced her process. "One of the things that's interesting about Andersen's fairy tales, at least in my opinion, is that they tend to feature ordinary people rather than aristocrats," she said, placing an illustration depicting a mermaid in a vivid underwater scene on the easel. "*The Little Mermaid* is one exception to that, I suppose, since she is supposed to be a mer-princess and her love interest is a prince.

But typically Andersen wrote about merchants and tradespeople, or even poor farmers or villagers, rather than royalty."

"Didn't he have sort of a love-hate relationship with the aristocracy?" Sandy asked. "I seem to remember reading that in a biography."

Lora nodded. "Some scholars have come to that conclusion. I mean, he often made fun of the wealthy and well connected, as you can see in *The Emperor's New Clothes* and *The Princess and the Pea*. Yet in real life, he also courted their favor. So yes—complicated."

"So many of his stories were sad." Linnea's gaze had focused on the *Little Mermaid* illustration on the easel. "She truly loves the prince yet ends up as sea foam. Doesn't seem fair."

"You expect life to be fair?" Arnie's voice was laced with amusement.

"Not always, but if someone deeply loves another person"— Linnea cast a glance at Zach—"I want them to have a happy ending, that's all."

Zach slammed shut his copy of the fairy tales, causing Linnea to jerk upright in her chair. "Anyway, getting back to your work, Lora—were you influenced by the Pre-Raphaelites? Because I think I see some evidence of that in your illustrations."

"Why yes," Lora said, her expression brightening. "I thought it fit the stories, since they are rather lush and dark and a bit mysterious."

Vonnie, who'd remained unnaturally quiet up to this point, shifted in her chair. "I like the illustrations you did for *The Snow Queen* the best. So magical, yet you captured the cold and gloomy aspects of the story perfectly."

"Thanks. Wait, let me put one of those up." Lora fished another illustration out of her portfolio and placed it on the easel.

This drawing depicted a young boy sitting at the feet of a mysterious woman who appeared to be as beautiful and regal as a queen but also as translucent and cold as ice. The pair was surrounded by a cave, with icicles dripping from the ceiling like crystals from a chandelier. The faceted walls of the cave shone like diamonds.

"Ah, the Snow Queen," Arnie said, crossing his arms over his broad chest. "A woman who chooses power and control over feelings."

Lora's smile faded. "I don't think that's exactly right. The Snow Queen isn't a person. Not in Andersen's original story, anyway. More like a force of nature."

"And the boy, Kai—wasn't he fascinated by logic and mathematics?" Zach said. "When I read it, I thought it represented the battle between logic and love."

"Which still goes on," Linnea said, under her breath.

"Exactly." Lora cast Zach a smile. "The Snow Queen isn't evil. She's just indifferent to human emotion."

Arnie dropped his arm and leaned forward. "But that still caused great harm. The boy is basically kidnapped and brainwashed, and the girl . . . what was her name?"

"Gerda," Ellen said, without looking at Arnie.

"Right." Arnie clasped his knees with both hands. "Anyway, she's forced to go on a mission to save the boy and nearly dies doing so. Which makes me say the Snow Queen, force of nature or not, has a lot to answer for."

"Oh, come on, Arnie, admit it—you just don't like women who wield any sort of power," Lora said.

I looked from her to Arnie and back again. There was definitely tension crackling between the two, which I found intriguing. *Has Arnie, as Lora's godfather, tried to tell her how to live her life too many times?*

Ellen stretched out her legs, wiggling rose-pink-painted toenails in white canvas sandals. "I have to agree with Lora on this one. There's nothing human about the Snow Queen. I think Andersen was contrasting the queen's—forgive the pun—*cold* logic with Gerda's warmth. Kai is caught between those two forces and only saved when Gerda's love melts his now frigid heart."

Arnie cast her a sidelong glance. "Interesting analysis, Ellie. I suppose I should concede to your superior knowledge on that subject."

Ellen shot him a side-eyed glare.

"Well, I'd certainly listen to her. Ellen is one of the smartest people I've ever met." Julie tossed her head, flipping her single braid behind her shoulder.

I could tell by Julie's bright expression that she wasn't picking up on any negative undercurrents in the room. Of course, she didn't know the history of Arnie and Ellen's relationship. "It's certainly a tale that can generate many different interpretations," I said. "What else do you have to show us, Lora?"

"Yes, I'd love to see more. I'm so impressed with your artistic talent," Sandy said. "Pete and I were just marveling at how anyone could so perfectly illuminate stories with illustrations."

Pete grinned. "Especially since I can't draw a straight line."

"That's actually difficult, at least freehand," Lora said. "And I'm not the only artist here, you know. Linnea is quite talented in her own right."

Happy that we seemed to have piloted the conversation into less turgid waters, I rose to my feet. "Please continue with your discussion. I just want to check with Alicia and see if there's anything I can help her with in the kitchen."

As I left the room, I heard Vonnie mention something about jewelry designs and reminded myself to check back with Linnea about the earrings I wanted her to create for Ellen.

When I headed back into the library, carrying the tray of hors d'oeuvres Alicia and I had made earlier, I noticed that Arnie was no longer in the room. "Did something happen to Mr. Dean?" I asked, setting the tray on the desk.

"Claimed he had a headache and was going to go up to his room to lie down," Linnea said. "I think he was just tired. He's rather elderly, you know."

"Ouch." Zach shot her a raised-eyebrow glance. "Getting a jab in at us older folks?"

Linnea made a face at him as Vonnie said, "Don't be disingenuous, Zach. Arnie's quite a bit older than you or me, even if we both have a few years on Linnea. Me more than you, of course."

"I'm sorry he's missing out on the food," I said, motioning toward the desk. "Speaking of that—I thought maybe this would be a good time to take a break from your discussion and grab some snacks and drinks. If that's okay with you, Lora."

"Of course," she replied.

As the guests stood and mingled near the linen-draped desk, I realized the pitcher of water that I'd placed in the refrigerator to cool was missing. "Oops, looks like we forgot the water. I know some people prefer that. Please, go ahead and dig in. I'll be right back."

I hurried into the kitchen. As I pulled the glass pitcher from the fridge, a noise from overhead caught my attention. "What's that?"

"Dunno," Alicia said, following my gaze up to the ceiling. "But I heard a few other thumps and bumps right before you came in. Is one of the guests upstairs?"

"Arnie Dean went up to his room. But he said he had a headache and was going to lie down."

Alicia frowned. "Doesn't sound like someone having a quiet rest. Do you want me to check on him? He is at the age where he might take a tumble and have trouble getting back on his feet, especially if he's not feeling well."

"No, I'll go. If there's a medical emergency, I should be the one to deal with it. Chapters is my property, after all."

"That it is." There was a sharp edge to Alicia's words that I decided to ignore.

After asking Alicia to carry the water pitcher into the library, I jogged down the hall, curling my fingers around the cell phone in my pocket. If Arnie had fallen, I wanted to be ready to call for help.

But when I reached the front hall, I noticed Lora descending the stairs.

"Charlotte," she said. "I thought you were in the kitchen."

"I was, but when Alicia and I heard some noises overhead, I was afraid Arnie might have fallen . . ."

"He's fine. I just checked," she said, cutting me off.

"That's good." I loosened my grip on my phone. "Thanks for looking out for him, but I imagine you want to get back to your event. I'll head that way too, if you're sure Arnie is okay."

Lora met me at the bottom of the stairs, her face calm as still water. "He said he was rummaging through his suitcase and it fell to the floor. I'm sure that's what you heard."

I wasn't so sure, but I decided not to contradict her. She was my guest, as was Arnie. If he had fallen but didn't want anyone except his goddaughter to know, it was none of my business. I motioned toward the hall. "After you."

We returned to the library, where the other guests were engaged in a lively discussion about the symbolism in Andersen's tales. Lora took a seat near her easel and immediately joined the conversation.

Crossing to the desk holding the drinks and snacks, I glanced upward as another thump reverberated from the beadboard ceiling.

"Everything okay?" Ellen asked, sotto voce, as she poured herself a glass of wine.

Glancing around to make sure no one was paying any attention, I said, "It's just . . . I don't think Arnie is quite so incapacitated as he made out. It sounds like he's rattling around upstairs rather than lying down."

Ellen filled another wineglass and handed it to me. "Curiouser and curiouser."

"It is, isn't it?" I raised my glass in a little toast. "We'll have to theorize why later."

"And down the rabbit hole we'll go," Ellen said, returning my salute.

Chapter Eleven

After cleaning up following the book club discussion, which stretched rather later into the evening than I'd expected, I overslept on Tuesday. Fortunately, Alicia said she didn't really need my help with breakfast, so after grabbing a cinnamon roll and some coffee from the kitchen, I retreated to my room to do a little online research on Stacy Wilkin.

There wasn't much to find—a few references to her on sites that forced one to pay to access court records and the like. I ignored those and kept searching, finally turning up a newspaper article that talked about Stacy opening her jewelry store in New Bern. There was a photograph of her, plus a few of the shop. One particular picture caught my eye—a display of jewelry from the store. The caption said the pieces had been fabricated based on Stacy's original designs, which intrigued me. I knew she'd sold estate jewelry as well as pieces designed by Lora and, I assumed, other artists, but I hadn't realized she'd designed anything herself.

Closer inspection of the photograph made me catch my breath. One of the pieces Stacy had claimed as her own design was a perfect match for the drawing I'd seen in Linnea Ruskin's sketchbook.

The one she seemed upset over, I thought, pondering this new clue. *Perhaps Stacy stole the design from Linnea somehow. And if she ripped off one concept, what's to say she didn't take others? She could even have commissioned Linnea to design some jewelry for the shop, then refused to acknowledge her artistic contributions.*

I had to admit it might be a possible motive for murder. Even though I'd have chosen another route, like a civil lawsuit, that didn't mean everyone would react in the same fashion to their original artwork being stolen. I knew from past experience that murderers weren't always thinking clearly when they committed their crimes. Anger and passion often overwhelmed common sense.

Examining the digitized newspaper again, I noticed a few comments listed under the original article. As I read through them, a couple sparked special interest, as they were from anonymous commenters who claimed Stacy was selling stolen goods at her store. I wondered if there was any truth to these accusations, which would certainly shine a new light on Stacy's business practices. *Perhaps she ran afoul of the wrong people,* I thought. *Cheated a criminal who then orchestrated her death.*

Shutting down my computer, I made a quick call to Detective Johnson to alert her to these new wrinkles in the case. Of course, it was up to her to decide if she wanted to question Linnea further or pursue the hot-merchandise angle. That wasn't my call, although I did file away the information to share with Ellen as part of our suspect file.

Finally taking my morning walk around eleven, I decided to stop by the Sandburg sisters' house on my way home. As longtime area residents, I figured they might know something about Samuel Joiner or one or another of my guests.

Their home, just around the corner from Chapters, was a charming bungalow with white clapboard siding and a covered porch. Tall windows with aqua shutters flanked the cobalt-blue front door. As I strolled up to the front porch, where white wicker furniture created an inviting seating area, I admired the flowers lining the concrete path. Since Ophelia Sandburg's gardening expertise was renowned in Beaufort, it was no surprise that her front yard consisted primarily of flower beds rather than grass. Her small backyard was also filled with shrubs and flowers as well as a few ornamental trees. She actually grew so many blooming plants that she made a little extra money supplying fresh flowers for local businesses, including Julie's bookstore and Pete and Sandy's café.

Bernadette greeted me at the front door. "Hello, Charlotte. So nice of you to stop by," she said as she ushered me inside. "Can I get you anything to eat? Ophelia made sticky buns this morning."

Although I loved Ophelia's baking, I refused the offer, having already eaten a pastry earlier. "But I'd love a glass of water," I said, taking a seat on a sofa covered in rose-patterned chintz.

Ophelia appeared in the open kitchen door. "We also have lemonade, and I'm happy to make coffee."

"Just water is fine," I said, allowing my gaze to wander for a moment. The bungalow's pale-jade walls and white cotton curtains edged with lace lent an airy quality to the living room, which was also filled with wicker plant stands and simple, whitewashed wooden furniture. An eclectic collection of vases overflowing with Ophelia's flowers and a few watercolor seascapes provided splashes of bright color.

"So sorry we couldn't be at the book club discussion last night," Bernadette said, as she sat down in one of the periwinkle armchairs facing the sofa. "Did anything interesting happen?"

"Yes, tell us all the gossip." Ophelia bustled into the room and handed me a tumbler filled with ice-cold water before settling into a matching armchair. "If there is any, I mean."

I took a sip from the glass before answering. "You mean, which of my guests do I think is a murderer?"

Ophelia shared a look with her sister. "It is another fascinating mystery, isn't it? Who'd want to kill a middle-aged lady who owned a jewelry store? I mean, I could see it happening at her store—during a robbery or something. But I doubt she'd carry her valuable inventory with her on vacation." Ophelia tugged the hem of her sunflower-print skirt over her bony knees. "The thing is, if you came looking for our input, I'm afraid we won't be able to offer much help."

"We don't know any of your current guests, you see," Bernadette added, stretching out her stocky legs. Unlike Ophelia, who was dressed for a garden party, Bernadette wore khaki shorts and a navy-blue polo shirt.

"I'm not sure about that," I said, before sharing Arnie Dean's story about visiting Chapters in the past. "Of course, Isabella gave so many parties, he may have attended ones you skipped."

"Let me think." Ophelia fiddled with the lace trimming the collar of her white cotton blouse before turning to her sister. "There was someone named Dean at a few parties we attended, wasn't there, Bernie? I vaguely remember a man with that last name. Couldn't be this guy, though, as this person was already late middle-aged at the time."

"Dean is the last name?" Bernadette kicked off her sandals and put her feet up on the tufted hassock in front of her chair. "There was a Claude Dean who was a big-time lawyer and politician in this area back in the sixties and seventies. I believe he was a regular at Isabella's parties." She rolled her eyes. "A real schmoozer, if you know what I mean. Good-looking guy, in a florid sort of way. Thick white hair, sparkling green eyes, and an exuberant personality. I remember he was far too hail-fellow-well-met for my taste, although others seemed to like him well enough."

"Oh, right." Ophelia widened her pale eyes. "I remember that fellow. He always reminded me of a sleazy Santa Claus."

I scooted to the front edge of the sofa. "That has to have been Arnie Dean's father. I wouldn't consider Arnie sleazy, exactly, but he does resemble a slightly slimmed down Santa."

"Come to think of it, Fee"—Bernadette tapped her chin with one finger—"wasn't there a young man who accompanied Claude Dean to one of the parties you attended when I was off nursing in 'Nam? I seem to recall you mentioning that in a letter."

"Oh heavens, that was so long ago." Ophelia patted down a flyaway strand of her fire-engine-red-dyed hair. "I can't remember all the details that far in the past." She scrunched up her rather beaky nose. "I may have mentioned something like that, but I'm not sure. The main reason I remember Claude Dean is because of his involvement in trying to solve that rash of jewelry heists in the seventies."

"Right." Bernadette snapped her fingers. "He was running for office on a law-and-order ticket."

"Jewelry heists?" I asked, my curiosity piqued. "What was that all about?"

Bernadette shrugged. "I wasn't here at the time, but I recall Fee telling me about some sort of cat burglar activity in the area."

"Someone, or maybe a group of thieves, robbed a lot of the wealthier homes, stealing mostly high-end jewelry." Ophelia's eyes sparkled at the memory. "Thefts also happened at some society parties, so of course Isabella told all her guests to be on their guard. Some people were frightened enough to avoid large events, but of course your great-aunt wasn't about to cancel a party because of some common thief."

"Did she ever lose anything to this burglar?" I asked, recalling photos of my great-aunt wearing some pretty spectacular jewelry. She'd stopped doing that in later years, when I knew her, choosing to wear inexpensive costume pieces instead. For good reason, although few people knew why, since she'd wanted that information kept under wraps.

Bernadette cleared her throat, drawing me out of my musings. "I never heard Isabella claim she'd been robbed, of jewelry or anything else."

"Wait, now I remember. It wasn't Isabella, but someone at one of her parties did lose a valuable emerald-and-diamond ring," Ophelia said, bouncing out of her chair. "You weren't here at the time, Bernie, but there was quite a flap about it. Isabella was pretty dismissive of the whole affair. Apparently the woman who lost the ring left it lying in one of the bathrooms. Isabella said that was careless, although I guess the guest took it off to wash her hands or something."

"You think it could've been stolen by the thief working the area at the time?" I asked, with a lift of my eyebrows. "I suppose it's possible, but it's more likely that it just fell down the drain or into a trash can."

"That was Isabella's theory as well. She actually refused to bring the police in on it. Which is a little strange, if you think about it." Ophelia wrinkled her brow. "In fact, I believe Isabella just paid the guest what the ring was worth, which wasn't an inconsiderable amount."

I bit back a comment, bobbing my head and muttering something about my great-aunt's generosity. I thought I knew why Isabella hadn't wanted to involve the police—she wouldn't have done anything that could've jeopardized her covert career as a spy for U.S. intelligence. It was even possible she'd been running some sort of information-gathering or surveillance operation during the party where the ring was lost and hadn't wanted the authorities to look too closely into the backgrounds of her guests.

"At any rate, the way Claude Dean comes into all this is that he made a lot of proclamations about the need to solve the thefts and arrest the culprit." Bernadette shrugged. "Even I heard about that, from the newspapers Fee sent me in 'Nam. Typical political pontificating. He swore that if he was elected, he'd bring people like the cat burglar to justice."

"And was he elected?" I asked.

"Oh yes, by a landslide," Bernadette said. "But did he ever fulfill that particular promise? No, I'm afraid not. That string of thefts was never solved."

"They just stopped," said Ophelia, who had remained standing. "Everyone assumed the thief or thieves simply moved on to another hunting ground." She pointed toward my tumbler. "Can I get you some more water?"

"Yes, thanks," I replied, handing her the glass.

When Ophelia left the room, Bernadette met my gaze with a wry smile. "I think Fee found the thief rather glamorous. She certainly went on and on about them in her letters. I suppose it may have had something to do with that movie that starred Cary Grant. She was a bit obsessed with that film when she was a girl."

"*To Catch a Thief*, with Grant and Grace Kelly?"

"That's the one. I tried to tell her that real thieves were never that handsome or charming, but I'm not sure she ever listened to me." Bernadette flashed me a grin. "She didn't, often."

"I think younger sisters are like that. I know I didn't always pay attention to my older sister, and as for Melinda"—I grinned— "she considered both Sophie and me to be hopelessly uncool."

Bernadette leaned forward and gripped her knees with both hands. "But still, we'd jump in front of a bullet for them, wouldn't we?"

"Take a bullet?" Ophelia asked, returning to the living room with my tumbler of water. "That would have to be for someone special," she added, as she handed me the glass. "I'd like to think I'd be the kind of person to do that for anyone, even a stranger, but I must confess I probably wouldn't."

"I was talking about family. Difficult as they may sometimes be, I expect we'd do anything for them," Bernadette said.

Ophelia cast her sister a smile before sitting back down. "I'd certainly take a bullet for you, Bernie. Even if you do get on my nerves sometimes, with all your logic and practical thinking."

"One of us has to stay tethered to the earth," Bernie said dryly.

Her sister settled back in her chair, the blue upholstery creating the perfect background for her vivid red hair. "Glad that's you."

"Me too," Bernadette said with a grin. "It means I get to enjoy your flights of fancy without actually having to live with the consequences."

Ophelia fluttered her pale lashes. "What consequences? I don't recall any terrible consequences stemming from my more creative lifestyle."

"Because I always sort things out." Bernadette dropped her feet to the floor and focused on me. "Anyway, tell us your thoughts about the guests, Charlotte. Anyone seem suspicious?"

"Actually, quite a few of them do." I mentioned Zach's conflict with the victim as well as his apparent problems with his ex-wife. "Vonnie Allen and Linnea Ruskin also seem to have had some sort of issue with Ms. Wilkin, and then there's Captain Joiner."

Ophelia waved her hand through the air. "He's a blowhard, but I've never heard of him being involved in any real violence. I think we would have, living in the area and having the connections we do."

"I suppose that's one point in his favor," I said.

Bernadette crossed her stocky legs. "What about your other guests? That Arnie Dean seems to have a tie to Chapters, at least from the past, although I don't know what that would have to do with this murder."

"True, it doesn't appear like that would have anything to do with Stacy Wilkin's death, although . . ." I closed my lips over the words that had almost slipped off my tongue. No sense in sharing my suspicions about Arnie borrowing photographs to make copies. If he didn't return the pictures before he left, it would be another matter, but for now I needed to give him the benefit of the doubt. *And you can't rule out Vonnie either,* I reminded myself. "Anyway, there's also the matter of the manner of death. Sodium cyanide isn't impossible to get, but you would need some sort of reasonable access. Since Zach Bell is a chemist, that's a mark against him."

Ophelia pressed her palms together. "Oh dear, he's a scientist? I guess he could get his hands on something like that more easily than some."

"But isn't one of your guests a jewelry designer?" Bernadette asked. "I think I remember you mentioning something about that when you were talking to our book club last month."

"Lora Kane is an artist who also designs and creates jewelry," I said. "And she's training Linnea Ruskin, another artist, in the craft. So two of the guests, actually." I tipped my head and studied Bernadette's thoughtful expression. "Why?"

"Because sodium cyanide is used in that work." Bernadette cast Ophelia a glance. "Remember, Fee? We learned about it when you and I took that jewelry-making course at the community college."

"Oh, right. It had something to do with gold plating." Ophelia shuddered. "I wanted nothing to do with that. Sounded so dangerous."

I slid to the edge of the sofa. "So it might be something a jewelry craftsperson would have in their studio?"

"Absolutely. Which means both of those guests could've had access to it," Bernadette said. "As well as that chemist fellow."

"Which doesn't narrow things down much." I glanced at my watch. "Shoot, I need to get back to Chapters. I'm supposed to be helping Alicia with some light cleaning today."

"Glad you could stop by," Bernadette said, rising to her feet. "Sorry we couldn't help you with any juicy gossip on your guests, but if we hear anything . . ."

"We'll definitely let you know," Ophelia chimed in.

It wasn't really their job to help me in my amateur sleuthing, but since I was eager to obtain any information that could help solve the murder, I didn't bother to dissuade them.

Chapter Twelve

When I got back to Chapters, I found Alicia dusting in the music room.

"You didn't have to tackle this," I said. "I was going to clean in here after lunch."

Alicia flipped her feather duster over the keys of the grand piano that dominated one corner of the room. "No problem. I'd rather dust in here than in the library, so feel free to take that on instead."

"I actually did that yesterday." I straightened a corner of a landscape painting hanging on one of the creamy plaster walls. "Maybe not as thoroughly as I should have, but close enough for government work," I added, wrinkling my nose as I realized the paradox of that cliché. In reality, the type of government work that my great-aunt and Ellen had done, and Gavin still did, required a great deal of attention and dedication.

"Then you can take a break." Alicia fluttered the duster over the side of the piano. "This might be a good day for that, actually. I think we have enough leftover snacks for tonight's smaller event. I can just supplement with some of the crackers and cheese we always keep on hand. It's only the five guests this evening, right? Not any of our local book club members?"

"That's correct."

"We should be fine, then." Alicia turned and tapped the handle of the duster against her palm. "Did you ever speak with Christopher?"

"Not yet." I met her expectant stare. "Which gives me an idea. Why don't I take this free time, until evening, anyway, and see if I can meet up with your cousin?"

Alicia bobbed her head. "Good thinking. He should be available. My aunt told me he had to take a few weeks off fishing due to a leg injury. I can call him to set up a time, if you want."

"That would be great, but first let me check with Ellen and see if she's free this afternoon."

Reaching Ellen on my cell phone, I confirmed her availability. Alicia headed into the office to make a quick call to her cousin. She returned in a few minutes, waving a scrap of paper. "Here's Christopher's address and phone number. He said anytime this afternoon was fine."

I spent the rest of the morning tidying the library in preparation for the event scheduled for the evening—a discussion focusing on *The Secret Garden* and a few other classic children's books from the early twentieth century. After a quick lunch, I changed into a gauzy turquoise tunic top and white cotton slacks for my trip into Morehead City.

Ellen had agreed to drive, with me acting as navigator. As we crossed the bridge that led to Morehead City, I brought up the issue of the missing photographs.

"I seriously suspect it was your old friend Arnie, borrowing them to make copies, but of course that's just my guess," I told her. "The only other possibility is Vonnie Allen, just because she seemed so fascinated with the history of Chapters and all its illustrious guests. But that's more of a long shot. Anyway, I just can't imagine anyone but those two having any interest in pictures from Isabella's old parties."

Ellen cast me a thoughtful look. "You could be right. I assume you plan to make sure the photos are returned before any of the guests leave?"

"Of course. I don't mind someone borrowing the pictures, but I certainly won't allow anyone to leave Chapters with them." I stared out the side window, taking in the view of the water sparkling in the bright May sunlight. Numerous boats dotted the calm waters of Beaufort Channel Creek, which could be navigated to reach Taylor's Creek and the Beaufort harbor. That wasn't surprising— there was a public boat landing nearby, as well as a marina. "Tell me a little more about Arnie. I find him rather hard to read."

"He always was," Ellen said, keeping her eyes fixed on the road. "I thought I knew him well, but then he did a total one-eighty on me."

I glanced over at her handsome profile. "He seems interested in reviving your friendship."

"Perhaps. I'm not sure I trust him enough to give that a try, though." Ellen met my questioning gaze with a smile. "Not really looking for a romance, you know, despite what Julie might think."

"Dear Julie," I said. "She's always trying to match people up. At least she's finally in a good relationship herself." Glancing down at Alicia's directions, I added, "We have to turn right in a few blocks."

"Onto Twentieth Street, I assume?"

"Yes." I peered down again at Alicia's scrawls. "Then we drive inland for a bit, which seems strange to me. I thought a boat captain would want to live closer to the sound, or at least Calico Creek."

Ellen shot me a raised-eyebrow glance. "Doesn't seem that odd to me. Property prices skyrocket the closer you are to the water. I doubt a charter boat captain, especially one who started his own business instead of inheriting it, could afford to live right on the water." She rolled her shoulders, as if loosening any tension. "You and I were lucky enough to be given our Beaufort properties. I doubt either one of us could've afforded to buy them on our own."

"Absolutely not." I offered Ellen additional instructions on where and when to turn before adding, "Speaking of Chapters, there's something I wanted to ask you."

"As the trustee of Isabella's estate, or as a friend?"

"Both, really." I fiddled with the strap of my purse. "It's just that I've been thinking . . ."

"About whether you want to continue to run the B and B?" Ellen turned onto a residential street lined with modest but well-kept homes.

I took a deep breath. "It's not that I would ever consider selling Chapters. I want to honor Isabella's memory and keep it in the family. But I have considered hiring someone to manage the place so I could return to teaching."

"It was this one, right?" Ellen said, slowing the car and pointing toward the house numbers painted on a mailbox mounted on an old anchor instead of a post.

I nodded and, as she parked in front of the single-story brick home, unbuckled my seat belt. "I would always keep Alicia on as housekeeper and cook, of course. I've reassured her about that."

"It would be impossible to replace her." Ellen swiveled to look directly into my face. "You should do what your heart tells you to do, Charlotte. I know you miss teaching, and I also realize that Chapters is too much of a full-time job for you to work elsewhere, even part-time. So I would totally understand if you wanted to hire someone to take over as manager. I just hope you'll continue to live at Chapters. I'd miss having you as a neighbor—and investigating mysteries with you too," she added, with a warm smile.

"That's my plan. I certainly think I could pick up a teaching job in the area. Experienced teachers are in high demand these days."

Ellen studied me for a moment before dropping her car keys into her purse. "Good to know you plan to stay, although I suspect things could change. But, speaking of sleuthing, shall we get to it? Mr. Freedman is expecting us, I believe."

"He said we could drop by anytime this afternoon, but yes, we should probably not loiter outside his house too long," I said, climbing out of the car.

The front yard was a neatly mown stretch of grass, devoid of trees or flower beds, although a row of boxwoods hugged the foundation of the house. *Probably too busy with his business to engage in much gardening*, I told myself as Ellen and I waited on the concrete porch after ringing the doorbell.

The door was opened by an attractive woman wearing denim shorts and a faded concert tee featuring a band I didn't recognize. "Hi, you must be Alicia's friends," she said, giving us the once-over with her thickly-lashed ebony eyes. "I'm Dana, Chris's wife."

"Thanks so much for allowing us to visit," I said, after we'd introduced ourselves and followed Dana into the house. "I know Mr. Freedman is recovering from an injury, so we won't keep him long. We just have a few questions."

"Oh, don't worry." Dana swept her hand through the air. "Chris is so bored and antsy he'll probably try to talk your ears off. You'll be looking for an escape route long before he wants you to go, I'm sure." Her laughter was bright as a string of bells.

"What's that?" asked a deep male voice from the adjacent room. "Are you talking smack about me again, wife of mine?"

"Of course not, dear. Just warning these fine ladies about how much you love a good conversation." Dana gave us a wink. "This way." She led us around the oval oak table dominating the formal dining room and into a combination family room and kitchen.

The great room gave off an air of well-worn comfort. A large leather sectional faced the brick fireplace, and an oversized TV screen hung above a rustic pine mantel. Christopher Freedman was lounging on the sofa, his leg propped up on an ottoman. A swathe of bandages encased the lower portion of one of his legs.

"Hello, you must be the two ladies Alicia mentioned over the phone," he said. "Sorry for not getting up, but I'm trying to get this darned thing to heal so I can get back to work sooner rather than later."

"No problem at all." Ellen crossed to the sofa and offered him her hand. "I'm Ellen Montgomery, and this is Charlotte Reed. Charlotte owns Chapters."

"So my cousin's boss lady, heh?" Christopher's deep-brown eyes reminded me of Alicia, as did his round face and thick head of curly black hair.

"Sorry about your injury," I said, sinking into one of the upholstered chairs that Dana had pulled up closer to the sofa.

"It's not too bad." Christopher tapped the side of his nose with one finger. "Mostly an inconvenience. I'm supposed to stay off the leg for a while, which is a problem when you run a fishing charter. You have to be on your feet constantly for that gig."

"This happened when you were out on your boat?" Ellen asked as she sat in the other upholstered chair.

"Yeah. Occupational hazard, really. I got tangled up in some tackle and fell, slicing my leg open."

"Because one of your customers left the tackle lying about," Dana said, shooting Ellen and me a swift glance. "Chris is vigilant about safety practices on the boat, but sadly, the people he takes out aren't always so careful."

Christopher held up his hands. "They're amateurs. It's easy to make a mistake when you get caught up in the excitement of a great catch."

"If you say so." Dana's pursed lips relaxed and curved upward. "Can I get you ladies something to drink? We have soft drinks, juices, and lemonade. And water, of course."

"I'm fine, thanks," I replied, at the same moment Ellen asked for a glass of water.

Dana headed into the kitchen. "Sure you don't want something, Charlotte?" she called out as she walked behind a butcher-block-topped island.

"No, I'm good." I turned my focus to Christopher. "Did Alicia explain why we wanted to chat with you?"

"Some questions about my old boss, she said." Christopher winced as he shifted the position of his injured leg. "Not sure what you're looking for, but I do have some stories. Joiner was an . . . interesting fellow."

Ellen tipped her head, keeping her gaze fixed on Christopher. "You didn't enjoy working for him, I take it?"

"Can't say I did. Not that I didn't learn a lot. The man is a great sailor and a better fisherman. But he's difficult. Arrogant, judgmental, and demanding. It was always his way or the highway." Christopher grinned. "I chose the highway."

"Thank goodness," Dana said, as she crossed the room. After handing Ellen the glass of water, she perched on the end of the sofa. "That man was the very devil to work for. Always docking Chris's pay for the least little thing."

"It did teach me how to run a shipshape boat," Chris said mildly. Stretching his arm across the back of the couch, he tugged one of the tight braids that hugged his wife's scalp. "Dana doesn't like him because he's a raging misogynist. Can't say I blame her. He doesn't treat woman well. One of those *I'm the man, so do what I say* types."

"Not my favorite thing," Dana said with a cheeky grin. "Certainly not something I find attractive."

Ellen crossed one ankle over the other, showing off her bead-embroidered leather sandals. "Neither do I, and I know Charlotte doesn't like that sort of man, so I'm sure we'd share your assessment of Captain Joiner."

"He's a person of interest in this latest murder, isn't he?" Christopher surveyed Ellen and me intently.

"Where did you hear that?" I asked with surprise. To my knowledge, the police hadn't shared any information about suspects with the media.

Christopher pulled his arm away from the back of the sofa and leaned forward. "I didn't. Just put two and two together when I heard the victim's name."

"You knew her?" Ellen asked.

"Only slightly. But I was still working for Sam when the lawsuit stuff happened, so I heard plenty. All from his side, of course."

"They had a fling, you know." Dana cast me a conspiratorial glance. "Sam Joiner and the victim. I bet he hasn't told the police that little tidbit."

I scooted to the edge of my chair. "We wouldn't know, either way, but he certainly didn't say anything about that when he told me about his past issues with Ms. Wilkin." Focusing on Christopher, I fought to keep excitement from sharpening my tone. "They really had an affair?"

Christopher shrugged. "I wouldn't call it that. It wasn't that serious. At least, I didn't think so."

"Not on Stacy Wilkin's part, maybe, but I believe Sam was more invested. Which is why he was so angry when she and that loser boyfriend of hers basically cheated him," Dana said.

"He was pretty furious." Christopher sat back, his expression growing thoughtful. "More so than I thought was normal. I mean, those two did mess up one of his boats and skip town without paying for the damage, but it's not like that hadn't occurred before." He met my surprised gaze with a wry smile. "It happens. People aren't always upstanding or honest, you know."

"I'm well aware of that," Ellen said. "So you think Captain Joiner's reaction in this case was more extreme than expected?"

"Definitely. And I agree with Dana that Sam was probably embarrassed and angry over the way Stacy Wilkin used him before unceremoniously dumping him." Christopher shared a glance with his wife. "Dana and I think the woman only seduced Sam to try to get a discount on the boat rental. Which apparently worked, from what I noticed on the books. The rental was not at the usual rate."

Dana shifted, bouncing the sofa cushions. "And Chris told me he thought the boyfriend's boat license was phony too. But Joiner didn't want to listen when Chris brought that to his attention."

"He was doing a favor for a woman he hoped to date after the boat trip, I suppose," Ellen said.

"Seemed like it to me. At the time I thought the boyfriend was really dense, since he seemed oblivious to the fact that Sam had hooked up with his woman, but after the fact"—Christopher tapped his temple with his index finger—"I realized he had to be in on the con all along."

I tipped my head and studied Christopher's sober face. "Do you believe Captain Joiner came to the same conclusion?"

"Absolutely. He told me as much."

"Chris thinks that's why Joiner's held a grudge for so long," Dana said.

Christopher held up his hands. "Not to spill all the guy's secrets. It's just . . . well, even though he's always had great luck catching fish, his track record with the ladies isn't so good."

"Which means being used and betrayed by someone he fancied might have really stabbed him in the heart." I met Christopher's gaze. "You should talk to the police. They already have him on their radar, and this information certainly gives him more of a motive."

"Financial grudges are one thing," Ellen said, "but add in anger over a lover's betrayal . . ."

As I shot her a quick glance, I couldn't help but notice the distant look in her eyes. *She's thinking about Arnie, I bet. Even though they weren't lovers, he probably felt betrayed when their close friendship didn't lead to more. Of course,* I reminded myself, *so did she, when he cut off that friendship because she didn't want what he did.*

"I guess I should call the Beaufort police?" Christopher sighed. "I don't look forward to getting involved. The fishing community is a very small world, and speaking out about Sam might make me some enemies. He's part of the old-boy network, and they already look at me with some suspicion." He lifted his hands. "Young and Black is not the norm for captains, you know."

"I'm sure the authorities can keep your information anonymous," Ellen said.

I wasn't so sure. "Ask to talk to Detective Johnson. We trust her to handle sensitive information more carefully than most."

"Okay, if you think she'll be discreet, I'm willing to share what I just told you," Christopher said. "I don't really want to get Sam in trouble, even though I'm not fond of him. But I also don't want to allow anyone to get away with murder."

"And if he didn't kill anyone, he has nothing to worry about," Dana said, patting her husband's thigh.

Christopher laid his hand over hers. "Guess you're right. Anyway, I imagine other factors will weigh equally as heavy, like how the victim was killed." He fixed his dark-eyed gaze on me. "According to the news I've heard, it was poison, right?"

"Yes, and that might be a factor in Captain Joiner's favor." I relaxed my back into the cushions of my chair. "It was cyanide, which I expect isn't something your former boss could get his hands on that easily."

Christopher's sharp intake of breath made me sit up straighter. "Sodium cyanide?" he asked, in a strangled voice.

"Yes, why?" Ellen shared a look with me before turning back to Christopher and Dana.

"Because Sam did have access to that. He wasn't supposed to, but he did." Christopher cleared his throat. "It isn't really something we're permitted to use, legally, but some older captains don't care. It's for the rats, you see. Always a problem on boats."

I opened my mouth but snapped it shut again when I couldn't think of any response.

"Captain Joiner kept sodium cyanide around to make rat poison?" Ellen asked. "You actually saw this?"

Christopher's grip on Dana's hand visibly tightened. "I saw him mix the poison, more than once. So he had it and knew where to get more."

"Well now, I think you have quite a few things to share with Detective Johnson." Ellen uncrossed her ankles and tapped the carpet with her sandaled foot. "All of which are rather important."

Christopher's eyes were shadowed with sadness. It was obvious to me that, despite his personal dislike, he still respected his old boss. "All of which might turn Sam into the number-one suspect," he said.

Chapter Thirteen

After exacting another promise that Christopher would share his information with the authorities, we left the Freedmans' house and headed back to Chapters.

On the way home I decided to avoid talking about the case and instead shifted the conversation to our latest garden exploits. This year I'd started a small vegetable patch, hoping to be able to supply some of the fresh produce that Alicia and Damian used for special dinners and other events as well as for our own daily consumption.

"Never really tried to grow tomatoes or anything like that before, so I thought you could give me some pointers," I told Ellen.

She was more than happy to share what she'd learned from her own gardening experiences, so we chatted about organic pest control and related subjects all the way home.

Ellen dropped me off at Chapters, saying she needed to run some errands. As I entered through the back porch, I heard Alicia speaking with someone in the kitchen. She didn't sound happy, which immediately put me on my guard.

"Hello there," I said, as I stepped into the kitchen to face Alicia and Lora. "Everything okay?"

"Just peachy," Alicia muttered, before spinning around and flipping the faucet to draw water into the sink. When she started banging a few pots together, I turned to Lora.

"Is there something you need? I'm happy to help if Alicia is too busy. I know she's probably trying to get everything ready for tonight's event."

"That's the thing." Lora offered me an apologetic smile. "I've decided to cancel the discussion for tonight, as well as the rest of the planned events for the week."

"I'm sorry to hear that," I said, observing the tension in Alicia's raised shoulders. "We're happy to facilitate, if it's a matter of your time . . ."

"Nothing like that. It's just that no one seems interested in group activities anymore." Lora lifted her hands. "With all the police questioning and news reports, I honestly think we're all starting to look at each other with suspicion. It seems everyone would just prefer to do their own thing."

"If you're allowed to leave town, I'm happy to refund a portion of your fees," I said, earning a loud grunt from Alicia.

Lora arched her thin eyebrows. "That's sweet of you, but the police are asking us to stay in town. So I think we'll continue to hunker down here, if it's all the same to you."

"Of course, of course, we're happy to have you," I said, hoping my voice didn't betray my white lie.

"Well, I believe I'll take a little walk and scope out more of the town," Lora said, before wishing me a good afternoon.

Alicia waited until Lora exited the kitchen before turning to face me. Hands on her hips, she surveyed me with an expression that radiated displeasure. "After we cleaned and fixed all the food, she tells us the thing is off."

"To be fair, we needed to clean anyway, and you did say that most of the food for tonight's event would consist of leftovers," I said.

Alicia sniffed. "It's the principle of the thing. I think it would've been much more polite to inform us as soon as she knew they weren't going forward with any more events."

Since I actually agreed, I didn't contradict this statement. "Changing the subject, Ellen and I did glean some interesting information from your cousin. From what Christopher told us, it seems Captain Samuel Joiner is a very likely suspect."

"Wouldn't surprise me." Alicia dropped her arms to her sides. "You said he showed up here uninvited the day of the murder."

"And Stacy Wilkin had her cup with her when he confronted her on the front porch. It was sitting on the buffet table too, so he could've had access to it while they were arguing."

"But that seems like a weird stroke of luck." Alicia's eyes narrowed. "For him, I mean. He'd have to have shown up with the poison, just hoping to catch her alone. How likely is that?"

Tugging on my dangling earring, I acknowledged the accuracy of her assessment. "It does sound like an unlikely string of coincidences. But stranger things have happened."

"I don't dispute that." Alicia rolled her eyes. "The longer I live, the less the world makes sense."

I studied her face for a moment, noticing the deep lines bracketing her mouth. "Since we don't have an event to manage now, why don't you take the evening off? I know you like to have dinner with your mom whenever you can. I can easily stay here and take care of anything the guests need."

Alicia's expression brightened. "Thanks, I think I'll do that." She whipped off her apron. "Starting now."

"Sounds good," I said. "You have keys, so you can let yourself in if you get back after eleven."

"Won't be that late. Mom goes to bed pretty early these days."

I smiled. "You could leave her house and enjoy a night on the town. I know, working here, you don't get too many opportunities to experience the local nightlife."

Alicia snapped the apron through the air. "I'm too old for such shenanigans. No, I'll just visit with Mom and head back. It'll probably be around eight or so."

I nodded my approval of this plan and left, making a beeline my bedroom to change clothes. I was determined to put in a few hours of work in the garden, which needed at least a cursory weeding.

Later, after taking a shower, I settled on the front porch with a glass of ice water and a copy of *The Secret Garden*, one of the books we'd planned to discuss at the canceled evening event. I'd read it a few times before and had recently skimmed it to refresh my memory, but I thought I might as well embark on a solid reread.

A few chapters in, I was distracted by footfalls clattering against the front steps of the porch. I glanced up to meet Julie's questioning gaze.

"Oh dear, I knew there was something I forgot," I said, as she crossed to my rocking chair. "I meant to call you about tonight, but it totally escaped my mind."

"Is the event off?" Julie asked, tossing her long hair behind her shoulders.

I snapped my book shut. "All of them are. Lora told me the guests decided they weren't up to any discussions or parties or anything. Honestly, I agree with what Lora told me about them all being a bit suspicious of one another at this point."

"That's not too surprising. When one of your compatriots is murdered . . ." Julie allowed this idea to drift away on the warm evening air.

"I agree. It would certainly put a damper on your enthusiasm for communal activities." I rose to my feet. "Listen, since you're here already and have obviously cleared your calendar for this nonexistent event, why not come in and share a glass of wine and a chat with me? I wouldn't mind the company."

"I did arrange for one of my part-timers to close up Book-waves, so I might as well make good use of my rare free time." Julie followed me into the house, the soles of her leather sandals slapping against the hardwood floors. "Where are all the guests, by the way? And Alicia?"

"Since the event was canceled, I gave Alicia the evening off. She's visiting her mother, and the guests are all out to dinner. Not as a group, I guess, although I think some of them are still friendly, like Arnie and Lora."

"And Zach and Linnea," Julie said, grabbing a couple of glasses as I pulled a bottle of white wine from the refrigerator.

"What makes you say that?" I asked.

Julie swung the two wineglasses by their stems as if she were ringing handbells. "Oh, just my intuition. I've seen them around town, looking rather cozy, if you know what I mean."

"Really?" I pondered this information in light of Zach's divorce and Linnea's rather questionable corroboration of his reason for searching the garden as I led the way into the library.

Julie plopped down in one of the leather armchairs. "Yep. And speaking of close friends or whatever you're calling it these days—heard from Gavin lately?"

"Actually, I have." I pulled the cork from the bottle and poured two full goblets of wine. "He just finished another job," I added, handing one of the glasses to Julie.

Settling back in her chair, Julie gazed at me, curiosity burning in her eyes. "Some research project, I take it?"

I made noncommittal noises as I sat down in the other armchair. "Something like that. He doesn't give me all the details. Some of the research is proprietary, you see."

"Hmm." Julie swirled the wine in her glass. "Scott's off as well. A camping trip with his daughter. He did invite me to go along," she added, with a little smile, "but I didn't think I could get away from the store, what with it being so close to the holiday weekend and all."

I took a sip of my wine and cast her a sly smile. "And then there's the whole camping aspect."

"Then there's that," Julie said, lifting her glass in a little salute. "You know me too well."

"I honestly can't picture you in the wilderness with all the bugs and snakes and things," I said.

Julie gave an exaggerated shudder. "And bears. Don't forget the bears."

"Always have to bear in mind the bears," I said, earning a well-deserved comical facial expression from Julie.

She pointed at the copy of *The Secret Garden* I'd laid on the wide arm of my chair. "I don't mind that it's just you and me chatting this evening, but it's a shame we won't get to talk about that book. I was looking forward to it. I remember when I was a kid, being mesmerized by the idea of bringing a garden back to life."

"We can still talk about it," I said, setting my wineglass on a side table and picking up the book. "Nothing wrong with a two-person book discussion."

"True." Julie sipped her wine for a moment as I flipped through a few pages. "I was also struck by how unpleasant the main character was at first. I get a lot of complaints from my regular customers about unlikable protagonists, even if the point is that they grow and change throughout the course of the book."

"Especially female protagonists, I bet." I held up an illustration of a very dour Mary Lennox. "She does start out as an entitled little brat."

"But it's kind of understandable, with her having lost her parents and entire way of life. I'm not sure I'd have been the most charming and gracious kid if that had happened to me."

"Me either," I agreed, lowering the book to my lap. "And it's not like her parents paid attention to her when they were alive. They pretty much ignored her, if I recall correctly."

Julie nodded. "That's right. I think that's one of the major themes—how neglected things, whether gardens or people, tend to grow stunted and twisted."

"But can be brought back to health and happiness if one simply makes an effort to work with them," I said, my thoughts drifting to my past experiences with certain students. "Paying attention and spending time does make a difference. I learned that while I was teaching."

"Nurture over nature?" Julie asked, with a lift of her eyebrows.

"I don't think it's all one or the other. Using this story"—I tapped the cover of *The Secret Garden*—"as an example, it really takes working with nature doesn't it? You can't fight against it."

"You just have to nurture it?" Julie asked, with a grin. "I see your point. And I also notice how your eyes light up when you talk about students and teaching. You really miss it, don't you?"

I took a long a swallow of wine before answering. "Yes, I do. And I'm actually considering . . ."

My words were cut off by loud banging and raised voices. Setting down my glass, I leapt to my feet to follow Julie out of the library.

"Coming from the kitchen," she whispered. "Do you think we should call the police?"

"Wait." I laid a hand over the cell phone she'd pulled from her pocket. "Let's listen for a moment. It could just be a couple of the guests having an argument. I don't want to involve the authorities in that."

But the next words rolling out from the kitchen disabused me of this notion.

"If you're innocent," Alicia said, her voice thinned like wire stretched to its breaking point, "you have nothing to worry about."

"Easy for you to say. You don't know what it's like, everybody poking in your business, looking to pin a murder on you just because you might've lost your temper now and then," said a gruff male voice.

Captain Samuel Joiner, I thought, sharing a concerned look with Julie. I held a finger to my lips and tapped her phone. "Go. Front porch. Make that call," I mouthed.

She nodded and slid her feet out of her sandals before tiptoeing to the front door.

"Don't know what you think you're going to accomplish, holding me here," Alicia said, as I crept toward the kitchen.

"I want you to admit you put that cousin of yours up to smearing my name. Not sure why, unless it was some sort of payback." A scraping sound made me wonder if Alicia was struggling to break free of Joiner's hold. "He told your family all sorts of tall tales about me, I bet. Just 'cause I was a little hard on him when he worked for me."

"It wasn't anything like that." Alicia's voice had gained an edge that told me she'd had just about enough.

Which could be dangerous, depending on whether Joiner had only his hands, or a knife.

Or a gun.

I shimmied along the wall, reaching the opening to the kitchen. Peeking around the doorframe, I noticed that Joiner had his back to me. His strong arms wrapped Alicia in a bear hug. Since she was shorter than him, all I could see was her legs and feet, but it was clear from the movement that she was struggling against Joiner's grip.

I slipped into the kitchen, my back against the wall. Sliding as quietly as possible, I reached the wall rack that held some of our sturdier skillets and pans.

"I'm not doing Christopher's bidding, if that's what you think. We aren't that close. Just mentioned that he'd worked for you at one time, and Ms. Reed and Ms. Montgomery went to his house to speak with him. But they sure didn't share anything he said with me. I just know they talked, that's all." Alicia squirmed free enough to twist and glance around Sam Joiner's body.

I pressed my hand to my mouth as she caught sight of me.

"Well, somebody sure set the authorities on me. They showed up just as I pulled in from a charter late this afternoon and didn't even let me properly stow anything on the boat before they hauled me off to the station for more questioning. Asking me about rat poison and all sorts of ridiculous stuff." Joiner spat out a vile epithet. "Acted like I was some sort of dangerous criminal."

"Doubt this little stunt will help clear your name," Alicia said, with a bravado that I hoped meant Joiner didn't have a weapon.

Surely she wouldn't be so reckless if he was holding a knife or gun, I thought, realizing with a sickening roll of my stomach that I couldn't be sure. Alicia didn't take nonsense from anyone, least of all a blowhard like Sam Joiner.

Afraid to risk the chance that he might strike Alicia, I rushed forward, iron skillet held high. Sliding into the back of his shoes, I slammed the skillet down on top of his head.

Joiner immediately released his hold on Alicia, who dashed to the other side of the kitchen and yanked a cleaver from the knife block.

But there was no need for her weapon. Clutching his head with both hands, Sam Joiner crumpled to the tile kitchen floor, swearing and moaning in equal measure, as a wail of sirens alerted me that backup had arrived.

I crossed to Alicia, still holding the skillet. She clanged a high five against the pan with her cleaver before thanking me. "He grabbed me right outside the back door and forced me inside. Claimed he had a knife, but I think that was a lie." Alicia strolled over to the boat captain, who was hunched over, still cradling his head. "Besides, I have a bigger one now," she told him, brandishing the cleaver.

He simply groaned. I noticed a trickle of blood oozing between his fingers and realized how hard I'd hit him. *Adrenaline, I guess,* I thought, as a few police officers burst into the kitchen and took charge of the situation.

While they pulled Sam Joiner to his feet and led him away, I told Officer Dennison about the skillet. "You might want a medic to check him over," I said, pointing toward the counter that held my impromptu weapon. "I hit him pretty hard."

Officer Dennison looked up from the notes he'd been taking to record my statement. "Used that? Good for you," he said, before turning to question Alicia.

Chapter Fourteen

After the turmoil caused by Sam Joiner's intrusion and arrest, I was looking forward to a quiet day at Chapters on Wednesday. But as I sipped my morning coffee, I received a phone call that changed my plans.

"Arnie has invited me to meet him at the aquarium," Ellen said, after we exchanged hellos. "He said he knew that you and I were doing a little amateur sleuthing."

"I wonder where he got that idea?"

"I think it's pretty common knowledge, especially after our conversation with Christopher Freedman sparked that violent reaction in Captain Joiner. Anyway, Arnie said he had some valuable information he wanted to share with me concerning one of the other guests. I suggested that we chat in the garden, either yours or mine, but he said he'd rather meet with me somewhere farther away from the others."

"That's interesting. I wonder if he's worried one of them really is a murderer."

"Could be, although Arnie isn't the fearful type. But perhaps he didn't want to cause another commotion at Chapters, which I appreciate."

"Me too," I said fervently.

"He suggested we meet around noon at the aquarium at Pine Knoll Shores. I said yes, but with the caveat that I would only come if you were free to accompany me."

"What, you need a chaperone now?" I asked, amused.

"Not exactly. I'd just prefer not to get into too much rehashing of the past." Ellen cleared her throat. "I told him I didn't like to drive to places by myself. You know, pulling the age card."

I snorted. "As if you're ever affected by such things."

"I know, but it sounds better than . . ."

"'I don't want to be alone with you'? Yeah, I can see how that might not go over very well. All right, I'll tag along. I don't have anything on my schedule today, and I'm really curious about what information Arnie has to offer."

"He said he'd meet us at the entrance. I'm not sure if that means the lobby or outside, but it shouldn't be too difficult to spot him either way." Ellen paused for a moment before adding, "I'm happy to pay for your ticket if we need to go inside. I have an aquarium society membership, so I can get in for free."

"As do I, so no worries," I told her, before we made plans to leave around eleven thirty.

Part of a state system that included two other aquariums and a large zoological park, the local aquarium was located in Pine Knoll Shores, one of the townships on the barrier island across Bogue Sound from Morehead City. We'd decided that I should drive my car, to back up the story Ellen had told Arnie about not liking to drive much herself. As we passed through Atlantic Beach on our way to Pine Knoll Shores, I looked over at Ellen. "You haven't actually talked to Arnie privately yet?"

"I didn't see the point." Ellen met my inquiring glance with a shrug. "So much has happened since we were in college. That girl feels like another person to me now. I don't think there's any way to revive our friendship, even if I had that desire, which I don't."

"It does sometimes feel odd to meet people you knew in the past," I said, thinking of Lora. "Especially when you've been through some life-changing experiences."

"Agreed. It isn't like all those romantic movies, where someone goes home after years away and rekindles friendships or even a romance."

I smiled. "I wouldn't have expected you to have watched such things."

"Oh, you know"—Ellen swept her hand through the air—"there are times when you just want something comforting. Like when the darker thoughts come calling and you don't want to grapple with them."

"Absolutely." I offered her a sympathetic smile. No doubt Ellen had accumulated a storehouse of unpleasant memories from her intelligence work. "I've often hunkered down on the sofa with a comfy blanket, cup of cocoa, and a lightweight romantic movie on the TV. We all need that occasionally."

"Turn's coming up," Ellen said, obviously looking to change the subject.

A forest of short, wind-sculpted trees lined the aquarium driveway. There were a few parking spaces carved out along the sides of the road, which would be filled with cars in season. But since this was before Memorial Day and, more importantly, prior to schools letting out for the summer, there weren't as many visitors. I was even able to park close to the building entrance.

"I don't see Arnie yet," Ellen said, shading her eyes with one hand as she surveyed the area. "Maybe he meant he'd be waiting inside, though. I did mention that I could get in for free."

As I glanced around the area, I didn't catch any sight of Arnie but did notice a familiar car—one I'd seen parked in the Chapters' lot over the last few days. "Looks like Arnie isn't going to escape his companions so easily. There's Zach Bell's car," I said, pointing toward a small SUV.

"You're sure?"

"It looks the same and has the sticker with his lab's logo. I guess it's a parking pass or something." I shrugged. "Of course, there's nothing wrong with him visiting the aquarium. It's a popular tourist destination. But the timing is a little . . ."

Ellen arched her brows. "Coincidental? Well, we can keep an eye out for him, I suppose. As you say, he's probably just here for a visit, not to follow Arnie."

"I hope so," I said.

Walking past a bog garden and a reflecting pool that featured a dramatic metal angelfish sculpture, Ellen and I climbed the stairs to the ticket booth, where a show of our membership cards allowed us to walk right into the building.

"Still no sight of him," I said, after looking around the rather barren lobby.

"That's odd. Unless he's changed dramatically, that isn't like Arnie. He was always very punctual." Ellen glanced at her watch. "And it's a little past noon now."

"Maybe he got unavoidably detained," I said. "I tell you what— why don't you wait here while I take a quick stroll through the rest of the building? You can keep a lookout through the front windows."

Ellen glanced around one more time. "That sounds like a plan. It does worry me that he might've had car trouble or an accident or something. He used to show up to things too early rather than late, so I would've expected to find him waiting for us."

"Did he give you a phone number?" I asked, bouncing on the balls of my feet. Ellen's concern had made me a little anxious. I'd already lost one guest this week; I certainly didn't want something bad to happen to another one.

"No, and I didn't think to ask." Ellen cast me a wry smile. "Despite using one myself, I still sometimes forget the ubiquitous presence of cell phones these days. I didn't have one for most of my life, you know."

"I'm sure he's fine." I briefly laid my hand on her arm. "But I'll take a look around, just in case. If he arrived early, he might've decided to scope out the aquarium before meeting us. Maybe he just lost track of time."

"Good point. Okay, I'll wait here. With this turned on." Ellen held up her cell phone.

"I've got mine as well," I said, patting the pocket of my loose cotton slacks. "If he shows up, give me a buzz. I'll do the same if I locate him."

The aquarium was laid out to show the progression of waterways and their aquatic life, from an artificial waterfall representing the start of a single river's origin in the mountains all the way to the wide-open sea. Looking for one white-haired older man wasn't as easy as I'd thought, though, since there were several grandparents ferrying children in strollers. Also, many of the galleries were dimly lit to allow better views of the illuminated tanks. But even with a couple of sweeps of each area, I didn't spot Arnie.

I didn't see Zach either, which was equally puzzling. But I did glimpse the back of a woman's head. *Strawberry-blonde hair—is Linnea here too?* I attempted to maneuver around a cluster of boisterous children and their weary parents to catch up with the woman, but by the time I'd made my way around the group, she'd disappeared.

I paused in front of a huge tank that featured a replica of a shipwreck and was home to several sharks and other large predators. Keeping a lookout for Arnie, Zach, and Linnea, I glanced at my phone and confirmed I had no messages.

Something stirred the hair lying against the back of my neck. I spun around, looking for the individual I thought must've been standing right behind me.

No one was there. I surveyed the area, observing only the normal aquarium crowd, until I caught a glimpse of a dark figure walking around the corner of the giant tank. Increasing my pace, I followed them.

In the dim light of the next gallery, I noticed someone in a black hoodie and dark jeans moving quickly in the direction of the adjacent halls. That was odd. Given the warmth of the late May day, I wouldn't have expected anyone to wear such heavy clothing.

Maybe it's just a teenager, I told myself, *either going through a Goth phase or simply sulking for some reason. Perhaps they resent being dragged along on a family outing.* I picked up my pace. *But what if it's Zach or Linnea, trying to hide their identity from Arnie? I didn't see what Linnea—if that was her—was wearing. Maybe she pulled up a hood to hide that distinctive hair.*

From other visits to the aquarium, I knew I'd almost reached the end of the indoor displays, which meant the hooded stranger couldn't have gone far unless they'd headed directly for the exit. I had no desire to tail them if that was the case. I decided my best option was to check the remaining sections of the aquarium, including the small gift shop. Seeing no sign of the person in black, and admitting to myself that it was possible they'd slipped by me and headed back to the lobby, I turned around and retraced my steps.

But as I walked past the otter display, which was crowded with excited children watching the antics of the charming creatures, I remembered that there was also an outdoor section attached to the aquarium. It featured a few animal displays as well as a wooded path and boardwalks that overlooked a natural marsh. Determined to check that area before returning to the lobby, I strode over to the nearby exit.

Steam hit my face as soon as I opened the door. *No wonder there aren't very many people wandering around out here*, I thought, before I was startled into stepping back as the stranger wearing the black hoodie brushed past me. With their head down so no part of their face could be seen, they rushed away while the door slammed behind them. I turned to stare after them but only caught a glimpse of their retreating back. Even their hands were obscured, shoved into the pockets of their worn jeans.

It struck me as peculiar, especially after having the feeling that they'd been tailing me earlier, but I realized I had no legitimate reason to chase after them. If the hooded stranger wasn't Linnea or even Zach, I would be accosting an innocent visitor. *And*, I reminded myself, *Linnea and Zach might be perfectly innocent as well*.

It would be more productive to search outside for any sight of Arnie. I pushed open the exterior door and stepped into the bright sunlight. Strolling out to the end of the first overlook without seeing Arnie, I continued along the boardwalk. It was very quiet outside. I passed only one small cluster of children and their parents.

Reaching the second wooden platform that overlooked the marshlands, I spied a heron flying overhead and an ibis perched in a bare-limbed tree that rose from one of the clumps of grasses studding the still water, but no human visitors. I turned around, convinced my quest to find Arnie was futile. But once I was back on the path, I paused, noticing the entrance to a nature trail that lay just beyond a small building housing a snake exhibit.

Surely Arnie didn't go on a hike, I thought. But I walked onto the trail nevertheless, peering down the tree-shadowed dirt path. "Hello," I called out. "Anyone there?"

A weak "Help" wafted up from the side of the trail. Dashing toward the sound, I slid my cell phone from my pocket, ready to call for assistance.

I found Arnie slumped in a tangle of undergrowth. "Are you all right?" I asked, squatting down to examine him. He appeared basically unscathed, except for a few scratches from vines and brambles.

Arnie sat up with a grunt, one palm pressed to his temple. "I think so. Nothing feels broken. May have bumped my head when I fell, but"—he pulled his hand away and stared at his palm—"it doesn't appear to be bleeding."

"Still, a hard knock to the head can be dangerous," I said. *Especially for someone of your age.* But I thought better of mentioning that point.

Arnie looked up at me, his normally bright eyes dimmed. "Could you help me to my feet? I feel rather foolish, sitting here among the weeds."

"Of course. If you're sure nothing is sprained or broken . . ."

"I'm sure," he replied, gripping my outstretched hand with surprisingly strong fingers. Once he was standing, he released his hold and used both hands to dust the leaf meal and other debris from his khaki pants and ivory polo shirt.

"Did you trip over a vine or stone or something?" I asked. "Don't feel embarrassed. It's happened to me more than once. It's a common hazard of walking through the woods."

Arnie lifted his head and stared toward the head of the trail. "Nothing like that. The truth is, I was being followed. Which was one reason I came outside. I wanted to see if I could force my pursuer to reveal themselves. But unfortunately, they got the jump on me instead."

"You mean this wasn't an accident?" I asked, my pitch rising.

Arnie fixed me with an intense gaze. "No, it wasn't. I didn't trip and fall. I was pushed."

Chapter Fifteen

I offered to help Arnie navigate the way back to the aquarium
building, but he waved me aside.

"Thanks, but I can manage," he said, with a little grunt as his
foot hit an uneven section of the path. "I may take things slow,
but I can get there under my own steam."

"That's fine, but if you need any assistance, I'm here." I followed his halting progress with concern. He did seem a bit wobbly. I was worried that he might've sustained a concussion. "Did
you see who shoved you? It will definitely help the police track
down your attacker if you can make a solid identification."

Arnie shook his head. "Unfortunately not. They pushed me
from behind, and when I caught a glimpse of them running off,
all I saw was someone in jeans and a black hooded sweatshirt of
some kind."

I inhaled a deep breath. "I also ran into that person. They
were rushing inside the building when I was heading out." I
didn't think it wise to mention my concern that it could've been
Linnea or Zach. I'd share that suspicion with the police, not one
of my guests.

"Did you get a better look at them?" Arnie asked, shooting me a sharp glance.

"Not really. I could tell it wasn't a large person, at least in terms of girth," I said, as I held the door open for Arnie to reenter the aquarium. "Not sure about height, since they were hunched over. And I didn't see their face, hair, or any glimpse of skin. So I can't provide much information, I'm afraid."

"Too bad." Arnie cleared his throat. "Now, Charlotte, I hope you won't mind if I don't want to talk to the authorities right away. I assure you I'll inform them about this incident, but I'd rather wait until tomorrow, when I'm already scheduled to speak with one of the detectives again." He lifted his hand when I began to protest this decision. "To be honest, I don't feel up to dealing with their questions right now."

"I'm not sure that's the wisest course of action. Let's face it—you might be in danger," I said, as we approached the lobby.

"Not at Chapters, surely." Arnie clutched my forearm, stopping me in my tracks, and fixed me with a pleading gaze. "I tell you what, why not ask your detective friend to add some extra surveillance tonight? Wouldn't that work? I really don't want to make a fuss, and if our hooded stranger wanted to try again, I'll bet they'll think twice if they notice a significant police presence around the B and B."

"I suppose." I frowned. I didn't like the idea that Arnie's attacker was walking around free, but I also didn't feel I could force him to make a report today. I, on the other hand, could certainly express my concerns to Amber Johnson and let her decide when she wanted to send officers to Chapters to talk to Arnie. *Whether he likes it or not*, I thought, tightening my lips. *The police could also quiz Zach and Linnea about their whereabouts today. I shouldn't do that—if the hooded stranger was one of them, it might just cause another attack. I need to play it cool and not let on that I suspect Zach or Linnea were at the aquarium today.*

Ellen hurried toward us as we entered the lobby.

"There you are. I was beginning to worry," she said, casting me a questioning look.

"Sorry. I forgot to call when I found him. I was a little preoccupied with the fact that someone had just hit him from behind, knocking him to the ground."

"What?" Ellen glanced from me to Arnie. "Who would do such a thing?"

"I'm not sure. I didn't actually get a good look at them. As to why"—Arnie shrugged—"I suspect it might be connected to Stacy's murder. Maybe someone thinks I know something."

"And do you?" Ellen's tone was razor sharp.

Arnie brushed a speck of dirt off his sleeve. "No. Nothing I haven't told the police, anyway. Why anyone would think otherwise is beyond me."

"So the next question is—are you all right?" Ellen asked, her gaze locked on Arnie's face.

Arnie waved his hands as if swatting away gnats. "Fine, fine. No need to fuss. Although"—he gave me a side-eyed glance—"perhaps it would be better if I didn't drive. I can just leave my car here, I guess, and have someone bring me back to pick it up tomorrow."

"I'm not sure that's wise. They may tow vehicles left here overnight. Why don't you ride back with Charlotte and allow me to drive your car?" It had apparently slipped Ellen's mind that she'd told him she didn't like to drive by herself.

Arnie obviously hadn't forgotten. He raised his bushy white eyebrows and gave her a speculative look. "I suppose that will work. If you're sure you feel confident driving a strange vehicle by yourself..."

After opening and closing her mouth without saying anything, Ellen squared her shoulders. "I think I can handle it."

"I'm sure you can," Arnie said, his tone indicating that he hadn't been fooled by Ellen's earlier lie. He fished a set of keys out of his pocket. "Here you go. Follow me—I'm parked right out front."

We walked outside, Ellen and me flanking Arnie, who shuffled along, appearing exasperated by our vigilance. I cast a glance toward the parking spot where I'd seen Zach's car earlier, but the space was now empty.

After Ellen unlocked the vehicle Arnie had pointed out as his, she turned to address him across the hoods of the cars that separated my older-model compact from his luxury-brand sedan. "Wait—you said you had something important to tell me. Shouldn't you do that here? You chose this meeting place so we wouldn't be anywhere near Chapters."

Arnie stared at her for a moment, his eyes narrowed. "I guess I'll just have to share that info with Charlotte. She can fill you in later," he said, before climbing into the passenger seat of my car.

He's unhappy that Ellen lied to him, I thought, as I slid into the driver's seat. I shot him a questioning glance as I buckled my seat belt. "You're sure you don't want to get checked out at the emergency room or a twenty-four-hour clinic or something?"

"I definitely don't want or need that," Arnie said, as he buckled up. "I think if I rest this afternoon and evening, I'll be perfectly fine."

A Fatal Booking

I wasn't so sure but felt I had to respect his wishes. After we drove in silence for a few minutes, I broached the subject of the information that had spurred him to set up this meeting. "Is it something you just found out about one of your friends?"

Arnie grimaced. It could've been a reaction to pain from his fall, but I suspected it was at least partly related to my question.

"They aren't really friends. Of course, Lora and I are close, but the others are more what I'd call acquaintances. I enjoy being in the book club, since some of them offer interesting input during our discussions, but we don't socialize otherwise." Arnie drummed his fingers against one knee. "To make a long story short, the reason I wanted to talk to Ellen, and now you, is because I thought you should know what I've found out about Vonnie Allen. I would've mentioned it sooner, but I didn't have all the facts until last night and didn't want to spread baseless rumors." Arnie tugged on the seat belt, pulling it away from his upper body. "Sorry, shoulder's a bit sore. Anyway, there's this fellow in New Bern, one of my boating buddies, and he confirmed a few facts for me."

I side-eyed him. "Okay. What's the story?"

Arnie coughed. "It's just . . . well, my friend told me I might be right to have suspicions about Vonnie, in terms of the murder."

I tightened my grip on the steering wheel. "She had a motive to kill Stacy Wilkin?"

"I'm afraid so. It's connected to Vonnie's son, Raphael," Arnie said. "He's nineteen and in college. But last summer, right after he'd graduated from high school, Raphael was working at Stacy's jewelry store. Apparently he was staying with a friend in New Bern, and Stacy offered him a summer job."

I glanced at my speedometer, realized I was driving too fast, and adjusted my pressure on the gas pedal. "And?"

"And Stacy accused Raphael of stealing from her. Or helping some of his buddies with a break-in, at any rate." Arnie lifted his hands. "It seems there was a robbery at Stacy's New Bern store last summer. Several valuable pieces of jewelry were taken and never recovered. It put Stacy in a bad spot, because those items were on consignment for one of her wealthier customers."

"Why did Stacy suspect Vonnie's son of being involved?" I asked, shooting Arnie a questioning glance.

Arnie sighed. "Possibly just because he's African American. That's my theory, anyway. To be honest, I've always thought Stacy possessed a bit of a racist streak. I've met Raphael and honestly doubt he was involved in any sort of crime."

"Was he charged with anything?"

"Fortunately not. There was no real evidence that he was involved, so the police just questioned him once or twice, and that was that. But because no one was ever arrested and the jewelry was never recovered, it remains an open case."

"I bet Stacy couldn't keep her mouth shut about her theory," I said, considering the implications of this. "Was she spreading rumors about Raphael?"

"Yes. That's what my buddy claimed, anyway." Arnie yanked on the seat belt's shoulder strap again. "Vonnie loves her son very much, so . . ."

"She may have had a motive to silence the woman who was spreading lies about him." I forced myself to focus on my driving despite my racing thoughts.

"Which is why I wanted to give you all the details concerning their ongoing conflict. I'll also mention this to the police, of course, but since Vonnie's staying under your roof, I thought it was only fair to warn you. I planned to do that by talking to both you and Ellen today, but obviously someone decided to shove me to the ground before I could do so."

"Do you suspect Vonnie?" I asked, as we crossed the bridge that led into Beaufort.

"I'm not sure. I mean, how would she have known I planned to talk to you and Ellen? Unless . . ." Arnie snapped his fingers. "I did catch Vonnie hovering around the library last night, right around the time I made my call to my friend. When I walked into the hall after I hung up, there she was."

"I suppose she could've followed you today. I know she has a car, because she had to register it with us when she arrived at Chapters," I said, judiciously not adding that I'd seen Zach's vehicle, not Vonnie's. Of course, she could've been parked in a far corner of the lot, so that wasn't conclusive evidence that she hadn't also visited the aquarium today.

"Yes, we all traveled separately. Rather wasteful, I suppose, and it does fill your parking lot, but it also allows us to do our own thing whenever we want."

"And perhaps keep tabs on one another," I said darkly, before throwing Arnie an apologetic glance. "I'm sorry. I probably shouldn't voice my thoughts so openly. Anyway, while I appreciate you sharing this information with me, I think it's best if we don't mention anything to the other guests. That could be either rude or dangerous. But I urge you to speak with the authorities as soon as you feel up to it. Let them sort it out."

"Of course," he said, settling back against the seat.

We chatted about innocuous things the rest of the way home. When we arrived at Chapters, Arnie refused the arm I offered and walked inside without my help, although I made sure to stay close behind him.

"Is there a problem?" Alicia stepped out of the kitchen as we made our way down the main hall.

She must've noticed the strain on my face, I thought, *or perhaps it's just the disheveled condition of Arnie's hair and clothes.*

"Mr. Dean took a fall. Nothing serious, thank goodness." I cast Alicia a warning look. "We probably shouldn't mention it to the others."

Alicia tugged her drooping apron strap up over her shoulder. "They're out anyway. To be honest, every last one of them's been gone all day."

"Everyone?" I asked. *That definitely means any one of them could've been our attacker in the hoodie. Zach might be too tall, but the stranger was hunched over, and I didn't get a good look, so it's wise to leave him, Linnea, and Vonnie on the suspect list.*

"All out since around eleven," Alicia said. "They drove somewhere too, because their cars were also gone."

When we reached the foyer, Arnie eyed the steps with a dubious expression. "I think I'll go up to my room and take a short nap. I do feel a little woozy at the moment. Would you accompany me upstairs, Charlotte? Just to be safe."

"Of course." I followed him up the steps, watching to make sure he didn't stumble, then trailed him into his room.

Arnie was in the Classics Suite, which featured bookshelves filled with the type of literature found on most English 101 reading lists. Many of the volumes were leather bound, with intricate tooling on their spines. Busts of famous authors served as bookends, and lithographs of Milton, Shakespeare, and the Brontë sisters as well as other well-known authors decorated the walls.

As Arnie plopped down on the edge of his bed, I stood beside one of the bookshelves, pressing one palm against a waist-high shelf. "I'm happy to sit with you if you still feel unwell," I said, my forefinger absently drawing circles in the light film that coated the polished wooden surface. I sighed. Alicia and I tried to keep the shelves free from dust, but with the number of older volumes filling the bookcases in every guest room, it was almost impossible.

"No, no, I'm feeling better now." Arnie cast me a warm smile. "Just a momentary wave of dizziness, that's all."

The door flew open, and Lora burst into the room. "Are you really feeling okay, Arnie? Ms. Simpson told me what happened." As she hurried over to the bed, I couldn't help but notice that her hair was mussed and her blouse buttoned up the wrong way.

"There's nothing to worry about," Arnie said. But he allowed Lora to come close enough to check his head. Her fingers brushed through the thick hair at his temple.

"There's a bruise, which means you did hit your head," Lora said, examining him with a critical gaze. "I heard something about you being pushed. Is that right?"

"Unfortunately. I was outside the aquarium, on the trail, trying to shake off someone who was following me for some unknown reason."

"Heavens." Lora cast me a concerned glance. "We should probably alert the police."

"That's what I suggested," I said, distracted by a section of books that had slid over on their sides.

"I plan to talk to them tomorrow." Arnie's tone was firm.

As I adjusted the fallen books, something glinted. I pulled the books to the side and discovered three silver-framed photographs that had been hidden behind the stack. "Wait a minute, what are these doing here?" I grabbed the pictures and spun around to face Arnie and Lora. "These went missing from the library. Why do you have them in your room, Arnie?" I adopted a stern expression. Although I thought I knew why he'd taken the photos, I still wanted to hear his answer.

Lora let out a little squeak as a flush of crimson stained Arnie's cheeks. "You caught me," he said, shooting Lora a look I couldn't decipher. "I'd hoped to return those before you missed them, but it seems you're too observant for me."

Lora clasped her hands, squeezing them so tightly her knuckles blanched. I stared at her for a moment, wondering why she seemed so upset over this discovery. *Has Arnie done this sort of thing before? Perhaps he's not quite as mentally fit as he seems*, I thought, as I studied her anxious expression. "It was actually Alicia—Ms. Simpson, that is—who first noticed they were missing," I said, after a short stretch of tense silence. "I didn't say anything right away because I did wonder if someone had simply borrowed them for some reason." I switched my focus, staring into Arnie's sea-green eyes. "Was that the case?"

He had the grace to look embarrassed. "I'm afraid so," he said, sharing another swift glance with Lora before looking back at me. "I wanted to make some copies. Just to have something to remember old times, when I was young and carefree."

I looked down, examining the top photo on the stack. It displayed my great-aunt Isabella with her arms around two men—one older, with dark hair slicked back from his high forehead, and one younger, whose fair hair flopped over his brow, almost veiling his bright eyes. I looked back at Arnie. "This is you, isn't it? Standing arm in arm with Isabella and some unknown gentleman?"

Arnie nodded. "I was in my midtwenties at the time. My dad brought me to a couple of parties at Chapters during that time."

"Where you met my great-aunt and developed, as you mentioned before, a major crush on her?"

"I did indeed." Arnie's face and posture relaxed.

Perhaps he's relieved to confess his obsession, I thought, tapping the glass on the top photo with my finger. "And you wanted a photograph of you two together, to remember her by? That's very sweet, but you should've just asked. I would have let you borrow these pictures if you'd explained why you wanted them. No need for subterfuge."

Arnie exhaled a gusty sigh. "Please forgive me, Charlotte. Sometimes I can be a foolish old man."

"Only sometimes?" Lora said, her face now exhibiting her usual composure. Whatever concerns she'd felt earlier seemed to have dissipated.

"Now, now, my dear. No need to rub it in." Arnie leaned back into the pillows stacked against the headboard. "I admit to being increasingly sentimental and foolish in my old age."

"Well, as long as you promise to return these before you leave, I don't mind if you have copies made." I shuffled the frames in my hands, glancing at the second photo, which again showed

Isabella standing next to a young Arnie, before focusing more intently on the third picture. This one was a glamorous portrait of Isabella. She looked to be in her early fifties, which made sense, since that was when Arnie had known her. Her rich brown hair was swept up into an elegant chignon decorated with a sapphire-and-diamond comb. A matching sapphire-and-diamond necklace glittered against her pale skin, complementing her silky ice-blue gown.

I'd seen that necklace in another photograph of Isabella. It was an extremely valuable piece. *No wonder the jewelry thief appeared at one or more of her parties*, I thought, before setting the three photographs on a bookshelf.

"I appreciate you lending me the pictures. I've made arrangements to have them copied at a local camera and framing shop tomorrow. I'll return them to the library after that." Arnie crossed his heart. "I promise to take good care of them."

"You'd better," I said, adding a smile to lessen the harshness of my words. Arnie was still a guest, even if he had taken something without asking.

"I've been thinking, and I honestly believe I should drive you to one of those minute clinics or something to get checked out," Lora said, fixing Arnie with an intent stare. "I just keep remembering those people who had head injuries and ignored them and later died."

Arnie met her gaze, his face radiating annoyance. But after a second, his expression softened and he exhaled gustily. "I suppose you're right. Don't worry," he added, with a swift glance at me, "you needn't be involved. Just point Lora in the right direction. I'm sure she'll be happy to take care of her silly old godfather."

I promised to locate the closest clinic and share the directions with Lora as soon as she came downstairs. "I'm happy to accompany you, if you think that would help."

"No, no." Arnie waved me off. "Lora will handle it, won't you, dear?"

"Always do," Lora said, with a tense smile.

"Okay. Just check with me before you head out," I told them before leaving the room.

They didn't respond, too busy talking in low tones. I couldn't hear what they were saying, but once again, it seemed like they were arguing.

That's interesting, I thought, as I descended the staircase. *They seem close and antagonistic at the same time. I wonder what that means?*

I mentally added that to my list of clues and anomalies before heading into my office to search for directions to the closest twenty-four-hour clinic.

Chapter Sixteen

Lora returned from the clinic, shepherding Arnie, who had a simple bandage plastered to his temple. "The doctor thinks he'll be okay but wants him to stay in bed for a bit and have me check on him from time to time. She said if he was to develop worsening symptoms, it would probably happen before morning." When Arnie protested, she added, "Now, don't be difficult. Someone needs to keep an eye on you, at least for a few hours."

Arnie begrudgingly agreed. Before they headed upstairs, I told Lora to alert me immediately if we needed to call an ambulance.

"It won't come to that," Arnie muttered as Lora guided him toward the steps.

"I'll be around if you need me," I told Lora, ignoring Arnie's glower. "Don't hesitate to ask for help if you need it."

Lora gave me a thumbs-up gesture before turning back to Arnie. I left them still arguing as they slowly climbed the stairs, then headed into my office.

I called Amber Johnson, filling her in on the attack on Arnie as well as my suspicions concerning Zach and Linnea. I also shared Arnie's information on Vonnie.

"Interesting," she said. "I'll send out some officers to question all of them, of course, but I think it can wait until morning. Just keep acting like everything is normal, please, so we don't scare the possible perpetrator into fleeing."

"That was my plan," I told her. "Maybe you could provide some extra surveillance tonight, though? Just in case the attacker was one of my guests. I'd hate for them to try to make another attempt. Maybe an obvious police presence will deter them."

"And that was *my* plan," Detective Johnson said. "Don't worry—your guests will know we're watching."

I thanked her before I hung up and wandered into the kitchen, where I filled Alicia in on the latest developments.

"I'm really starting to wonder who's the most likely culprit," Alicia said. "That Captain Joiner is probably in jail, so he couldn't have been involved in this latest attack."

Realizing I was still gripping my cell phone, I laid it on the kitchen island. "Unless he made bail. But even so, you'd think he'd try to keep his nose clean."

"And what beef would he have with some old gentleman who's simply visiting Beaufort?" Alicia pursed her lips. "It's not like that Arnie fellow has history with Joiner like my cousin does."

"That we know of," I reminded her. "The truth is, Arnie has visited Beaufort in the past, although I guess Sam Joiner would've been just a kid when Arnie was last at Chapters. There is also his father, though. He had some dealings in the area, as a lawyer and politician. Maybe there's a connection between him and someone in Joiner's family."

"Seems pretty farfetched." Alicia looked me over and sniffed. "I think you're getting carried away with this amateur detective stuff. Not everything is a mystery. Isabella threw a lot of parties back in the day, and it wasn't unusual for her to invite high-society lawyers or politicians. Arnie Dean's dad would've fit right in."

But you don't know why she might've invited him or what sort of political shenanigans he might've been embroiled in. I nodded my head instead of voicing that thought. Alicia didn't know that my great-aunt had been a spy for U.S. intelligence, and I wasn't about to tell her. The fewer people who were aware of Isabella Harrington's true past, the better.

My cell phone dinged, the vibration causing it to skitter over the smooth soapstone top of the island. I scooped it up and glanced at the screen. A new text. I clicked on the message icon.

Garden was all it said. I stared at the number, realizing who'd sent the text. "If it's okay with you, I think I'll head outside for some fresh air," I told Alicia, who was watching me with interest. "I'll just be in the garden, though, so if Lora or any of the other guests comes looking for me, just give a yell and I'll come right back in."

"I will if necessary, but don't worry—I can probably handle any of their requests, and I'm sure you'd enjoy a little time to yourself after all the excitement today." Alicia frowned. "Do you think it's wise wandering around outside at night by yourself? What with me and then a guest being assaulted over the last day or so, it might not be safe."

"I'll be fine. I won't go any farther than the garden, and anyway, Mr. Dean wasn't attacked here. Besides, I can't imagine that Sam Joiner would come back, even if he's out of jail already."

"If you say so. Just keep that phone with you." Alicia's expression reminded me of my mother's stern face when I'd headed out of the house as a teenager.

172

Of course, I knew there was someone waiting for me outside, but I wasn't about to mention that. I held up the phone and reassured Alicia that I'd keep it handy. "Just in case someone's lurking in the garden," I said, keeping my tone light.

Heading out through the back porch door, I quickly crossed the flagstone patio, which was illuminated by an outdoor floodlight. I knew I could easily be seen by anyone hiding in the shadowy garden, but I wasn't concerned. I wanted my visitor to know I was alone.

Slipping through the gate, I paused on the main path, surveying the garden for any sign of movement. The vegetation, lacking the light it needed to reflect color, appeared washed in shades of gray, while the fragrance of roses mingled with the spicy scent of herbs and the rich odors of mulch and earth.

A shadow slid from its hiding place behind the lilac bush and moved toward me. As the figure approached, it coalesced into the form of a man of average height and build, whose curly light-brown hair appeared tipped with silver in the moonlight.

"Hello, Charlotte," Gavin said, his eyes as bright as his voice was warm.

I eyed him, noticing that he looked rather tired and a bit thinner than I remembered. "I can't really tell for sure in this light, but you appear more tanned than usual. Does that mean you've been working in a location with a lot of sun?"

"You look as lovely as ever," Gavin replied, not rising to my bait. "It's so good to actually get to see you in person."

"Agreed, but why the secrecy?" I stepped forward to meet him and clasp the hands he'd extended to me.

"I'll explain, but first . . ." Gavin pulled me into a close embrace. "That's better," he whispered in my ear. "Don't you think?"

"Hmm, not really thinking at the moment," I said, earning a chuckle.

We'd talked so often, over video chat as well as phone and text, that I felt I knew him well, even though we hadn't been in physical contact over the past year. But it was different to feel his arms around me and his body pressed close to mine. I had to confess that while I'd envisioned such a thing many times, the actual sensations were better than my imagination.

Gavin's next words tickled my ear. "I would very much like to kiss you. Would that be okay?"

"Absolutely perfect," I said, before his lips stopped me from saying anything else for quite some time.

When he finally stepped back, he looked me over with a smile. "Now that we've enjoyed that delightful diversion, how about sitting down to talk about this latest murder of yours?"

"It's not *my* murder," I said, trailing him over to one of the garden benches. "Ellen and I are just seeing what we can do to provide some help to the police."

As Gavin sat down, he shot an amused look up at me. "Uh-huh. That's not what I've heard."

"How have you heard anything?" I asked, sitting next to him. "It's not like the stuff Ellen and I have been doing has been plastered all over the evening news."

"I have my ways." Gavin's expression sobered. "Anyway, you did ask me to dig into the backgrounds of your guests, among others."

I leaned into him. "And?"

"And, if you're going to drape yourself over me like that, I'm going to lose my train of thought," Gavin said, without making any effort to move away.

"Well, then . . ." Sliding forward, I attempted to stand up, but Gavin grabbed my arm and pulled me down again.

He slid his arm through mine and pulled me close to his side. "I didn't say I didn't like it. Now, listen—one thing you should know is that your victim, Stacy Wilkin, was not squeaky clean."

I thought about the jewelry I'd seen in the newspaper article—the designs that I'd suspected were stolen from Linnea Ruskin. "That doesn't exactly surprise me."

"The truth is, there's speculation that she was selling stolen goods in her stores. Not openly, of course." Gavin cast me a side-eyed glance. "Apparently there wasn't enough evidence to charge her with anything, but she was mentioned in reports on some known fences and other suspicious characters."

"I saw comments about that on an article about her store. I wasn't sure if that was just some anonymous people being catty, but it sounds like there was substance to the rumors. Which means she really could've been mixed up with thieves or gangsters. That does put a different spin on possible motives for her murder. Although means would be another matter."

Gavin absently caressed my bare forearm as he stared out into the shadowed garden. "Because she had to have been poisoned at the tea party?"

"Yes. Only so many people had access to her. The other guests, of course, and perhaps Captain Samuel Joiner. But there weren't any strangers lurking about."

"That you saw," Gavin said. "What if she wasn't poisoned before she entered the garden?"

I raised my eyebrows. "You think someone could've been lurking here, grabbed her, and forced the cyanide on her?"

"It isn't outside the realm of possibility, although I admit it's a stretch." Gavin pulled his arm back and lifted it so he could slide it around my shoulders. "It does seem more likely that one of the other guests, or even your spurned captain, spiked her tea."

Looking up into the sky, its stars hidden by a drift of dark clouds, I considered my list of possible suspects. "Other than Joiner, who obviously hated Stacy for a couple of reasons, there's also Vonnie Allen, who seems to have nursed a grudge because Stacy accused her son of being a thief."

"Pot, meet kettle," Gavin said, shooting me a smile. "It seems Ms. Wilkin may have been deflecting to excuse her own less than legal behavior."

"Could be." I tapped my lips with one finger. "Then there's Zach Bell. He felt his mother was cheated when she sold some family heirlooms to Stacy. Also, I have my suspicions about Stacy stealing jewelry designs from Linnea Ruskin." I described the jewelry I'd seen pictured online, credited to Stacy as designer. "But I'm pretty sure she didn't create the original designs for those pieces, since I saw some of Linnea's drawings that matched them exactly."

Gavin rubbed my shoulder. "Which could also bring Lora Kane into the picture."

"How so?"

"Well, if Stacy stole designs from Linnea, what's to say she didn't also pilfer a few from Lora?"

"That's true." I pressed closer to his side. "I don't have any evidence of that, but it certainly wouldn't be an impossibility."

"Which just leaves the older gentleman, Arnie Dean." Gavin turned his head to look into my eyes. "Anything about him seem suspicious to you?"

"Maybe not in terms of Stacy Wilkin, but he did take some of Isabella's photos out of the library without my permission. I saw them, hidden on a bookshelf, when I was in his room today. He said he planned to return the pictures once he made copies, but"—I shrugged—"it does show a rather devious side to him, don't you think?"

"It certainly proves he's not above deception and keeping secrets. Although I'm not sure how that would tie in to the murder."

"I know. It doesn't appear that there's any connection. But he was attacked today. I wonder . . ." I sat up, dislodging Gavin's arm from my shoulders. "You know, what if one of the guests was working for or with someone? Like the type of person you mentioned earlier. If a guest with a grudge was approached by a thief or other criminal who knew enough to play on their vendetta against Stacy . . ."

"They could've leveraged their access to her, using the criminal's ability to plan a murder and perhaps access the cyanide?" Gavin sat forward, gripping his knees with both hands. "That does sound like a possible scenario, although you said some of the guests could get their hands on that poison anyway."

"Also true." I rubbed the back of my hand across my forehead. "Lora and Linnea because of their jewelry craft and Zach because of his scientific research. And apparently Captain Joiner used it to make rat poison in the past, at least according to Alicia's cousin." I swiveled my legs to shift my body toward Gavin. "So they didn't all need a partner, at least not for that reason."

"No, but it's still possible they had one. It might explain the attack on Mr. Dean." Gavin met my questioning gaze with a wry smile. "Maybe the killer thought Mr. Dean saw something or knew something and asked their partner in crime to help silence him."

"It's as good a theory as any." I sighed. The truth was, there were too many theories, and a lot of them sounded like they could be the truth. "As far as the attack on Arnie Dean today, it could've been one of the guests or someone else. I didn't get a good look at them, although I think I did see Linnea earlier, and I know Zach's car was parked at the aquarium."

"Could they have been working together?"

"Maybe. They do seem to be close. Julie thinks they might be involved in a romantic relationship."

Gavin's lips quirked. "Julie looks for romance everywhere."

"True, but she may be right in this case. Of course, there's also Vonnie Allen. She was out today too, according to Alicia." I frowned. "Actually, Alicia said all the guests' vehicles were gone for a while, so as far as someone driving to the aquarium, it could've been any one of them."

"Not really narrowing the field of suspects."

"Unfortunately not. Oh, by the way, I meant to tell you this sooner, but it just flew out of my mind in the midst of everything else that's been happening. Anyway, Bernadette and Ophelia Sandburg shared some info with me about a rash of jewelry heists in this area back in the seventies. I don't imagine it has any connection to the murder, but it is tied to Isabella in a way, since a theft occurred at one of her parties. A valuable emerald ring went missing."

"Isabella reported it to the police?"

"No, and I think you can guess why. She just paid off the woman who lost the ring and that was that, according to Bernie."

Gavin's thoughtful expression told me he'd made the same leap of intuition that I had. "She wouldn't have wanted to involve the authorities if she was running some sort of intelligence operation at the time."

"Exactly. But the theft at Chapters was only one of many. There was a span of time when a cat burglar was targeting several of the well-to-do homes in Beaufort and the surrounding areas. Which is a connection to Arnie Dean. It seems his father, who was a prominent lawyer and politician, swore to bring the thief to justice."

Gavin laid one hand on my knee. "I'm guessing he didn't make good on that vow?"

"No. The thefts ceased as abruptly as they'd begun, and from what the Sandburg sisters told me, the perpetrator was never caught." I lifted my hands. "I know the only connection to our current situation is Arnie Dean's peripheral association, and the whole stolen jewelry aspect in terms of Stacy Wilkin perhaps selling illegal goods, so maybe it means nothing."

"But you'd like me to investigate that chapter from the past anyway?" Gavin patted my knee. "I'm sure that's where this is leading."

"You guessed it." I cast him a look from under my lowered eyelashes. "I like to tug on every thread, no matter how thin and frayed."

"Which is why you would've made a great agent. Although"—Gavin lifted his hand, palm out—"don't get any ideas. I really don't plan to recruit you."

"Good, because I would refuse. I like doing a bit of amateur sleuthing with Ellen, but I don't think I want your job."

"Sometimes even I don't want it," Gavin said ruefully. "As a matter of fact . . ." He glanced away, obviously thinking better of whatever he'd been about to say. "Sorry, let's not discuss that yet. I need to be sure about a few things first."

"Okay." My curiosity was piqued, but I knew I shouldn't press him to offer any information about his job that he didn't feel comfortable sharing. "By the way, where are you staying? Did you dock your boat in the Beaufort harbor again?"

He shook his head before looking back at me. "No, I berthed her at the marina near the bridge into town. I thought it might be best to stay incognito for a while."

"Why? You aren't on an official assignment or anything, are you?"

"I'm not, but people in Beaufort know me. At least as Ellen's cousin," he added, smiling. "Your friend Julie, for one, as well as the Sandburg sisters and the rest of your book club friends."

"You don't want them to know you're visiting me?" I asked, fighting to keep any tinge of disappointment from my tone. If Gavin didn't want anyone to know he was in town, what did that say about our relationship?

"It isn't that." Gavin took hold of my hands. "I'd like to announce our relationship to the world, if it comes to that. But I just thought . . . perhaps I could do more to aid you and Ellen, and the police, if no one knew I was around. Except you, of course. And Ellen, if you want to tell her. I know she can keep such things under wraps."

I looked into his amber-flecked eyes. Finding nothing but honesty there, I nodded. "Good point. You could follow my guests, or keep tabs on Samuel Joiner, and they probably wouldn't suspect they were being watched."

"They definitely wouldn't know." Gavin smiled at me again. "And since you can identify my boat, you can pop by the marina from time to time to keep me up to date on the investigation without involving anyone else."

"Just to keep you informed about the investigation?" I asked, arching my eyebrows.

Gavin grinned. "Maybe also to share a friendly chat—or something."

"I suppose, since you said I could tell Ellen you're in town, that she could accompany me."

"You're old enough to be alone with me without a chaperone, don't you think?" Gavin dropped my hands to gently cup my chin with his strong fingers.

"I suppose that depends upon your intentions," I said, not drawing back as he pulled my face closer to his.

"Only the best," he replied. "At least I hope you'll think so," he added, before kissing me again.

"This is definitely a good start." I flashed him a smile when he released me and sat back. "I'll be interested to see how you improve upon it."

"And I'll be delighted to show you," he said, with an answering smile.

Chapter Seventeen

After Gavin used one of the benches to hop over the fence, I left the garden as well, quickly crossing the patio to reach the back door. But the sound of crunching gravel in the driveway caught my attention, drawing me around to the side of the house.

"Damian," I said, when I recognized the tall, lanky young man in shorts and a T-shirt. "What are you doing out at this hour?"

Damian lifted one foot, displaying a sleek track shoe. "Running. I like to go out when it's cooler."

"In the middle of the night?" I offered him a smile, acknowledging that I was out at the same time.

"Couldn't sleep." Damian pulled a small towel from his pocket and wiped the sweat from his face. "Too many things on my mind."

"Such as?" I looked him over, noticing the excitement brimming in his eyes.

Dabbing the front of his neck with the towel, Damian shot me an apologetic look. "Well, I wasn't going to mention this yet, but I may have landed a permanent chef gig."

"That's great news." I lifted my hands. "Not necessarily for me, since it would mean you probably couldn't freelance at Chapters anymore, but I know how long you've tried to get a decent full-time position."

"Thanks. I'm glad you understand." Damian stuffed the towel back into his pocket. "The thing is, I paused my run here because I noticed the extra police cars on this block and was worried something else had happened at Chapters. But one of the officers reassured me that they just had extra surveillance on tonight because one of the guests got attacked at the aquarium today."

"Yes, Detective Johnson said she was arranging extra patrols. Not something you need to worry about, though. Just a precaution."

Damian fiddled with the end of one of his long dreadlocks. "Maybe so, but then I looked up and thought I saw something strange, and it seems I wasn't wrong. See the side window, under the eaves? There shouldn't be a light on in the attic, should there?"

I followed his gesture to stare at the illuminated window. "Certainly not. Especially in the middle of the night." As we watched, a shadow blotted out the light for a second. "That can't be right."

"There's definitely someone moving around up there." Damian cast me a questioning look. "I thought you always kept the attic locked."

"I do." I turned and strode away, heading for the front of the house.

Damian jogged up beside me. "Hold on, I'm coming with you."

"It's not necessary," I said, as we both bounded up the steps to the porch.

"I'm not letting you check out the attic alone."

I glanced over at him as I unlocked the front door. "I have a houseful of people."

"Yeah, and one or more of them might be looting your attic," Damian said, his black eyebrows drawing together.

"All right, let's check it out." I held up one hand. "But I don't want to make a scene. If one of the guests is rooting through stuff in the attic, I want to assess the situation before we call the police or anything like that. It might just be someone who's nosy, not a thief."

Damian nodded. "Gotcha, boss."

Entering the house, I paused at the bottom of the staircase as the sound of footsteps echoed off the floorboards of the hall above.

"Let's stay as quiet as possible," I told Damian in a whisper. "Maybe we can catch whoever it is sneaking back into their room."

I hurried up the steps, Damian right on my heels. When we reached the second floor, I pressed a finger to my lips while I surveyed the hallway.

The suite doors didn't offer many clues. They were all closed except one, and that was the Classics Suite, where Arnie was staying. There was a light on in his room as well.

But Arnie's been ordered to rest in bed for the evening. Can't imagine him risking a serious danger to his health to rummage through the attic. And surely, if he had, he would've made certain his door wasn't left open.

And as for the others . . . I narrowed my eyes. I had to rule out Zach, since he was staying out in the carriage house, but Linnea, Vonnie, or Lora could've easily slipped back downstairs and into their rooms before Damian and I entered the house.

I followed Damian over to the attic door, which was closed but unlocked.

"Let me lead the way," Damian whispered.

I nodded, following as he carefully made his way up the steep set of stairs. Damian paused at the threshold of the attic to allow me to join him. "Don't see any noticeable destruction," he said, keeping his voice low.

Stepping around him, I surveyed the area. The dust on the floor was once again disturbed, but like last time, it appeared that the intruder had shuffled their feet to obliterate any obvious footprints. Glancing over toward the window, I noticed that one of the trunks wasn't closed properly and spied the edge of a lace doily poking out of one of the boxes. Otherwise, it seemed that whoever had been digging through things had made sure to return them to their proper places.

"I guess I should make a more thorough examination at another time," I said. "Just to be sure nothing was taken. Not that there is anything of great value stored up here."

"Which is the weird part." Damian sent me a sidelong glance. "I know you have some rare antiques and books downstairs, so why would any thief bother digging around up here?"

I shook my head. "I have no idea. Maybe they're just an inveterate snoop, especially when it comes to old papers and stuff. Some people are like that, always thinking they're going to run across some amazing historical information or something."

A thought about my great-aunt's connection to espionage flitted through my mind, but I dismissed that idea almost immediately. Surely no one staying at Chapters right now—except me—knew about that part of her life. Even Alicia didn't know. *Or at least, you don't think she does*, I reminded myself.

"It seems no one is still lurking up here," I said, after Damian and I took another look around. "I guess we can turn off the lights and head back downstairs."

"I'm not sure I like the idea of you and Alicia staying here with someone who has no qualms about breaking into the attic," Damian said as we descended the stairs.

"There's the extra police surveillance, as you saw. And Alicia always locks her door, as do I. Besides, I really think it was just one of the guests being nosy," I said. "Granted, one of them may be a murderer . . ."

Damian narrowed his eyes. "Yeah, there is that."

"But I doubt this is connected to that in any way," I said, "even if someone did also take some photographs from the library."

"You think it was the same person?"

"Unlikely. The guy who took the photos claims he just wanted to make copies of them, and I believe him. Anyway, he was ordered to stay in bed by his doctor, because he suffered a fall earlier today."

"You aren't going to talk to him, though? I think I would," Damian said.

I cast a swift glance at the sliver of light spilling through the door to the Classics Suite. "You're right. Maybe I should check." I touched Damian's arm. "Tell you what—why don't you go on home? No need for you to hang around while I talk to the guest in question. And no," I added, "I won't be in any danger. The guy is seventy-five years old, for heaven's sake."

"Okay, if you're sure." Damian's dubious expression warmed my heart. It was nice of him to be so concerned.

I offered him a bright smile. "I am. Just use the back door and make sure it locks behind you when you leave."

He flipped his dreadlocks behind his shoulders. "Will do. And if we're giving directions—you'd better turn on your phone and have it at hand, at least."

I slid my cell phone from my pocket and held it up. "Thanks again," I told him, before he bounded downstairs.

Turning away from the steps, I walked over to the door of the Classics Suite and rapped gently on one of its thick oak panels. "Mr. Dean?" I called out softly. "Arnie? Are you awake?"

"Charlotte, is that you?"

"Yes. I was just . . . checking some things up here and noticed your door was open. Would you like me to close it for you?"

"I would, but first, could you come in for a moment? I need someone to turn off the blasted light, and I was ordered not to try to get out of bed on my own until morning."

"Okay," I said, slipping into the room.

Arnie was in the bed, wearing a navy-and-white-striped pajama top, with the suite's fluffy white bedding pulled up above his waist. He sat up a little straighter. "Sorry to bother you, but Lora went off without taking care of that lamp in the corner. I've been trying to sleep despite the light, but it hasn't been easy."

"She also left your door unlocked," I said, frowning. "Is she always so forgetful?"

"I'm afraid so. Brilliant artist, you know, but sometimes she's very scattered about everyday things." Arnie shifted against the pillows piled behind his head and back. "I guess I'd drifted off for a minute or two and she just decided to escape to her own room, thinking I was sound asleep."

"I'm glad you followed doctor's orders and stayed in bed." As I headed for the corner to turn off the standing lamp, I noticed that the three framed photographs were stacked on Arnie's bedside table. "You really did have a crush on Isabella, didn't you?"

"Oh my, yes." Arnie's jovial smile lit up his face. "Let me tell you . . . listen, why don't you leave that for a minute and come sit down. I'd love to share a few of my memories of her."

"And I'd love to hear them," I said, deciding that a few more minutes away from my own bed couldn't hurt. "I only knew her later, when she was older. That was after she stopped throwing all those amazing parties I've read about. She was fascinating, even then, but I'd certainly enjoy hearing your impressions of her in her prime."

"What can I say—she was spectacular." Arnie's sea-green eyes sparkled like gems. "She always made an entrance, sauntering into the music room, which is where most of the partygoers congregated." Arnie cast me a conspiratorial glance. "But I confess I used to hang out in the hall, wanting to catch a glimpse of her gliding down the stairs, one slender hand on the rail and her head, crowned with all that lovely rich brown hair, held high."

"You attended several of her parties, then." I settled against the cane lattice back of the rocker placed beside the bed.

"As many as my schedule would allow. I guess it was maybe three or four times? My dad attended many other parties here, but I was in college and then law school during that time."

"In that photo of you two"—I motioned to the stack of framed pictures—"you look quite chummy."

Arnie rolled his eyes. "I wish. We weren't really that close. Isabella just had a way of making you feel like a dear friend, even on short acquaintance."

"Don't tell me you didn't try to flirt with her," I said with a sly smile.

"Oh, for sure. But like I said, I was in my twenties and didn't have much game, I'm afraid." Arnie's expression grew distant. "We did dance together once or twice. I was fairly light on my feet back then, and Isabella was easy to partner. That's a memory I cherish—her in my arms, with her laughter as sparkling as the glorious jewels adorning her ears and throat . . ." He pressed his palm to his forehead and shot me an apologetic smile. "Sorry, I didn't mean to drift off into the past like that. Old man's folly."

"It's really quite sweet." I rose to my feet. "But I think I should go now and let you get some sleep. You settle back and relax. I'll make sure the light's off and the door's locked when I leave."

Arnie reached out to clasp my hand. "Thanks for listening, Charlotte. You know," he said, staring up into my face, "you would look quite lovely in some of the jewelry Isabella often wore. You have her hair and eyes."

I shook my head. "I'm afraid I don't attend any events where such accessories would be appropriate." He dropped my hand and I moved away, crossing the room to turn off the lamp before heading for the door.

"Shame," Arnie said, as I paused in the doorway. "About not having a reason to wear such jewelry, I mean. You should have the opportunity to attend at least one glamorous event. Perhaps I could arrange that, once I'm back home in Cary. I still know some people who throw those sorts of parties." He winked. "You could be my date."

"I'd be honored," I told him, before exiting the room. Making sure the door was locked behind me, I headed downstairs.

I wasn't worried about my promise—I was sure Arnie Dean was simply flattering me, as he would any female he hoped to charm. I suspected he was the sort of man who often said such things, with no intention of following through. Which was fine with me, of course.

But as I walked into my bedroom, passing by the portrait of Isabella, I had to wonder if Arnie was telling the absolute truth. Had my great-aunt been as oblivious to his youthful charms as he seemed to indicate? From his photo, I could tell he had been a handsome young man, and I suspected he'd been more successful with the ladies than he'd claimed. Had there been more to their relationship than one or two dances? Was that why Arnie was so invested in her memory?

"You'll never tell, will you?" I asked the photograph.

As usual, Isabella's enigmatic smile was her only reply.

Chapter Eighteen

The next morning, I decided to work in the garden. Feeling groggy, I hoped the fresh air would clear my head. Fortunately, I was free to do so, since my guests had once again scattered after breakfast. Even Arnie, assuring me he felt perfectly well, had gone out—to get the photos copied, I assumed. So I thought I'd take advantage of their absence to don some casual clothes and get my hands dirty.

But no sooner had I started weeding the two herb beds than my cell phone alerted me to a text. After wiping my hands on my faded cotton shorts, I slid the phone from my pocket and read the message. It was from Julie.

Thought you and Ellen might want to meet up to discuss stuff, it said. *This afternoon, around four, at the Sandburgs? Pete and Sandy's idea. They have some info.*

I texted back my agreement with this plan, then called Ellen to make sure she'd also been invited.

"I think the Irregulars are excited to help with the case," Ellen said, after confirming her plans to attend the impromptu gathering. "Which is fine by me."

"The more the merrier," I agreed. "Anything they can add to our knowledge about the guests, or anyone else, will certainly be appreciated." I hesitated for a moment before adding, "Gavin's in town."

"And hasn't stopped by to visit me?" Ellen's voice was filled with mock outrage. "What a thoughtless cousin he is."

"As if you're actually related," I replied. "Anyway, he doesn't want anyone to know he's in the area, so keep that on the down low, please."

"Ah, is he doing some incognito investigating to aid us with our sleuthing?"

"Exactly."

"That should be helpful. He is quite competent in the field, at least from what I hear."

"So you do still have connections in the intelligence community," I said. "How would you know such a thing otherwise?"

"I still have friends. We have to be discreet, of course, but they keep me posted on things that might affect my life. Like an agent showing up last year under the cover of being my cousin."

"Oh right," I said, distracted by the iridescent dragonfly zooming from the crimped petals of a clump of pinks to a majestic stand of purple irises. "Well, I should probably get back to my weeding, especially since we plan to meet up with our book club friends later."

Ellen wished me a good day before hanging up.

I spent the rest of the morning in the garden, then grabbed a shower and changed into white linen slacks and a coral cotton blouse. After lunch, I called Detective Johnson about the mysterious incursions into Chapters' attic. She said she could send someone out to dust for prints if I wanted but suggested that might be a waste of time.

"Best bet would be to change the lock," she said. "Or better yet, put a padlock on the door."

After finishing the call and making a note to buy a padlock, I dug into the paperwork piled on my office desk—confirming future reservations and reconciling accounts. Not my favorite activity, but years of dealing with teaching plans and other administrative work had taught me the value of keeping up with such things.

Around four, I grabbed my purse and headed outside. Since the Sandburg sisters lived just around the block, it was barely a five-minute walk to their house.

Strolling into the living room, I noticed that everyone but Julie had already arrived.

"She called and said she'd be a few minutes late," Bernadette told me when I asked. "Grab a drink and snack before you sit down," she added, pointing toward the buffet placed against one wall.

Settling down with a tall glass of lemonade and one of Ophelia's famous sugar cookies, I surveyed my friends' interested faces. "Julie said you might have news?"

Sandy scooted to the edge of her seat. "Well, I don't know how important it is to the case, but Pete and I have observed two of your guests getting pretty lovey-dovey."

"On more than one occasion," Pete added. "In the café, but also when we took a break and walked to the waterfront park."

As Ellen crossed her legs, I caught the glimpse of a golden ankle bracelet. "Let me guess—Zach Bell and Linnea Ruskin?"

"Yes, how'd you know?" Sandy asked.

"It seemed the most likely pairing." Ellen leaned back against her chair's plump cushions.

"That might explain why they both seem to vanish so often," I said thoughtfully. *As well as why they might've worked together to attack Arnie. But perhaps I should keep that to myself until the police have a chance to question them.* "I know Zach's going through a contentious divorce, so I'm sure they're trying to keep their relationship under wraps."

"Not doing such a great job of it, if that's their aim," Sandy said with a little laugh. "But I know how it is when you're in love, especially in the beginning. It's hard to keep it a secret."

Feeling Ellen's gaze on me, I shifted in my chair. "They probably saw this trip as a good opportunity to spend time together without as many prying eyes on them. Which could explain their tendency to disappear for hours at a time. But in terms of our suspect list, we definitely can't rule them out."

"Because Linnea, like Lora Kane, makes jewelry?" Bernadette gave me a nod before turning to face the others. "Sodium cyanide is sometimes used in plating jewelry, which means both women could've had access to it."

Sandy gasped and reached for Pete's hand. "Heavens, that's unnerving."

"But so could Zach, since he's a research scientist," I said. "And Alicia's cousin told Ellen and me that he saw Captain Joiner use sodium cyanide when concocting a rat poison."

Ophelia fanned her face with her napkin. "Oh dear, that's practically all of them, then. Except Ms. Allen and Mr. Dean."

"Arnie is Lora's godfather, though. He could've had access to her jewelry studio." Ellen wiggled her toes, flashing her ruby-painted toenails. "The real outlier, in terms of the poison, is Vonnie Allen."

"True," I said, after taking a sip of my lemonade. "But on the other hand, Vonnie has the most substantial motive. Sure, Lora and Linnea may have been upset if, as I suspect, Stacy Wilkin stole their jewelry designs and passed off the finished pieces as her own. And Zach was angry over the way Stacy treated his mother. Not to mention, if he's involved with Linnea, he might've also been willing to aid her in a plan for revenge over the jewelry design thefts. But"—I took another sip of my lemonade—"I think all that pales in the light of Vonnie's reason to hate Stacy."

All eyes turned to me.

"So Arnie shared his information with you?" Ellen asked, with a lift of her eyebrows. "I thought he might."

I straightened, heat rising in my face as I realized my mistake. "On the ride home. I should've called you last night . . ."

Ellen swept this apology away with a wave of her hand. "It's not important. You can tell all of us now."

As I shared what Arnie had told me about Stacy's accusations about Vonnie's son, Sandy *tsk*ed her disapproval while Pete narrowed his eyes.

Of course they would understand the implications of such behavior better than most, I thought. *They are the only parents in the room.*

"I can sympathize with Ms. Allen's anger," Pete said, when I'd finished speaking. "I'd be furious with anyone who falsely accused my child."

"Absolutely." Sandy bobbed her head. "What an awful thing to do to that young man."

"It is a compelling motive, but to be fair, we must remember that Vonnie is the only one without ready access to sodium cyanide," Ellen observed.

"There is that." I slid one finger around the rim of my glass. "With her, it's motive over means."

"And some of the others do have motives. Even if we don't consider them quite as serious as Ms. Allen defending her son, we've all heard of people driven to murder over the tiniest things," Ophelia said, with a delicate shiver.

Bernadette plopped her sneaker-clad feet on the hassock in front of her chair. "But I don't see much, if any, motive for Mr. Dean. Even if he could've grabbed the poison from Lora Kane's studio, why would he kill Ms. Wilkin? The others on our list have some sort of reason to have hated her. So far we haven't heard about any motive associated with Mr. Dean."

"Protecting someone else?" Ellen tapped her chin with one finger. "Lora is his goddaughter, and the child of one of his closest friends."

Bernadette shot her a sharp look. "Who was that, by the way? I suppose it couldn't have been anyone with ties to Isabella and Chapters, like Mr. Dean and his father. I mean, I don't remember anyone named Kane at any of Isabella's parties, but I was out of town for a while when I was an Army nurse."

"It wouldn't be Kane, though," I said, straightening in my chair. "Lora's maiden name was Lester. I remember that because I attended her wedding back when we were teaching colleagues. It was a grand affair; rather over-the-top, actually. One of those expensive extravaganzas which turned out to be ironic, since the marriage only lasted a few years." I glanced over at Ellen. "Her father was a lawyer and businessman, just like Arnie's dad. That's how they met."

"My goodness, you mean Marvin Lester." Ophelia leapt up. "Remember him, Bernie? He attended a lot of Isabella's parties."

Bernadette dropped her feet to the floor with a thud. "What I remember is you talking about him. You were a bit smitten with the guy, I think."

Ophelia blushed. "Oh, now, he was charming. He liked to flirt with all the women, young and old."

"And of course you didn't mind that," Bernadette said with a wry smile. "Anyway, I never met the guy, but I recall he was quoted in one of the articles you sent me when I was in 'Nam. There was something about a valuable emerald ring that was stolen during a party at Chapters. Lester claimed to have caught a glimpse of the thief fleeing the house but then couldn't provide a detailed description to the police." She shrugged. "Always thought he was probably grandstanding."

I shared a glance with Ellen. "Would there have been a picture of him taken at Chapters? I mean, could he have been in one of those silver-framed party photographs Isabella displayed in the library?"

Ophelia sat back down with a flounce of her full skirt. "Yes, indeed, I believe he was in at least one of those photos. Isabella always preferred to have a couple of handsome men flanking her when pictures were taken."

I thought about the photographs hidden in Arnie's room and the way both he and Lora had reacted when I'd discovered them.

Could the dark-haired man in the photo of Arnie and Isabella have been Lora's father? If so, was it actually Lora who stole the pictures and was Arnie merely covering for her, using his tale of a long-ago infatuation with my great-aunt to deflect from her guilt?

The front door slammed as Julie rushed into the room. "So sorry I'm late," she said. "I had a customer who needed to place a special order. It was complicated, and I didn't want to leave my part-time staffer to handle that on their own."

Bernadette grinned. "Sorry, you missed it. We solved the whole thing just now."

Julie rolled her eyes. "I doubt that's true."

"No, no, you haven't missed too much. Charlotte can fill you in later on most of our musings," Ellen said, patting the cushion beside her. "Come and have a seat."

Ophelia jumped up again. "I can get you lemonade or tea, or water. Whatever you want."

Julie shook her head. "I don't need anything, thanks." She glanced around the room, her eyes sparkling. "I do come bearing gifts, or at least some information that might help your sleuthing," she said, plopping down on the sofa.

Ellen widened her eyes. "Do tell."

"Yes, please share," I said.

"Well"—Julie flashed a triumphant smile—"I just met one of Stacy's former employees. Someone Stacy fired, as a matter of fact. Her name is Caitlin Chiba, and she still lives in New Bern. She was visiting Beaufort today and popped into Bookwaves. When we got to talking, the subject of Stacy Wilkin's murder came up. Caitlin had quite a bit to say about that, believe me."

"After being fired, I assume she wasn't overly fond of the woman," Pete said.

"Hardly." As Julie leaned forward, her single braid flopped over her shoulder. "She told me the firing was just a way to get rid of her after she raised some concerns about Stacy's business practices."

"You mean Ms. Wilkin fired her in retaliation for raising the alarm over some red flags?" Sandy made a face.

Julie nodded. "She didn't have anything nice to say about Stacy, that's for sure. But she also didn't want to go into detail about her concerns with me. To be fair, there were other people in the store at the time. I guess that made her uncomfortable." Julie side-eyed Ellen. "However, I did ask if she'd be willing to talk in private to a couple of my friends who were looking into the murder. She seemed open to that idea, especially once I mentioned that one of them owned the B and B where the death had occurred. I think she was sympathetic to your need to clear things up in order to protect Chapters' reputation," she added, with a glance in my direction.

"Shouldn't she talk to the police first?" Ophelia asked as she sat down again.

Bernadette frowned. "Suggesting that might just scare her off. A lot of people don't want to get involved with the authorities, for one reason or another."

"That's what I thought," Julie said. "She seemed very reluctant to go public with any information on her former boss. I mentioned that maybe Charlotte and Ellen could listen to her concerns and figure out whether they were anything important— I mean, anything that could possibly be connected to the murder.

She said that might work, even though she was very hesitant when I mentioned speaking directly to the police."

"That makes sense," Ellen said. "After all, why involve an innocent person if all she has are suspicions or stories about Stacy that may ultimately have no bearing on the case?"

I cast Ellen an inquiring glance. *She just wants to talk to this Caitlin Chiba before the police do, but why? Despite her protestations over her relationship with Arnie being in the past, is she trying to protect him or his goddaughter?* After clearing my throat, I said, "We can certainly speak with her. But if she has information that might point to a culprit, we'll have to urge her to talk to Detective Johnson or someone else on the investigative team."

"Of course." Ellen kept her gaze locked on Julie. "But I'd like to vet her first, for her sake if nothing else. What if going to the authorities targeted her as a suspect? She is a disgruntled employee, after all. If she doesn't have a solid alibi for the time of the murder . . ."

"Good point," Julie said. "I'd hate to see her dragged into the investigation if there's no official need to involve her."

I straightened in my chair. "I suppose that's okay, but if we do get any inkling that she had any connection to Stacy's murder, I'm going to immediately share that fact with Detective Johnson."

"Fair enough. But let's just wait and see, shall we?" Ellen finally met my stare and gave a little shake of her head. "No use making up our minds ahead of time."

We discussed the case for another half hour before calling it a day. Leaving the house after obtaining Ms. Chiba's phone number from Julie, I jogged to catch up with Ellen, who'd hurried away as soon as our impromptu sleuthing group had disbanded.

"Why are you so intent on speaking to this woman before the police have a chance to interrogate her?" I asked, as Ellen paused in front of her house.

She shaded her eyes with one hand, her gaze fixed on her front porch. "I simply fear that bringing in the authorities too soon might spook her, that's all."

"Really? It doesn't have anything to do with Arnie Dean or his close connection to Lora Kane?" I asked, tapping my foot against the sidewalk.

Ellen leveled her piercing blue stare on me. "Why would it?"

"I don't know. I thought perhaps you were worried that this Caitlin person might know something about Stacy's dealings with Lora. Not just in terms of selling Lora's jewelry, but maybe some other, more nefarious, connection?"

"What makes you think I would care about what happens to Lora Kane?" Ellen asked, her eyes narrowing.

"I don't believe you do, at least in terms of Lora herself. But it occurred to me that you might care how it could affect your old friend, Arnie . . ."

Ellen cut me off, slicing her hand through the air. "As I've already told you, that friendship is relegated to the past. I have no interest in protecting Arnie or, by extension, his goddaughter. My insistence that we speak with Ms. Chiba before she talks with the police is simply based on years of experience dealing with informants. They tend to clam up if they believe their words may bring too much scrutiny to bear on their own actions."

"You think she'll spill more useful info if she doesn't feel she's being interrogated?"

"I'm sure she will. The minute she's sitting across from a police officer, she's going to realize her own situation is tenuous at best. As mentioned earlier, she's a disgruntled ex-employee. Someone Stacy Wilkin fired. That could easily be seen as a motive for murder, don't you think?"

"I suppose." I looked Ellen up and down. "You hope she'll feel she can speak freely to us, which she might not do if she's already been questioned by the police."

"Exactly." Ellen reached out to pat my arm. "Don't worry. I have no intention of keeping anything from the authorities. I just want to see what this former employee is willing to share with us before she realizes that she could be seen as a possible suspect."

"Very well. I'll trust your judgment on this." I tapped my foot again. "I did want to let you know a few things I've already shared with Detective Johnson—involving Arnie's possible attacker, and someone rummaging through my attic again last night."

Ellen's lips thinned into a straight line. "Another thing you forgot to call me about last night?"

"I'm telling you now," I said firmly. As much as I liked Ellen, sometimes her interrogative tone irked me. Clearing my throat, I proceeded to fill her in on my thoughts about Zach and Linnea being possible suspects in the aquarium incident as well as on Damian's and my discovery that someone had once again been searching the attic.

"It had to be one of the guests staying in the house," she said. "Which leaves out Zach Bell."

"But what if he and Linnea are working as a team? Anyway"—
I patted my pocket, where I'd stashed my cell phone—"Julie gave
me Ms. Chiba's phone number. I'll call when I get back to the
house and see if we can set up a meeting for tomorrow."

Ellen flashed a warm smile. "Perfect. Now I'd better get
inside so I can let Shandy out, or I might have a different sort of
mess to clean up."

Chapter Nineteen

M y phone vibrated in my pocket as I walked back into the kitchen at Chapters. It was a text from Gavin, asking if I could meet him on his boat later in the evening.

"Is there anything you need help with tonight?" I asked Alicia, who was covering a plate of freshly baked muffins with plastic wrap.

"Nope. Just need to clean up a few things, and we should be set for tomorrow's breakfast." Alicia looked me up and down. "Are you headed out for dinner or something?"

"No, I'll just grab a sandwich. But I am going out to visit a friend in a bit." I picked up some clean utensils Alicia had set on a towel on the counter and carried them over to one of the drawers in the kitchen island. "I may be back late. Just wanted to let you know so you don't worry."

The clatter of the utensils as I dropped them back in the drawer almost, but not quite, covered Alicia's dismissive snort. "You're a full-grown woman. If you want to stay out till the wee hours or even all night, it's really none of my business." She caught my eye and shook her finger at me. "Just don't forget your key. I don't want to be woken up at three in the morning to let you in."

"I won't be that late," I said, not entirely sure this was true.

Alicia waved me off. "Whatever. Have fun. Heaven knows we could all use a break after the nonsense of this week. Honestly, today was almost as bad as the day of the murder, what with the police running all over the place, questioning the guests again."

"They wanted to follow up after the attack on Mr. Dean," I said, hoping she wouldn't ask me anything else. I didn't want to get into a discussion concerning Zach, Linnea, or any of the others. As Amber Johnson had said, it was best if we treated the guests normally, and I wasn't sure Alicia could do so if she knew all my suspicions.

Alicia just huffed. "Tracked in dirt all over my clean floors, but I guess they're just doing their jobs." She turned away, signaling that our conversation was over.

Happy to avoid any further discussion, I left the kitchen and did a little more work in the office while I ate my sandwich—checking the clock every ten minutes, of course. When it grew closer to the time I was to meet Gavin, I headed into my bedroom. Mainly to brush my teeth, although a glance in the mirror made me reconsider my outfit. Even though I knew I technically didn't need to change clothes again, I perused the options in my closet, settling on a full-skirted tropical-print sundress topped with a white bolero jacket. I also decided that a pair of canvas flats with gripping soles was the best choice for trekking around a marina and boat. Finally dressed, I dashed back into the bathroom to check my hair one more time.

Honestly, I'd think you would've outgrown the butterflies at your age, I chided myself. My reflection just made a face at me, reminding me to touch up my lip gloss.

Slipping out the back door, I reached my car just as Arnie and Lora exited the garden. They were arguing about something. I paused, one hand on the driver's side door handle, before deciding that I should simply drive away.

I couldn't hear what they were saying anyway.

The marina wasn't far. I reached it in under ten minutes. After parking my car, I made my way along the boat slips, searching for an older cabin cruiser with a white-painted hull.

The boat wasn't hard to find. Although not the largest in the marina, its vintage charm and the chrome fittings gleaming against its rich wood decking and trim made it stand out. Confirming that the boat was named the *Anna-Lisa Marie*, I knew I was in the right place.

"Hello," I called out. "Anybody home?"

Gavin stepped out of the covered upper cabin. "Come aboard," he said, striding over to stand across from me. He held out his hand and helped me step over onto the wooden decking. "You look like you're ready for a party," he said.

I held out the skirt of the dress with one hand. "Is it too much?"

"Not at all. I'm flattered you took so much effort. And afraid you'll think me a slouch," he added, sweeping his hand over his plain navy T-shirt and ivory cotton shorts.

"You look just fine. Very nautical," I said, leaning in to kiss him on the cheek.

Gavin pulled me closer to return the kiss. "Perhaps we should head inside," he said, when he finally released me. "We don't want to create the sort of spectacle that could draw unwanted attention."

"In case our murderer is keeping tabs on me?" I asked, arching my eyebrows.

Gavin's expression sobered. "There is that possibility."

"Seriously? I suppose I should trust your judgment on that," I said, as I followed him into the covered section of the boat.

"You should. As a matter of fact"—Gavin's gaze swept over the docks—"we'd probably better head down below. Just to be certain no one can see or hear us."

"Are you sure you aren't just asking me to see your etchings?" I asked with a smile.

Gavin grinned. "No room for such things on a boat like this. But it is where I sleep. If that worries you . . ."

"Not at all. Lead on. I think I can trust you to behave like a gentleman," I said, following him through a small door that led down a short flight of stairs.

"You probably can, blast it," Gavin called over his shoulder. "I'm too decent for my own good sometimes."

"Hmm, what makes me think that is a bit of an exaggeration?" I said, surveying the bottom level of the boat. As in the upper cabin, polished wood covered most of the surfaces. A small kitchenette filled one end of the space, while the opposite end was taken up by a full-sized mattress on a wooden platform. Lining the walls between the bow and stern were two bench-style bins that I suspected could be used for extra sleeping quarters as well as storage. Between the cushioned benches, a small pedestal table anchored to the floor sprang up like a metal mushroom.

"Very cozy," I said, as Gavin opened the mini fridge and pulled out a bottle of wine.

"It's sufficient. I don't live on her full-time, of course. Usually just when I'm between assignments."

"And then you're camping out in hotel rooms? That still sounds challenging to me. I guess you can't collect too much stuff, either way."

"It's a simple life." Gavin plucked two tumblers from a cabinet over the saucepan-sized metal sink. "Please, sit down, madam. Your waiter will be right with you."

Sliding behind the table, I took a seat on the saffron-yellow bench cushions. "It's really lovely, though, all things considered. You've kept this vessel in excellent condition, especially considering her age."

"I'm kind of a stickler for cleanliness and keeping things tidy." Gavin crossed the short distance between us and placed two rubber coasters on the table before setting down the tumblers. "I guess it's because so much of the rest of my life is messy, and often out of my control," he added, sitting down across from me.

"That makes sense." I sipped my wine and studied his face. "Why do I get the feeling that you're getting tired of this life?"

"Because you know me pretty well by now, it seems." Gavin took a long swallow of his drink. "And because I'm not getting any younger. I'm beginning to feel my current occupation is strictly a younger man's game."

I stretched my left arm across the small table and laid my hand on his wrist. "What would you rather do?"

"Not sure. Although"—he cast me an amused glance—"perhaps a job you've done in the past."

My eyes widened. "Teach?"

"Something like that. More like training, I suppose," Gavin replied, turning his hand so that he could clasp my fingers. "Instructing new agents in the finer points of espionage and survival."

"That certainly sounds less dangerous than your current position, which would be an improvement, in my opinion." I tightened my hold on his fingers. "I'm being selfish here, but that sort of change would definitely make me happy, if only because it would keep you safer. But is it really an option?"

"Maybe." Gavin gave my fingers a squeeze before pulling his hand away and settling back against the bench cushions. He examined me with an intent gaze that made me squirm. "There's an opportunity opening up. I've put in for it, but we shall see." He lifted his glass in a little salute. "The wheels of bureaucracy grind slowly and all that."

"Where would this be, if you got the job?" I asked, before gulping down more wine. "I mean, you'd finally have a home base, I guess. Which would be nice, but hopefully it wouldn't be in California or Europe or somewhere else that would be difficult to . . ." Heat prickled the back of my neck. "I mean, that's far away."

"Don't worry. I wouldn't even have applied if that was the case." Setting down his tumbler, Gavin leaned forward, resting his arms on the table. "I'd be based in Virginia, fairly close to Washington."

"Good for docking the boat, then," I said, keeping my tone light. "There are lots of harbors not far from DC."

"Good for visits to this area too," he said, his light-brown eyes fixed on my face. "Only about six hours without stops. Just a day trip."

I carefully placed my own glass on its coaster. "I see you've checked into that too."

"Of course. I'm a planner, you know."

"And it seems your plans include visiting Beaufort."

"As often as possible." Gavin reached across the table to clasp both my hands. "I hope that meets with your approval."

"Absolutely. And I wouldn't mind making a few trips to the DC area either. I mean, all those museums . . ."

Gavin rose to his feet. Still holding my hands, he stepped around the table and sat down next me. "That's better," he said, after kissing me. He tapped my nose with one finger. "I suppose I'd better get that job now. Don't want to let you down." He grinned. "You know, about visiting all those museums."

"Whatever happens, I'm sure we can work something out," I said, sliding closer to him. "Now—how about I fill you in on some news on the Stacy Wilkin case. That is why I'm here, right?"

Gavin slipped his arm across the top of the cushions behind my head. "No, but I do have some information to share with you, so I guess we should get that out of the way first."

I didn't respond to that *first*, instead launching into what I'd learned about Linnea and Zach, Vonnie, Caitlin Chiba, and the connection Lora's father may have had with Isabella and Chapters.

"You're planning to meet with the ex-employee, then?" Gavin asked, when I'd finished my report. "Don't you think that could be risky?"

"Ellen will be there as well. And I think I'll suggest that we meet in the office at Bookwaves, so Julie will also be nearby."

Gavin's arm dropped down around my shoulders. "Still, if this Caitlin person had any involvement in Stacy Wilkin's death, she could turn volatile. Maybe I could pretend to be a bookstore customer or something."

"Except Julie will recognize you and I thought you wanted to avoid that, at least for now."

"I could loiter outside, then." Gavin hugged me closer to his side. "I just don't want you, or Ellen, to be put in danger."

"If you can stay out of sight, outside might work."

Gavin reared back and looked me in the eye. "*If* I can stay out of sight? Have you forgotten who you're talking to?"

"Okay, double-oh seven, calm down," I said, patting his arm. "I'm sure that will be fine. I'll text you once I know what time we're meeting, and you can take it from there. Now—what is the info you wanted to share with me? Some relevant background on one of the guests?"

"Not exactly. It's actually connected to those old jewelry heists you mentioned." Gavin stood up and grabbed the tumblers off the table. "More?" he asked, holding up the glasses.

"No, I'm good." I scooted down the bench, away from the table, so I could stretch out my legs without hitting the pedestal. "What did you find out?"

"That there was a file on the heists at the agency, for one thing. Mainly because they didn't only happen in this area." After setting my tumbler beside the sink, Gavin poured a little more wine in his glass. "There was a series of jewelry thefts with a very similar MO that occurred in a few other U.S. cities, as well as in London, not long after the robberies around here ceased."

"Really?" I rose to my feet. "When was this? The London heists in particular?"

Cradling his glass, Gavin strolled toward me. "Does that mean something?"

"It could. I've learned that Lora Kane's father, Marvin Lester, attended a lot of parties at Chapters around the time the thefts were happening here."

"And?" Gavin tipped his head to study me, his expression filled with interest.

"And he and his family also lived in London in the early to mid-eighties. Lora mentioned that to me just the other day, so I know it's true."

"Interesting. That does match the time period when the jewelry thefts occurred in London. You suspect a connection?"

"Don't you?" I moved close enough to take the tumbler from his hand and set it on the table. "Think about what we know—those photographs that went missing from the library included one with a dark-haired man who could've been Marvin Lester. Then Arnie Dean tells me he took them because he wanted to make copies due to some old crush he had on Isabella."

"But he could've simply been covering for Lora, the daughter of his good friend, Marvin Lester . . ."

"Who just so happened to be a frequent visitor to Beaufort around the time the jewelry heists were occurring here."

"And who lived in London when similar thefts happened there." Gavin took hold of my hands. "I see where you're going with this. You suspect Lora Kane is covering up the misdeeds of her father." He shook his head. "But even if that was the case, why kill Stacy Wilkin? There appears to be no connection."

"Jewelry," I said, tightening my grip on his hands. "Jewelry is the connection. I'm not sure how, but I bet there's some link between her father possibly being involved in a jewelry theft ring and Lora subsequently creating jewelry that was sold at Stacy's stores." I dropped Gavin's hands and stepped back as another realization hit me. "Lora also told me that her father passed away about seven years ago. I know her mother died when Lora was a teen and she's an only child, which means she could've inherited his entire estate."

"Perhaps including some ill-gotten gains."

"Yes, and according to a few comments on an article I read, there were rumors about Stacy selling items with questionable histories. Maybe she was helping Lora get rid of some hot merchandise that was part of her inheritance?"

Gavin tapped his jaw with two fingers. "It's certainly a possibility. Especially since Marvin Lester was in a position where he had access to parties and other events that included a number of wealthy guests."

"Which is why talking to Caitlin Chiba feels more important than ever. What she knows about the interactions between Lora and Stacy could be the key to this case."

Gavin crossed his arms over his chest. "But conversely, isn't that why you should let Detective Johnson and her team take over at this point?"

"No, because if Ellen is right, Caitlin could be scared off by the police and clam up. I mean, what if she was involved in selling stolen goods? She isn't going to want to say much about the situation if that's the case. Whereas if she tells Ellen and me something useful, we can urge her to go to the authorities and turn state's evidence for immunity or something."

"I see your point, but whatever happens, I think you should talk to the Beaufort police as soon as you hear anything even the least bit relevant to the case."

"We will, of course. Neither Ellen nor I want to hamper the investigation in any way." I placed my hands on Gavin's shoulders. "You should know that."

"I do. It's just . . . it's a tricky situation. I understand Ellen's reasoning, but the police might not view it the same way." Gavin dropped his arms so he could slip them around my waist. "Anyway, I'll be keeping an eye on things, discreetly and from a distance, during this convo with Ms. Chiba. Just know you can call on me if necessary."

I laid my head on his shoulder. "Thank you. That will make me a lot less anxious. And Ellen too, once she knows."

"I'm not sure Ellen will feel the same way about it, but then again, I also don't care." Gavin leaned in until his lips were at my ear. "Now, having completed our little business meeting, how about we get to the real purpose of this visit?"

I lifted my head to look into his face. "Which is?"

"Me demonstrating my true intentions, as we discussed last night," he said, before proceeding to do so.

Chapter Twenty

Although I'd sent a text to Caitlin Chiba Thursday, after the meeting with my book club friends, she didn't contact me until Friday morning.

I was standing at the kitchen island, drinking my third cup of coffee while I waited for my guests to finish breakfast so I could clear the dishes. Having gotten in late the night before, I needed all the caffeine I could guzzle to jump-start my day.

I'd just set down my empty mug and headed for the dining room when my cell phone jangled.

"Hello, is this Charlotte Reed?" asked a pleasant woman's voice.

"Yes, it is." I said, pausing outside the half-open door into the dining room. "Is this Ms. Chiba?"

"Caitlin is fine." There was a brief pause. "The lady at the bookstore told me that you and your friend might want to speak with me. I guess that will be okay, although I'm not sure what it has to do with the murder at your inn."

"We simply want to ask you some questions about working for Stacy Wilkin. Just the three of us—no police involved. I thought we could meet at Bookwaves, in the back office, some-time this afternoon. If that works for you, of course."

"All right." Caitlin's voice was edged with suspicion, which I felt was perfectly normal. "How about two o'clock?"

"Two it is," I said, before wishing her a good day.

As I pocketed my phone and pushed open the dining room door, I realized that all of the guests were on their feet, staring at me.

That was foolish, I told myself. *Now every one of them may have heard you set up that meeting with Caitlin Chiba.* I shook off my apprehension over this mistake and forced a smile. "Excuse me, I need to clear the tables. As long as you're all finished with breakfast, of course."

"Good timing," Arnie said, his eyes shining with what looked like suppressed excitement. "We just heard the most interesting news from these two." He waved one hand toward Zach and Linnea, who were huddled together behind one of the room's circular tables.

Lora met my gaze with a lift of her chin. "Apparently they're engaged. Who knew?"

"I'd guessed," Vonnie said, with a swift glance at Lora. "Not that they were engaged; just that they were dating. But I honestly didn't think it was my place to say anything."

"Well"—I offered Zach and Linnea a sincere smile—"congratulations are in order, then. We'll have to break out some champagne later."

Zach, whose arm was draped around Linnea's shoulders, straightened to his full height. "Thank you, but that won't be necessary. We're trying to keep everything low-key, since I am still finalizing my divorce. We wouldn't even had said anything yet, except some people"—he shot a furious glance at Lora— "seem to be overly interested in other people's business."

Lora lifted her slender hands. "I couldn't help it. You two were chatting pretty loudly about your future lives together."

"You were eavesdropping." Linnea's blue eyes glittered like shards of lapis.

"Not at all. You were talking in the garden, quite loudly," Lora said. "Since that's a public space, at least for any of Chapters' guests, I had as much right to be there as you did."

Zach hugged Linnea closer to his side. "Anyway, it's out in the open now. And I'm certainly not ashamed to admit that Linnea and I are getting married, as soon as we legally can. It's just that I don't want my wife getting wind of it. She might delay things even longer if she knew."

"Don't worry." Arnie's tone projected his typical good humor. "None of us are going to contact your soon-to-be ex. I don't even know her, for one thing. She never attended any of our book club events, did she?"

Vonnie rolled her eyes. "Heavens, no. That would've been such a bore for her." She cast a smile in Zach and Linnea's direction. "I did meet her once."

"And assessed her accurately, it seems," Zach said, relaxing his hold on Linnea.

I surveyed my guests, struck by their appearance of normality. Yes, they might snipe at one another occasionally, as all such groups sometimes did, but surely none of them had murdered Stacy Wilkin. *Wouldn't it show on their faces?* I thought, as I wished them a good day before they exited the dining room.

But, I reminded myself, *from past experience I know it isn't always that easy to identify a murderer.*

* * *

Having confirmed the time with Ellen earlier, I met her outside her house at quarter to two.

"Gavin's going to be joining us?" She handed me Shandy's leash as she adjusted the ribbon ties of her wide-brimmed straw hat.

I leaned over to pat the Yorkie's head, getting a lick of his tongue across my hand in return. "Not officially. But I let him know when we'd set the appointment so he could hang out in the general area and keep a lookout."

"That makes me feel better, especially since you said that your guests may have overheard our plans to meet with Ms. Chiba." Ellen took back Shandy's leash.

"Actually, I thought it might be interesting to see if any of them show up," I said. "And Gavin will be able to tell us that."

We set off, allowing the little dog to bounce along in front of us. Of course, we had to pause so Shandy could sniff some sprigs of grass that had sprung up between cracks in the sidewalk and bark at a butterfly flitting through flowers in a curbside garden, but we kept up a fast pace otherwise and reached Bookwaves a little before two.

I glanced around the boardwalk but didn't see Gavin. Which didn't really surprise me. I assumed he was somewhere nearby, just keeping out of sight.

Julie met us at the door. "Your packages are in the back," she said, gesturing with a bob of her head toward the customers milling around the shop.

I nodded and followed Ellen and Shandy into the office behind the sales counter, knowing Julie would keep an eye on things. I'd sent her a text earlier warning her to keep anyone from crashing our meeting. If any of my guests slipped past Gavin's notice and entered the store, I was sure Julie would keep them at bay.

"Oh, what a sweet pup," said the young woman waiting for us in the office. Petite and dark haired, she stepped around a stack of book boxes to greet Ellen and me.

"His name's Shandy," Ellen said, as Caitlin Chiba bent down to get closer to the dog. "He might lick you to death, but he won't bite."

Shandy sniffed Caitlin's hand for a second before looking up at her with his bright black eyes, his stubby tail wagging.

"I love dogs," Caitlin said, patting his head.

I'd already figured that out, since I'd learned that Shandy had a sixth sense about people. He seemed to be able to instantly tell if someone disliked dogs and would either snap at the air or bark furiously at such misguided individuals.

Ellen rolled Julie's task chair back from the desk. "Here you go, Caitlin. Make yourself comfortable."

"Where are you going to sit?" she asked, straightening and stepping away from Shandy, who strained at his leash as if trying to reach her again.

"There's a couple more chairs around here somewhere." I surveyed the small room, which was lined with shelves and cluttered with boxes. "Here we go, behind this stack." I pulled out two folding chairs and popped them open.

Caitlin glanced at Ellen, who was taking off her hat. "Why don't you sit here, Ms. Montgomery? I can use one of those harder chairs."

"Nonsense. I may be the oldest one in the room, but I can handle a folding chair, at least for a short period of time." Ellen laid her hat on the desk before sitting down.

I'd set up the folding chairs so that we could face Caitlin across the desk. Sitting down in the chair next to Ellen with Shandy curling up in the space between us, I met Caitlin's wary gaze. "Getting right to the point—Julie tells me you used to work for Stacy Wilkin. Was that in her New Bern shop?"

Caitlin nodded. "Yeah. I know she also used to own a jewelry store in Cary, but she'd closed that one down before I ever went to work for her. She'd just opened the New Bern store, as a matter of fact. I was an assistant manager there for about a year or so."

"But she fired you because you questioned her about some things?" Ellen asked.

"About some of her business practices, yeah," Caitlin said, her expression darkening. "I mean, she claimed that my work performance was inadequate, blah, blah, blah, but I knew it was really retaliation for me questioning her business dealings."

I crossed my ankles and leaned forward, resting one palm against the desk. "Like what, exactly? Was she selling stolen property or something?"

"Not sure, but I suspected she was. She handled a lot of estate jewelry on commission as well as original pieces. I just thought, well"—Caitlin squinched up her nose, as if she'd smelled something unpleasant—"a few of the clients she dealt with didn't appear to be the type to have that sort of stuff. Not that only wealthy people could've inherited valuable jewelry; I don't mean that. But some of these guys just seemed sketchy to me. Furtive, you know?"

Ellen leaned back in her chair. "Like they were dealing in hot merchandise?"

"That's exactly the feeling I got," Caitlin said, her dark lashes fluttering over her ebony eyes. "And the paperwork seemed a little . . . incomplete sometimes."

"Interesting. But to play devil's advocate—maybe she knew, and maybe she didn't. If she was taking things on commission, she might not have been aware of the provenance of every piece," Ellen said.

"She didn't look too closely into that, for sure," Caitlin said. "I don't even think she bothered to ask where stuff had come from most of the time. Which I thought was weird. When I'd worked at another jewelry store, they were very careful about establishing a line of ownership for any estate jewelry." Caitlin ran her fingers through her shoulder-length dark hair. "That's why I was surprised Stacy didn't seem to ask too many questions or demand paperwork on the pieces or anything like that."

I shared a glance with Ellen. Caitlin's words solidified my suspicion that Stacy had been selling stolen jewelry and that she absolutely knew what she was doing. "Then there were original pieces, from what I've heard. Stacy's store also carried jewelry designed by regional artisans, didn't it?"

"Yeah. She had quite a few designers who supplied the shop with unique items." Caitlin frowned. "That was another thing that bothered me. There was this one young artist who sent Stacy some sketches. I saw them, and it was really gorgeous work. Sadly, I think Stacy just appropriated them. She had a few pieces made off the designs and sold them, even though I never saw any evidence that the artist was paid or even credited."

Linnea Ruskin, I thought, wondering how many others Stacy had ripped off. Perhaps she had stolen a few designs from Lora as well. "Stacy also sold some jewelry from well-known designers in her stores, didn't she? Like Lora Kane."

Caitlin's lips tightened at the mention of that name. "We sold her stuff, which was fine, but Stacy also got other, odd deliveries from her. I mean, we'd get these heavily insured packages with items designed by Kane, and nestled in the box there'd be one or two pieces of jewelry that I was sure had to have come from somewhere else."

"How so?" Ellen's eyes narrowed.

As Caitlin tossed her head, the office's fluorescent light fixture streaked her silky black hair with blue highlights. "I knew Kane's style well enough to know that she'd never design a piece like that. They looked vintage to me. More like the estate jewelry."

"And Stacy sold those pieces in the store?" I leaned over to stroke Shandy's head as he snuffled my bare ankle, all the while keeping my gaze fixed on Caitlin's face.

"Not always. That was the other weird thing. Sometimes Stacy had those items reworked. She had a couple of craftsmen on retainer. They'd come by to reset pieces for customers. Once or twice, I caught her asking them to take the gems out of an item Kane had sent us in order to use them in a new setting. There was this one emerald-and-diamond ring . . ."

As I shoved back my chair, the screech of the legs against the wood floor startled Caitlin as well as Shandy. Ellen cast me a knowing look before turning back to address Caitlin. "You think Lora Kane was supplying Stacy with questionable goods along with her own designs?"

"Pretty sure of that." Caitlin frowned. "I think Stacy believed she could put one over on me because I was young. And, to be brutally honest, she had these ideas about anyone who wasn't, well—white."

"I've heard she was a bit of a racist," I said, my mind still processing the thought that Lora may have had a stolen emerald-and-diamond ring in her possession. A ring that could've gone missing during one of Isabella's parties years before. *A ring that might've been stolen by, or at the behest of, Lora's father*, I realized, remembering my conversation with Gavin.

Caitlin's sharp burst of laughter made Shandy bark in response. "A bit? She was totally on the 'only white is right' train. Me being Asian American was bad enough; she was even harder on anyone brown or black. That's why she went after Raphael Allen the way she did."

"We did hear that she accused him of stealing from the store," Ellen said, picking up Shandy and cuddling him in her lap.

"To be exact, she said he helped his friends with a break-in. Still a lie." Anger vibrated through Caitlin's voice. "I think it was one of her shady dealers or someone like that. Stacy just wanted to pin it on Raphael."

"But the police could never find any evidence that he was involved," I said.

"Because he wasn't." Caitlin made a derisive noise. "But that was Stacy all over. She kept repeating that false claim even after Raphael was completely cleared by the authorities." A wicked smile curved her lips. "And eventually had to pay for it too. Justice served, for once."

"What do you mean?" I asked.

"Most people don't know, 'cause it was a private deal, but Stacy had to pay a settlement to Raphael and his mom. To avoid a more public civil suit for slander, I think. Anyway, she was paying them something monthly. I'm sure of that, because I saw her writing Raphael a check once, not long before I was fired."

I leaned forward until my back wasn't touching my chair. "She set up a private arrangement with them?"

"Yeah, and I'm pretty sure it was ongoing." Caitlin frowned. "I guess the payments will stop now, which is a shame. Raphael deserved all the money he could get, after what Stacy put him through."

"I think perhaps you may have protested Ms. Wilkin's treatment of your colleague," Ellen said. "If so, good on you, even if it did contribute to your firing."

"It didn't help," Caitlin said with a shrug. "But, to be honest, I was glad to be free from that situation. I was out of a job, but at least I wasn't mixed up with someone I suspected of buying and selling stolen property."

I shared a look with Ellen, who nodded her approval of my unspoken thought. "You should tell the Beaufort police everything you've told us," I said. "Ellen and I did want to hear you out first, but now that it's obvious that you had no connection to the murder . . ."

"You thought I might?" Caitlin asked, jerking her slender shoulders.

"No, not really," Ellen said, in a soothing tone. "We just didn't want to place you in an awkward situation. But after hearing you speak, I think it is safe for you to take your story to the authorities. It might help with the case, if only to raise the possibility that some of Ms. Wilkin's less than savory connections should be questioned and checked out."

"I hadn't thought of that. I figured all my information on Stacy was irrelevant to the murder case. But maybe not." Caitlin pressed her palms together and rested her chin on her templed hands. "I'll talk to the authorities as soon as possible, if you think that's wise."

"Ask to speak to Detective Amber Johnson." I rose to my feet. "She's the best one to contact."

"And tell her everything, even if you don't think it's important," Ellen said, setting Shandy back on the floor before standing. He danced on the end of the leash, obviously ready to take another walk. "Thank you so much for speaking with us today, Caitlin. It was quite illuminating."

"Thanks for listening, and giving me some good advice." Caitlin stood up to face us. "Can I just pet Shandy again before you leave? That would make my day."

"Of course." Ellen led the dog around the desk. "Maybe wait ten minutes after we leave the office before you make your exit," she told Caitlin, as Shandy reveled in the attention from the young woman.

"So no one sees us leave at the same time?" Caitlin arched her thin black eyebrows. "If I didn't know better, I'd suspect you two were secret agents or something."

Ellen's bright laugh gave nothing away. "Now, dear, that's quite a stretch, don't you think?"

We made our way through the store and out onto the boardwalk before I dared to say what was on my mind. "It doesn't seem that Vonnie Allen would've wanted to kill Stacy, not if her son was receiving monthly payments from the woman."

"Yes, that would be like killing the golden goose." Ellen popped her straw hat back over her short white hair. "Gavin's lurking over in the shadow of that doorway, if you want to go fill him in on what we've learned today."

I squinted and peered in the direction of her gaze, but it still took me a moment to notice a male figure in dark clothes and a fisherman's cap pulled down low over his brow. "You're good. And so is he, I guess. I wouldn't have noticed him without you pointing him out."

"That's what we wanted, isn't it? Why don't you tell him to meet us later, somewhere we can actually talk, like my house. Just text me the details." Ellen patted my shoulder before heading off, Shandy trotting at her side. She didn't acknowledge Gavin as she walked past him.

I waited until she'd disappeared around the corner before I strolled over to the doorway to greet Gavin. "Got some useful info today," I said, keeping my voice low after he pressed two fingers to his lips.

"Good," he said, surprisingly not making any move to touch me.

Oh, right, we need to be discreet, I reminded myself, crossing my arms over my chest. "See any of the guests?"

"All of them," he said. "At one point or another."

I sighed. That didn't narrow anything down. "Ellen wants to meet. Tonight, her house. I'll text you the details." I gave his bare forearm a swift brush with my fingers before turning and striding away.

Chapter
Twenty-One

After dinner, I slipped away from Chapters to join Gavin at Ellen's house. Over texts, we'd coordinated a meeting to discuss some of the day's information and events.

Taking a seat at the round oak table, I surveyed Ellen's kitchen. Unlike Isabella, who had given Chapters a more modern upgrade, the previous owner of Ellen's house had opted for a quasi-Victorian look. It wasn't entirely successful. As Damian, after working one of Ellen's parties, had once succinctly said, it was "neither fish nor fowl." A black reproduction stove that mimicked an old wood burner and a white refrigerator rigged out to look like a turn-of-the century icebox anchored the space, which included cabinets designed to look more like free-standing furniture than standard built-ins.

"You haven't renovated yet, I see," Gavin said, as he entered the kitchen through the back door. "If I remember correctly, you were talking about doing that the last time I was here."

"I haven't felt a strong enough inclination to change anything. It's just me living here, after all, and I don't hang out in the kitchen that much. Not really into cooking, to be honest."

Ellen set a crystal pitcher on the table. "If you want something more than water, just let me know."

"This will be fine," I said, filling one of the glasses Ellen had placed on the table.

Gavin chose the chair next to mine. "Water is all I need."

"You're easy guests." Ellen looked Gavin and me over with a critical eye before taking a seat across the table from us. "So—are you officially a couple now, or do I have to continue to tap-dance around that issue?"

"You don't," Gavin said, pressing his fingers over the hand I'd laid on the table.

Ellen poured a full glass of water and took a sip before replying. "Good. Now, on to more urgent matters. Charlotte tells me you saw all of Chapters' current guests in the vicinity of Bookwaves earlier, Gavin. What did they appear to be up to?"

"Hard to tell. I can say that there were three distinct groups—Linnea Ruskin and Zach Bell arrived as a couple and hung out by the boardwalk railing, making a great show of looking at the boats docked in the slips." Gavin lifted his hand and ran his fingers through his curly light-brown hair. "Then Vonnie Allen showed up, on her own. She spent her time window-shopping at the stores adjacent to Bookwaves. The last to arrive were Arnie Dean and Lora Kane. They sat at one of the outdoor tables at a nearby restaurant and ordered wine and some sort of cheese platter. They drank the wine but didn't eat much," Gavin added, with a sidelong glance at me. "It appeared to me that they were arguing, but I wasn't close enough to hear what was being said."

I absently tapped the rim of my glass. "That's interesting. I caught them having a disagreement in the garden when I went out to my car last night. Seems like they've been arguing a lot recently."

"Maybe Arnie's having second thoughts about protecting Lora, goddaughter or not." Ellen, whose elbow was propped on the arm of her heavy wooden chair, rested her chin on her hand. "If Lora is our murderer and he knows something, it could also be why he was attacked at the aquarium."

"You think the hooded stranger was Lora?" I asked, widening my eyes.

"Maybe. Or someone she hired. If she's been dealing in stolen goods, she may have made some not-so-upstanding acquaintances."

"From what Caitlin Chiba told us, Lora had to be in on Stacy's little side gig. Selling jewelry with murky provenances," I added, when Gavin cast me a questioning look.

"You'd better bring me up to speed," he said.

Ellen complied with this request, detailing what we'd learned from Caitlin.

"That does bolster our suspicions about Lora and her father," Gavin said, when Ellen finished her report. "If Marvin Lester truly was the mastermind behind the jewelry heists here as well as in London and elsewhere, Lora could've inherited a cache of stolen items."

"Maybe she knew all about it," I said thoughtfully. "They were very close, from what I've seen and heard, which means he may have eventually told her about the stolen loot. Perhaps he even stored some of it away so she could sell it after his death. Sort of a bonus inheritance," I added with a wry smile.

Gavin rested his arm across the back of my chair. "You don't think she would've exposed him? I love my parents, but I still wouldn't cover for them if they engaged in illegal activities."

I shook my head. "Her mother passed away when she was fairly young, and it was just her and her dad after that. I got the feeling, especially when I observed them at Lora's wedding, that she pretty much worshiped her dad. I really doubt she would've turned him in, no matter what."

"Fortunately, Caitlin Chiba has agreed to talk to the Beaufort police, sharing what she told us, so I imagine they'll be pursuing a similar line of reasoning," Ellen said. "I expect Ms. Kane will find herself under a very bright spotlight soon enough."

"In the meantime, she's still in your house." Gavin dropped his arm around my shoulders. "Not sure I like that very much."

"You can always camp out here, if it makes you feel better," Ellen said. "No one needs to know I have a guest, as long as you're careful leaving and entering the house. Hold on"—she rose to her feet and crossed to the hutch where I'd found the dog biscuits—"let me give you the extra key."

"Thanks. Honestly, If you don't mind me crashing here, it would definitely make me feel better about the situation." Gavin tightened his hold on my shoulder blade. "I'd like to keep an eye on Lora Kane, as well as the other guests, until the police either arrest someone or give them clearance to leave town."

Ellen returned and slid the key across the table to Gavin. "Of course I don't mind. As long as you're looking out for Charlotte, as well as Alicia and any of the innocent guests, I'm happy to have you."

"I'll watch out for you too," Gavin said, offering her a warm smile. "I have to make sure all my favorite ladies stay safe."

Ellen arched her pale eyebrows. "I can take care of myself, but thanks. Now—if you two would like a little alone time, feel free to head into the front room."

"You're not going to chaperone?" I asked with a smile.

"Heavens, no." Ellen walked over to the back door. "I'm going to bring Shandy in from the backyard and head upstairs. I have a very intriguing book I'm longing to get back to." She gave us a wink before calling for Shandy.

"Now I feel like a teenager," I told Gavin. "It reminds of the time Great-Aunt Isabella stayed over, promising my parents she'd keep an eye on me and my sisters."

Gavin grinned. "Don't tell me she let you run wild."

"Not exactly. But she did let me have my first sip of champagne and allowed my sister Mel to dye her hair purple."

"Sounds like Isabella, all right." Holding Shandy to her breast, Ellen wiggled her fingers at us. "Good night. Make sure you lock up if you go out to grab a few things from your boat, Gavin."

"Aye, aye, Captain," he replied, giving her a salute.

Ellen just laughed and headed upstairs.

* * *

On Saturday morning, I got a call from Detective Johnson, who informed me that Captain Sam Joiner had been cleared of any involvement in the murder.

"We found no evidence of him purchasing sodium cyanide in the past couple of years, and there were no traces of it on his boat or at his residence," she said. "Of course he's still facing charges from the attack on you and Ms. Simpson at Chapters, but he's no longer a suspect in the death of Stacy Wilkin."

"Did Caitlin Chiba stop by to talk to you?" I asked.

"She did, and yes, we are planning to talk to Ms. Kane as soon as possible. As well as Mr. Dean, since it's possible he's an accomplice." There was a brief lull on the line. "By the way, would you happen to know where Kane is? I sent someone to Chapters last night to bring her in for further questioning, but she wasn't there."

"I'm afraid I have no idea," I said, silently cursing myself for not having an answer to this query. The truth was, I'd returned to Chapters late the night before and hadn't bothered to check in with Alicia about the status of the guests. I'd noticed that Lora wasn't at breakfast but hadn't questioned that either, since she hadn't always shown up for that meal. "Let me check with Alicia. I'll call you back if she knows anything."

Immediately upon hanging up, I hurried into the kitchen to find Alicia, who was stacking the last of the breakfast plates and utensils in the dishwasher.

"Have you seen Lora Kane this morning?" I asked.

"Afraid not." Alicia glanced up at me, her eyes shadowed under her black lashes. "To be honest, I haven't actually laid eyes on the woman since early yesterday afternoon. She went out a little before two, along with Mr. Dean. I saw him come back in later—that was after dinner. Ms. Kane wasn't with him at that point."

"She stayed out all night?" I clutched my hands together.

Alicia straightened and met my intense stare with a lift of her chin. "Not sure about that. I know she wasn't here when the police arrived, looking to talk to her, but she could've come in later, before I locked up. I don't keep tabs on the guests that closely, you know. If she slipped in after the police left and then stayed up in her room, I wouldn't have known any different."

"True enough." I released my tight grip and shook out my fingers. "So she may still be in her suite."

"Could be. Do you want me to check? I need to grab something from my own room anyway."

"That would be fantastic," I said, my enthusiasm sparking surprise in Alicia's brown eyes. "I mean, I'd hate for her to have fallen ill or something, with none of us aware of her distress."

"Sure thing. Let me just go and see." Alicia wiped her hands on a dish towel before leaving the room, casting me a questioning glance as she passed by.

She was back within a few minutes, her face now expressing concern. "No one's in the room. I knocked and called out, then entered with my key. I'd figured I'd better check, since you mentioned the possibility of her being ill. But the suite was empty."

"That's very odd," I said, after swallowing back an epithet.

"Even stranger, her suitcases were gone too, and the room key was sitting on top of the dresser. Looks like she just took off." Alicia made a face. "I hope she paid in advance."

"She did, but that isn't my real concern." I stopped myself from saying more, not wanting to drag Alicia any deeper into the situation. "Listen, can you do me a favor?"

"If it isn't anything illegal," Alicia said, with a twist of her lips.

"No, of course not. It's just . . . please don't inform any of the other guests about Ms. Kane's disappearing act. I'm going to call the police and let them know, but I think it's best if we keep this to ourselves otherwise."

Alicia shrugged. "No problem. I'll just tell people I have no idea where she is. Which is true."

"Thanks." I flashed a smile before dashing out of the kitchen. Reaching my bedroom, I called Amber Johnson and let her know about this latest development.

"You have the right idea—don't mention anything to the other guests," the detective said. "Like Ms. Simpson, you should simply claim you don't know where Ms. Kane is at the moment. Let us handle looking for her. But please call or text if she shows up."

"Of course," I replied, before wishing her good luck and ending the call. I then immediately texted both Ellen and Gavin to let them know what was going on.

Gavin called me back.

"Ellen's going to be out all day," he said. "Or at least, that's what she told me earlier this morning. Something to do with her garden club. She also said she might be meeting a friend afterwards. So don't be surprised if she doesn't reply right away."

"What about you? Do you have plans for today?"

"Nothing much. I need to grab an overnight bag and a few things off the boat, though. Since I didn't quite make it back there last night."

I smiled. "You were sleeping so soundly on the sofa when I left, I didn't have the heart to wake you."

"I hope you remembered to lock up when you left. I completely forgot about that."

"I did. Luckily, I happen to have my own key to Ellen's house—for emergencies, or if she gets delayed somewhere and needs someone to check on Shandy. By the way, did she take him with her today?"

"No, he's in his crate right now. I'll make sure to take him out, though, so don't worry about that. I'm just going to dash over to the boat and get a few things and then hurry back. I want to stay here most of the day to keep an eye on Chapters. Especially now, with Lora Kane in the wind."

"Thanks, that makes me feel better." I stared out my bedroom window and observed Linnea and Zach emerging from the garden, hand in hand. "I plan to stick around here today too. It's probably a good idea if I keep a watch over the rest of the guests, now that I've lost one of them. No, two, actually," I added, in a grim tone.

"That's not your fault," Gavin said. "Okay, I'm heading out. I'll text you when I'm back in case you need to go anywhere—that way one of us will always be around to keep an eye on things."

"Will do," I told him.

The rest of the day passed without incident, although a couple of police officers stopped by to talk to the guests. They brought good news for Zach, Linnea, and Vonnie, who were told they were cleared to leave town, although they still needed to be available for questioning in the future. Unfortunately, I had to inform the officers that Lora was still missing and that Arnie had left before their arrival. "He didn't tell me where he was going either, I'm afraid," I said.

Before leaving Chapters, Linnea sought me out and pressed a business card in my hand.

"I still want to create those earrings for your friend," she told me. "Just get in touch when you're ready to discuss some designs."

"That sounds great," I said. Looking over her and Zach, who was standing at her side, I added, "Can you clear up a couple of things for me before you leave? I'm just curious."

Zach's expression turned sheepish. "About why I was searching the garden the day after the murder?"

"That's one thing," I said.

"The truth is"—Zach cast a swift glance at Linnea, who nodded—"we were in the garden late Friday night. Then, after Stacy was found dead, Linnea realized she was missing an earring."

"One of my designs," Linnea said, as Zach slid his arm around her waist. "Easily traceable to me, especially if Lora ever saw it. I found it later, in my suite, but that morning it was still missing."

"So you were actually looking for an earring, not a pin?" I shook my head. "Why didn't you just say that? Were you afraid that Linnea was involved in the murder and wanted to cover her tracks?"

"No, no." Zach pulled Linnea closer. "I didn't think that. I know Linnea would never harm anyone. But I was afraid that others might suspect her. You see, Stacy . . ."

"Stole Linnea's jewelry designs? Yes, I know about that."

Zach's eyebrows rose above the rim of his glasses. "You really are an amateur detective, aren't you? But yeah, that was my concern."

"He was protecting me, not himself," Linnea said, glancing up at her fiancé with an adoring look. "Even if it put him under more of a spotlight."

"Well, to be honest, I've had my suspicions about the two of you being involved in something together," I said, meeting their suddenly wary gazes. "You were both at the aquarium the day Arnie was attacked, weren't you?"

Linnea lifted her chin. "We were. But that means nothing. We were simply visiting the site, as most tourists do."

"I suppose that's possible," I said, not entirely convinced. But it wasn't my place to accuse them. If the police found more evidence to link them to any crimes, I was sure they'd be hauled back in for questioning, even though they were cleared to leave Beaufort now.

"Just coincidence," Zach said, his expression hardening. "And honestly, I'm not sure why you seem to think Linnea, or I, had any connection to Arnie's attack, much less Stacy's murder."

"Because you had a motive too, as did Vonnie," I said, earning a surprised look from Linnea. "But I suppose it's not really any of my business at this point. You're leaving Chapters, and apparently the police aren't focusing on either of you."

Linnea shrugged. "They said they would contact us if we were needed for questioning again, so we aren't completely off the hook, but I guess they aren't worried that we're going to flee the country or something."

"That would be foolish, no matter what," I said, wanting to slip in a little warning just in case they actually were somehow involved in Stacy's death. "I trust the Beaufort police, with help from the state authorities and others, to close the case and arrest the proper suspect or suspects."

"I'm sure they're quite capable," Zach said, shifting his weight from foot to foot. Neither he nor Linnea looked me directly in the eye as they muttered their good-byes before leaving the house.

I had a more pleasant encounter with Vonnie, who confirmed her anger over Stacy's treatment of her son. "But, as I think you've learned, I had no reason to murder Stacy, since her death doesn't benefit Raphael. In fact, it actually hurts him, at least financially," she said.

"I know you had arranged a settlement with her." I tipped my head to study Vonnie's calm face. "Perhaps Raphael will receive something from her estate?"

"If there is anything." Vonnie offered me a wry smile. "I think she had a lot of creditors. But in the end, what matters is that justice is served." She wished me a good day before heading out the front door.

I stared after her, wondering if she meant she really wanted Stacy's killer to be caught—or felt Stacy's murder had been a sort of justice in itself.

Shaking my head, I decided to clear my mind by spending some time working in the garden. I finished weeding the vegetable beds before heading inside to grab a shower. As I towel-dried my hair, I noticed my cell phone, which I'd placed on vibrate, skitter across the nightstand.

I plopped down on my bed and checked the phone. A new text had just arrived.

It was from Ellen. *Meeting a contact who may have info to crack the case. Can you join us?* it said. *New Bern, at the waterfront park with the gazebo. Eight PM.*

I peered at my bedside clock, noticing it was already six thirty. Tapping the phone against my palm, I considered Ellen's request, which I found exceedingly worrisome. For her to agree to meet someone so late, in a city that was a good forty-minute drive from Beaufort, struck me as peculiar, if not dangerous.

I texted back a confirmation, before calling Gavin and telling him to crate Shandy, lock up Ellen's house, and meet me at my car.

"Where are we going?" he asked, after saying yes.

"To New Bern," I said. "To make sure Ellen hasn't gotten herself into trouble."

"Should we alert the police?"

"Not yet. I don't want to bring them in on this if it's just Ellen following a lead. But"—I scooped up my keys, ID, and cell phone and shoved them in my pockets—"we should probably keep them on speed dial."

After I'd reached the stretch of highway outside Morehead City, Gavin patted his pockets and swore. "I planned to try contacting Ellen again, but I left my cell back at the house. Must've set it down when I was slipping on my shoes and forgot to pick it up again."

"Here, use mine," I said, sliding it from the car phone holder and handing it over to him. "Just tap in forty-two for Ellen's number."

On the ride to New Bern, Gavin alternated calling and texting but received no response.

"Maybe she doesn't want to scare off her informant," I suggested, when Gavin expressed his frustration over her silence.

"Let's hope that's all it is," he replied, worry lines creasing his brow.

It was getting dark as we crossed the bridge that linked the highway with downtown New Bern. The historic city, founded in 1710 by Swiss and Platine colonists, was named after Bern, the region from which many of the colonists had emigrated. With its strategic location at the confluence of the Trent and Neuse Rivers, it had been a powerful colonial settlement and had served as the capital of North Carolina from 1770 to 1792.

Pulling into one of the lots near the convention center, I noticed the ghostly shapes of sailboats and other vessels looming off to our left.

"So that's where the boat slips are," Gavin said, as we climbed out of my car. "I've never been here before, but some of my boating acquaintances have mentioned it as an option if other marinas in the area are full."

"I bet this is where Arnie docks his boat."

Gavin cast me a sharp glance. "You don't think Ellen's informant is Arnie, do you?"

I gnawed on the inside of my cheek, embarrassed that I hadn't considered that option. "She would've said if that was the case, wouldn't she?"

"I don't know. It depends on if he asked her to keep his identity under wraps. You know, in case you decided to alert the police." Gavin stared out over the river. "I didn't realize Dean was keeping his boat here, or I would've brought up that possibility sooner. It's an odd place to meet otherwise."

"I should've mentioned that, I guess. Arnie wasn't at Chapters when we left either." As I turned to face Gavin, a fleeting shadow caught my eye. "Who's that?" I pointed at a dark-clad figure lurking only a few feet away.

Gavin turned and strode toward the stranger, who stopped in their tracks. Dressed in a black hooded sweatshirt and dark jeans, they practically blended into the shadows.

A Fatal Booking

As Gavin approached, the stranger spun around as if preparing to flee. At that moment, their hood fell back, exposing a dark sweep of hair and pale skin. They ran, passing under a streetlight long enough for me to realize who they were.

Our missing guest, Lora Kane.

Chapter
Twenty-Two

Lora disappeared into the darkness, sprinting away from the waterfront. As Gavin took off after her, he called out, "Speed dial!"

I fumbled for my phone, realizing he meant I should call the police, before the truth struck—he had my phone.

I inhaled a deep, steadying breath and considered my options. I finally decided it would be best if I followed the sidewalk that skirted the river to reach the waterfront park and gazebo Ellen had mentioned in her text. The area was brightly lit enough for me to feel relatively safe, and once I reached Ellen, we could use her phone to notify the authorities about Lora's presence in New Bern.

Of course, I didn't know who might be meeting with Ellen, but surely they weren't a threat. Ellen was fearless but not foolish. She wouldn't have agreed to meet with someone, especially at night, if she felt they would pose a serious danger.

Someone like Lora, who I was more and more convinced was a murderer.

The narrow waterfront park at this point was basically a sidewalk separated from the shore by a metal railing. I couldn't see much of the river as I jogged toward the larger section of the park, but the sound of the lapping water reminded me of the danger of this section of the riverbank. From previous visits, I knew that once you got beyond the boat harbor, the waters near the shore were studded with jagged stones and the broken columns of old wooden moorings.

After passing the convention center and bridge, the slender ribbon of the park opened up to a view of a large white gazebo in the middle of an expanse of grass and trees. I slowed my pace to a walk, squinting to see if I could recognize the person who was standing in the gazebo, facing Ellen.

It was odd. Ellen stood ramrod straight, her attention so focused on the individual in front of her that she didn't even acknowledge my approach. Moving closer, I realized that the other person in the gazebo was Arnie Dean. *Of course*, I thought. *Despite their issues in the past, Ellen would trust him.*

He must have more information on Lora. Perhaps he's decided to stop protecting her and wanted to share the information with Ellen and me before going to the police.

Choosing New Bern for the meeting made more sense now. Arnie's boat was undoubtedly docked nearby, so he had a legitimate reason to be here, and he probably felt it was a safer location to share information on his goddaughter than anywhere near Chapters.

But it isn't, I realized, breaking back into a jog. *Lora is here.*

I needed to reach Ellen and Arnie and ask one of them to immediately call the authorities. While I knew Gavin could handle himself in a confrontation, I wasn't convinced that he'd be able to catch Lora, especially since he didn't know the area.

If she escaped his pursuit, she could still pose a danger to Arnie and Ellen.

Or me. As I clattered up the wooden steps to reach the interior of the gazebo, Ellen's gaze shifted in my direction.

"What are you doing here?" she asked, her tone sharp as the rocks in the river.

I stopped in my tracks, my eyes widening in surprise. "You asked me to come."

"I didn't." Ellen refocused on Arnie, her mouth working as if she were chewing over several words before she spat out, "You."

Following her stare, I noticed Arnie's grim expression first. No longer the jovial, out-of-season Santa, his eyes were cold as an Arctic sea. I dropped my gaze to his right arm, which he held close to his side, bent at the elbow, with his forearm extended. A flicker of light from a nearby streetlamp glinted off the object in his hand.

A gun.

I gasped and stumbled into Ellen, who threw one arm around my shoulder to steady me.

"Hands down where I can see them," Arnie said.

Ellen dropped her arm. "You didn't need to involve Charlotte."

"Oh, I think I did. She's your sleuthing partner, isn't she? I'm sure she knows just as much as you do. And maybe more of what *I* want to know."

Ellen cast me an apologetic side-eyed glance. "He greeted me outside my garden club meeting with the revolver. I thought I'd better get in his car rather than risk anyone at the meeting getting hurt. He took my cell phone, of course."

"Which I subsequently used to text you. Worked out perfectly." Arnie frowned. "Speaking of phones, hand over yours, Charlotte."

"Don't have one," I said, patting my pockets. "You can search me if you want."

"No, I think I'll take your word for it. But if you try anything, well . . ." He tapped his gun against his palm before pointing it toward the benches that encircled the inside of the gazebo walls. "Go sit down, both of you. No sudden moves, or I'll randomly choose who to shoot."

"That would be a mistake," Ellen said, as she and I stumbled backward. "Might draw unwanted attention."

My heel hit the support on one of the benches. "Yes, gunshots are noisy," I said, as I slumped down onto the hard wooden seat.

"Silencer," Arnie said, holding up the gun so we could see that it did indeed feature that attachment. "This isn't my first rodeo."

"Apparently." Sitting next to me, Ellen reached for the hand I'd pressed against the bench.

"All this to protect Lora?" I asked, clasping Ellen's fingers like a lifeline.

Arnie's chuckle held no cheer. "Heavens, no. In fact, that ungrateful little liar is next on my list."

"You aren't covering for her or her late father?" I considered mentioning something about Gavin accompanying me but decided it was better if Arnie didn't know we had any possibility of backup.

"Why would Marvin come into it? I admit that Lora and I have had a rather uneasy partnership for some time now, but her dad had no involvement, God rest his soul."

"I thought"—I shared a quick glance with Ellen—"that he was the thief, or at least the mastermind, behind a series of jewel robberies back in the seventies and eighties. In this area as well as elsewhere. Like London, where he was posted by his company at one time."

Arnie made a dismissive noise. "Marvin was a wonderful fellow, but he couldn't have organized the theft of a pack of cigarettes from a convenience store. He didn't have that sort of mind."

"But you did." Ellen raised her head and fixed Arnie with her piercing blue-eyed stare. "I should've seen it sooner. You used to dazzle me with your intelligence in the past, so I didn't see it then, but time has shown me the truth. I should've realized that you lacked empathy when I observed how often you liked to display your superiority over everyone else."

"What can I say. It's a gift," Arnie said. "And yes, at first the heists were only a game. I was young, and restless, and bored. I went to law school to please my father, but I found it all so . . . tedious. Rules and regulations and all those cases one had to memorize. And at the end of it, what? Eventually taking over the administration of my family firm? What an incredible bore it all was."

"So you decided to spice things up by becoming a jewel thief?" I thought about Ophelia Sandburg's fascination with the debonair characters portrayed by Cary Grant and others and wondered if those glamorous depictions had also influenced Arnie.

"Yes, and it was exhilarating." Arnie's smile did nothing to calm my racing heart.

"Using your father, with his legal and political connections, as your entrée into exclusive social circles, I suppose." Ellen shook her head. "It seems I didn't know you well at all, Arnie. I would never have suspected such duplicity from you."

"Perhaps not, but then, you were always a little closed off from reality, weren't you, Ellie? So trapped in your own head, it's a wonder you noticed anything at all."

Ellen tightened her lips but didn't respond to this jibe. "Charlotte has learned that there were thefts with a similar MO in London a few years later. Was that Lora, already acting as your apprentice?"

Arnie's eyes flashed. "Certainly not. She was just a child at the time. No, that was me as well. It was always me, and only me. I didn't have any help. I didn't need it."

I shifted uneasily on the hard bench. "You were in London too?"

"Yes. Lora wouldn't have mentioned this to you, since she doesn't think it's wise to point out that connection, but after I finished my degree and before joining the family business, I interned with Marvin's company. We were law school pals, you see, even though he was a couple years ahead of me. He actually got me the position in London." Arnie lightly tapped the muzzle of the gun against his temple. "Once I finagled it, of course. I needed to get out of the States for a bit, after having pulled off one caper where the cops were a little too close for comfort. Good thinking on my part, hmm?"

"Very clever," Ellen said dryly. "Is that why you're telling us all this?" she added, tightening her grip on my fingers. "To brag about your brilliance?"

"No, simply to fill in the gaps in your little amateur investigation. Of which there are many, I'm afraid." Arnie strolled a few steps closer. "Although I must say, you were on the right track, suspecting Lora of being somehow involved. She is, but only because, in recent years, she's helped me turn some of my stolen goods into cash."

"I'm surprised you hadn't sold them on the black market long before this," Ellen said.

Arnie shrugged. "Like I said, it was mainly about the thrill. For many years, I simply stashed most of the jewels. I wasn't really interested in the money. Not then." His expression hardened. "I had plenty when the family firm was doing well. But I'm afraid I wasn't quite as careful about managing things as I might have been. After my father died, I lived off my inheritance and occasional legal fees, but when the firm took a nose-dive and the money dried up . . ."

"You turned to selling off the jewelry you'd stolen years before," I said. "With Lora's help."

"Exactly. And of course, Stacy Wilkin proved to be an asset too."

"Until she wasn't?" Ellen lifted her eyebrows. "Is that why you killed her? Because she refused to continue to sell your stolen goods?"

Arnie's bark of laughter hit me like a punch in the chest. "You're assuming Stacy had a conscience, which is quite a stretch." He rested the gun against his other palm. "She had no qualms about selling hot merchandise, I can assure you."

"So why murder her?" I asked.

"Who says I did?" Arnie pointed the gun back at Ellen and me. "Anyway, that isn't relevant right now. What I actually want to know—and why I lured you to this meeting, Charlotte—is where Isabella Harrington stashed all that jewelry she used to flaunt so openly at her parties. Ellie seems to be clueless on this point, or at least she's playing dumb. So I thought perhaps you could provide me with an answer."

"Jewelry?" Thoughts of the disturbances in the attic and the photos removed from the library whirled around in my mind. "You wanted your group to stay at Chapters so you could search for my great-aunt's jewelry?"

"Clever, eh? I mean, who would suspect an old codger like me?" Arnie's grin looked more like the barred teeth of a rabid dog. "I know Isabella had some very valuable pieces. There was a necklace she wore . . ."

"Sapphire and diamonds," I murmured. When Arnie shot me a fierce glance, I held up my free hand. "I've seen it in photos."

"Like the one from the library," Ellen said.

"Yes." I stared into Arnie's cold eyes. "That's why you took them. Not because you wanted to make copies. Not to protect Lora or her late father. You hoped to hide your real intention by grabbing three, but you really only wanted the one to confirm your memory of that necklace."

"It was given to her by some aristocratic fool," Arnie said. "Or at least that's the story I was told, when I asked around. It would be worth a small fortune today, and unfortunately, I find myself rather short of funds at the moment, so if you'll just tell me where it is . . ."

Amusement swamped me like a wave. I knew the humor was misplaced, but I couldn't help myself. I pulled my hand free of Ellen's grasp and doubled over, my shrill laughter sounding mad even to my ears.

"Sit up, sit up," Arnie snapped. "Stop that caterwauling and tell me what I want to know."

Ellen rose to her feet. "You've frightened her into hysterics. Good luck getting an answer out of her now."

"Stay still," Arnie said, leveling the gun on her. "She'll tell me, or I shoot you."

"So much for that great love and friendship you once professed to have for me." There was no mistaking the anger edging Ellen's voice.

Of course, he's betrayed her once again. I straightened and wiped the tears from my cheeks with the back of my hand. "I will tell you, but you won't like my answer."

Arnie pointed the gun barrel at my chest. "Let me decide that. If the necklace and other jewels are in a safe-deposit box, I'm sure you, as Isabella's heir, have access to it. Or you"—he swung his arm until the gun was leveled at Ellen's forehead—"as the trustee of the estate. You see, I do know quite a few things."

"But not everything." I stood up and moved closer to Ellen. "Unfortunately, I didn't inherit my great-aunt's jewelry, valuable or otherwise. Oh, she left me and some other family members a few costume pieces. But the bulk of her collection? I never even saw any of that."

Ellen crossed her arms over her chest. "Neither did I, to be honest. Granted, I met Isabella in person later in life, but she never mentioned owning any truly valuable jewelry. I think she would've included that in the instructions she gave me about her estate."

"What are you talking about?" Arnie's panicked gaze flew from Ellen's stoic face to mine. "I know she owned the necklace and that there were at least a few other priceless pieces in her possession. They weren't something you'd discard. What happened to them?"

I lifted my chin and stared directly into Arnie's eyes. "She did the sort of thing only Isabella would do. She gave them away."

Chapter
Twenty-Three

"That can't be true," Arnie finally spat out, after letting loose an inventive string of swear words.

I squared my shoulders, hoping my trembling wasn't visible. "Sorry to disappoint you, but she donated it all to charity. I was actually in the room when she told my grandmother and mother about it during one of her family visits. She explained that she'd sold everything that was worth any real money. All done quite legally, by the way. The funds from the sale went to help refugees displaced by various wars."

"That makes sense." Ellen's voice remained perfectly calm. "Isabella always had a soft spot for those who found themselves at the mercy of circumstances beyond their control."

"There's nothing?" Arnie clutched the grip of the gun with both hands, making me wonder about his own steadiness. "She sold it all?"

"Every bit of it, from what I understand," I said, sharing a swift glance with Ellen, who gave a little shake of her head. In that moment, I knew I should've lied. Now there was nothing to bargain with, no reason for Arnie to keep us alive. "That I know of, anyway. My great-aunt was rather secretive, so maybe . . ."

"Don't try to barter now." Arnie's expression shifted from despair to something more dangerous.

Cunning and cold, I thought, as I sidled up closer to Ellen. *He's calculating what to do with us. What course of action will benefit him the most.*

"I suppose this calls for a change of plans," he said, dropping one hand off the grip but keeping the revolver fixed on us. "I was going to demand that you drive me back to Chapters and force you to hand over the jewels, if they were stashed there. Or make you give me the keys to the safe-deposit box or wherever else they were stored. But since those options are gone, I'm afraid I need to take you to my boat and secure you there, at least until I can safely leave the country."

Ellen nudged me with her elbow, which I took as a signal to stay quiet and allow her to negotiate. "That sounds reasonable. No one will think to look for us on your boat, at least not for some time. No one else knew I was supposedly meeting someone here tonight, and your disappearance could be blamed on Lora, who I understand has gone missing herself."

"Lora's not at Chapters?" Arnie's tone betrayed his surprise at this news.

"You didn't know she'd taken a powder?" Ellen pressed her forefinger to her jaw. "Apparently she disappeared yesterday afternoon. I thought you would've known all about that, since you were still at Chapters last night."

"I knew she was away in the evening, but I didn't realize she'd never returned." Arnie's cheeks paled to match the color of his beard. "She never said anything to me."

"Oh dear, your accomplice seems to be in the wind. That can't be good. Not for you, anyway. Perhaps she had a change of heart." Ellen's lips twitched. "Which is even more reason to get out of town, and quickly. If you hurry, you might be able to escape, especially if you've already set up a foolproof exit plan, which I suspect you have."

I looked over at Ellen from under my lowered eyelashes. *Good for her. She knows just how to play him—exploit his superiority complex.*

Arnie jutted out his chin. "I do. The problem is, you two are sure to raise the alarm as soon as I leave. So I think I'll still have to tie you up on my boat to prevent that from happening."

I exhaled. It seemed that Arnie wasn't set on killing us. But as I sneaked another glance at Ellen and noted the tautness of her jaw, my confidence wavered. "We can go quietly, if that's what you want. The boat slips aren't that far a walk, and it seems no one is around to notice anything amiss." *Unless Gavin returns,* I thought, hoping against hope that might happen.

"I suppose that's my only option," Arnie said, baring his teeth in another rabid-dog grin. "All right, enough chitchat. Head down to the water. We'll follow the river walk to the boat. But no funny business, or I swear I'll shoot at least one of you."

As we left the gazebo, Ellen leaned into me. "Follow my lead," she whispered.

Arnie called out, "No talking."

I dutifully followed Ellen, Arnie trailing close behind. When we reached the sidewalk that ran along the river bank, Ellen stumbled.

"Are you okay?" I asked, before Arnie once again warned me to be quiet.

Ellen stopped walking and clutched her right knee. "Not sure. I might have sprained something. Give me a minute."

"You can hobble, for all I care," Arnie said, stepping around me to face Ellen.

Ellen abruptly straightened and mouthed *run* at me over his shoulder.

I knew she wanted me to take off while Arnie was preoccupied. Leaving her behind, and at his mercy.

The logical part of my brain realized this was a decent plan— not only to ensure my safety, but also to allow one of us to alert the authorities. But . . .

He'll shoot her, I'm sure of it.

As I dithered over this moral conundrum, Arnie moved close to Ellen, demanding a look at her knee. "Very well," she said, lifting her hand in a karate-style chop that almost connected with his gun.

But Arnie must've sensed something at the last minute, because he blocked her hit by swinging the gun up and away. In the next second, he brought it crashing down against her shoulder.

Ellen stumbled backward, falling into the metal railing. I let out a strangled shriek as Arnie rushed forward and, still clutching the revolver, shoved his entire weight against her upper body. Ellen's legs flew out from under her right before Arnie slammed into her again, sending her careening back over the railing.

There was a dreadful splash. I flew at Arnie's back, making unintelligible sounds. "She's in the water. Too many rocks. She'll die," I finally managed to squeak out.

"And what's that to me?" Arnie turned on his heel to face me, his expression transformed into a macabre mask by his anger. He pressed the revolver against my forehead. "Looks like a fortunate accident to me. One down, only one to tie up. Now—march. And you'd better not try anything else, or I'll throw you in after her."

"We can't just leave her," I sputtered, my concern for Ellen overcoming my fear of the gun.

"I'm afraid we can, and will. Move."

I cast one more desperate glance at the dark waters of the river before following his brutal instructions. *The only hope she has is for you to somehow survive and find Gavin or someone to get help*, I told myself as I staggered along the path. From time to time, Arnie popped the barrel of the revolver between my shoulder blades. I pressed my lips tight. *As if I might forget it's there.*

We reached the boat slips without seeing anyone I could alert to my dilemma. My thoughts consumed by the image of Ellen, knocked unconscious by the river rocks and sinking down in the dark water, I shuffled onto the boat dock indicated by Arnie and made my way to a sleek cabin cruiser.

Larger and more modern than Gavin's boat, Arnie's vessel was, I assumed, also much more expensive. With Arnie dogging my steps, I climbed onto the boat deck.

"Inside," Arnie said, pushing me toward the covered upper cabin. I stared longingly at the ship-to-shore radio as he forced me through a door and down several steps. *The lower deck, of course. Far from the radio or any way to signal for help.*

As on Gavin's boat, this lower-level cabin was outfitted with a kitchen and dining setup, although they were much more expansive. In fact, it resembled a suite in some fine hotel, complete with lounge seating, a large-screen television, and a walled-off space I assumed held the main bedroom.

"Sit," Arnie commanded, pointing the revolver at the sofa built into one wall.

I complied, my mind racing with thoughts of Ellen drowning and my own possible demise. My only ace-in-the-hole was the fact that neither Ellen nor I had mentioned Gavin. If he investigated the gazebo and found no one, he might think to check Arnie's boat.

Although he doesn't know which one it is, which will delay things, even if he does consider that possibility. I exhaled loudly, earning a fierce glare from Arnie.

"I suppose it's time to tie you up," he said, holding up a coil of rope he'd pulled from one of the storage cabinets. "I don't want to kill you," he said, as he bound my ankles and arms with the ropes. "I'm really not into murder."

"You could've fooled me," I said, as he stood back for a moment to admire his work. "I suppose it was all an act, wasn't it? Including that incident at the aquarium." I thought of the dark clothing Lora was wearing when I'd glimpsed her earlier. "Lora pushed you and ran off, pretending to be some dangerous stranger, didn't she?"

"The better to set me up as a victim rather than a perpetrator." Arnie grabbed a sheet from another cabinet.

Another thought occurred to me. "Were you hurt at all? I know Lora took you to the doctor . . ."

"She didn't, actually. We drove around and then picked up a large bandage at the drugstore." Arnie ripped a strip of fabric off the sheet. "I wasn't actually injured. I simply dropped down on the ground and pretended while Lora played the mysterious, escaping attacker. It was a setup, and you fell for it. Hook, line, and sinker," he added, tearing the strip in half.

"Perhaps because I actually have some concern for my fellow humans," I said. "So the clinic visit was all a ruse too? I guess to allow you the opportunity to rummage through the attic again while everyone thought you were laid up in bed."

"Well, not *again*, exactly. Lora was the one who searched up there the first time. I did try one other time, during the book club discussion, but then Lora came upstairs and cautioned me that you could hear noises downstairs, so I stopped." Arnie advanced on me, holding the wide ribbon of fabric. "I was surprised that you didn't question any of us guests about that, to be honest."

"I didn't want to accuse anyone without any real proof. I guess you were searching for the jewelry?" I wiggled my fingers, glad at least that Arnie had tied my hands in front of me rather than jerking my arms behind my back.

"Of course. We didn't realize it was a futile effort at the time. Now enough of your chatter," Arnie said. "I've answered far too many of your questions as it is."

I swore, earning a smash of the revolver against the side of my head. As I blinked, my vision swimming, Arnie shoved the strip of fabric between my teeth. He tied the gag tightly behind my head, ignoring my moan of pain. "Now, now, let's not get testy. Here I am, letting you live. At least for now," he added, stepping back to look me over.

Trussed up and with my head throbbing, all I could do was glare at him.

"That will do. Now I must go and see if I can speed up the arrangements I've put in place to allow me to quietly leave the country. You can stay here all nice and comfy until I get back."

I futilely chewed on my gag as he saluted me with the gun and headed topside.

That "until I get back" worried me. If Arnie was simply going to keep me on the boat, unable to alert the authorities, while he fled, why would he need to return? I struggled against my bonds, hoping to loosen them, to no avail.

There had to be something I could do. Sitting meekly, waiting for a man without a shred of human decency to return, didn't seem like the most intelligent choice. As I contemplated my situation, despair set in. *Sure, he'll be back. And he'll probably take the boat out into open water, shoot me, and dump my body.*

Unbidden, the memory of my late husband rose in my mind. Brent had shown incredible courage in the face of terror, saving an entire schoolroom of children from a tornado. Surely I could display at least a scrap of his courage. I straightened and relaxed all my muscles. Taking deep breaths, I called up memories of Brent's face.

Need your help, if you can spare it, I told him in my mind. *I know you're in heaven, if anyone is. Maybe you can ask one of your angel pals to be my guardian, just for today?*

Foolish as it might've seemed to others, this thought calmed me.

"And send down one for Ellen too," I added, hoping that request wasn't too late.

I settled back against the sofa cushions and surveyed my surroundings, looking for anything in the vicinity that was sharp enough to cut rope. If I could somehow free my hands, I could release my other bonds and escape.

With nothing useful in view, I considered other scenarios. Flopping to the floor and somehow scrambling my way to the kitchen's lower cabinets, where I could possibly find a knife or other sharp object, was all I could come up with. I shifted on the sofa cushions, sliding my body forward, then bounced off the bench, landing on my behind. The jolt amplified the pain from the blow Arnie had given me with the gun, and I blinked rapidly to clear the stars from my eyes. *The pain doesn't matter*, I chided myself. *Don't think about that. Focus on somehow maneuvering your body so you can reach the kitchen, even if that means inching along like a caterpillar.*

Rolling over, I shoved the heels of my bound hands against the hard planks beneath me. It took several attempts, but I finally pushed myself up so that I was on my knees, my palms pressed against the floor. Unfortunately, that motion brought on a wave of light-headedness that blurred my vision and clenched my stomach.

I felt like retching, but knew I had to fight that urge with every fiber of my being. Being gagged, I could easily choke. I swallowed back the bile and scooted forward far enough to fall against the wooden platform supporting a dining bench. The floor seemed to tilt as I dropped my head back against the edge of the seat cushion.

Aware that my life depended on my ability to free myself, I fought the desire to give in to despair. *But still*, I thought, *if I could rest for a minute, just to clear my head and stop everything from spinning . . .* Closing my eyes, I slipped into a state of half consciousness. Spangles of light flashed, like schools of tiny silver-scaled fish darting through dark water, while visions from the past danced through my mind. There was a sense of time speeding up and slowing down until I couldn't tell whether I'd been drifting for minutes or hours. Lost in a fog, I relived moments from the trips Brent and I had taken to Italy and elsewhere. There was the glint of light off Ghiberti's golden doors in Florence, and the jangle of bells as a herd of cattle clattered up the road in a quaint hill town. The scene shifted to a car, were I was singing along with the radio as we traveled Route 66 from one end of the United States to the other. Another flash of light and we were sitting on a blanket under the stars while the magical strains of a Mozart overture, played by an orchestra on an outdoor stage, wafted over us.

Then it seemed as if Brent were kneeling in front of me, urging me to look at him, telling me I had to stay awake, and aware. Struggling against the seductive pull of memories, I opened my eyes.

As I lifted my head and adjusted my body into a more upright position, I felt something that made me again question whether I was asleep or awake. But a quick press of my palm against the floorboards confirmed my suspicion.

I wasn't imagining things—the boat was moving.

Chapter
Twenty-Four

Arnie had obviously returned and, as I'd feared, was taking the boat out into open water. I worked my jaw, trying to dislodge the gag, but only succeeded in scraping both sides of my mouth. Closing my eyes again for a moment, I sent up another prayer for help.

"Now would be a good time for that guardian angel," I told Brent.

My eyes flew open as I again sensed someone kneeling in front of me. But this was no angel or spirit. I wasn't complaining, though, and sent a silent *thanks* heavenward.

Gavin tapped two fingers against his lips before reaching around to untie the gag. He pulled it away and tossed it aside before pressing a swift kiss against my mouth.

"How did you . . . ?" I asked, before following his downward hand gesture and lowering my voice to a whisper. "Find me?"

"Ellen told me about the boat," he whispered back, as he worked to loosen the rope binding my hands.

"She's alive?" I realized I'd spoken too loudly and bit my lower lip.

Gavin nodded. "Beaten up, but yes. She was able to crawl up the bank, where I found her. Called 911." He slid my cell from his pocket and laid it on the bench cushion. "Sorry, your phone."

"Glad you had it. Especially since Ellen needed help." After he unwrapped the rope and tossed it aside, I flexed my wrists. "You went to find us at the gazebo?"

"Yes. With Lora."

I widened my eyes. "She helped you?"

"She was in New Bern to warn Ellen. She knew about the meeting and wanted to stop Arnie. Had a change of heart," Gavin said, as he turned his attention to the ropes binding my ankles. "She planned to surrender to the police," he added, looking up to meet my surprised gaze.

"She told you how to find this boat?"

"Before the police arrived."

"You didn't wait for them," I said, realizing he must've immediately run off to find me.

Gavin nodded. "I was afraid to wait. I told Ellen to inform the police about Arnie dragging you to the boat, and then I just took off. Snuck aboard hoping to free you before he returned, but . . ." He sat back. "Blast, this knot won't let go."

Footsteps overhead made us both look up. "Leave it. I can work it loose eventually. Maybe you'd better . . ."

"Go topside and try to stop Arnie? My thoughts exactly." Gavin jumped to his feet. "Get those ropes off and be ready to run if necessary." He turned away.

"Careful, he has a gun."

Gavin glanced over his shoulder. "I'm aware, and plan to remedy that situation, if I can." He strode over to the stairwell, then slowed his pace to creep up the steps.

Worried about his safety, I frantically dug my fingers into the remaining knot, pulling to loosen it enough to free my ankles. If I could get to my feet, I'd find some heavy object and join Gavin topside. *Even the odds a bit*, I thought, hoping Gavin would be able to grab the revolver or at least knock it into the river so we'd have a fighting chance.

Even two against one was no match for a gun.

The boat motor sputtered to a stop, followed by the sound of running feet. Curses and thumps soon followed. Gavin was obviously grappling with Arnie. Fumbling with my bindings, I finally untied the knot as a gunshot rang out, followed by a resounding splash.

Frantic, I threw the rope across the cabin and attempted to stand. But as soon as I managed to make it to my feet, the wooziness I'd experienced earlier swamped me again, forcing me to slump down onto the bench cushions.

I couldn't allow my wobbly legs to defeat me. Spurred on by the knowledge that Gavin might need my help, I shoved my palm against the wooden panel behind the bench. Leaning into the wall, I hoped I'd be able to regain my balance.

But before I attempted to stand again, my gaze fell on the cell phone. I grabbed it and punched in 911, praying we were close enough to shore for my phone to retain a signal.

When a voice answered, I spilled out as much information as I knew, which wasn't much. We were on a boat. No, I didn't know its name or model or anything else. Traveling on the Neuse or Trent River. I wasn't certain what direction Arnie had taken, so no, I couldn't be more specific.

The dispatcher told me to stay on the line.

"Sure thing" I said. Finally able to stand, I clutched the phone in one hand and shuffled forward, my gaze searching the area for any object I could use as a weapon.

Before I could find anything, a clattering from the stairs told me that someone was heading down into the lower cabin. I grabbed the edge of one of the storage cabinets built into the wall and straightened my back. If that gunshot had hit Gavin and Arnie was coming to finish me off, I wanted to meet him face-to-face.

Gavin burst into the cabin, shouting something about staying where I was. Arnie appeared behind him, waving one arm. Something glinted in his hand. I staggered backward, dropping my cell phone, which hit the floor. The sound of the screen shattering barely registered as I remained fixated on the object in Arnie's hand. Its metal surface gleamed, just like the revolver.

But brighter. I blinked. That wasn't right. The whole scene didn't make sense. Why would Gavin still be on his feet if Arnie had some way to shoot him? I looked closer and realized what Arnie was holding was a large wrench, not a gun.

Gavin must've knocked the gun from Arnie's hand and into the river, forcing Arnie to grab a new weapon. That's still dangerous, but at least it means hand-to-hand combat, and Gavin is the younger man . . .

I took a few steps toward them, until Gavin yelled, "Stay back. I have this."

It looked like he did, too, as he advanced on the older man, fists raised. But then Arnie stepped back and lowered his arm. Hoping he planned to surrender, I remained frozen in place.

Arnie flashed a maniacal smile before he raised his arm again. He swung the wrench down, smashing it into the top of a white cylinder before turning and dashing back up the steps.

Gavin, his gaze fixed on the tank, didn't follow. He rushed forward to swiftly examine the top of the cylinder. Swearing loudly, he crossed the cabin, reaching me in three long strides.

"We have to move," he said, grabbing my free arm. "Can you run?"

I looked into his ashen face. "What is it?"

"He's banged open the propane tank." Gavin threw his arm around me as I wobbled on my unsteady legs. "Can't be closed. Could blow eventually."

I made some unintelligible noises before blurting out, "He hit my head with the gun. Don't know if I can stay on my feet, much less run."

Gavin swore again as he adjusted his arm to prop me up against his side. "Lean on me. I'll drag you if I have to, but we need to move."

"You go," I said, as we shambled toward the stairs. "Save yourself."

"Don't be foolish. I'm not leaving you." Gavin maneuvered me closer to the handrail. "Pull yourself up, step by step. I'll balance you on this side."

Determined not to let him die because of me, I gritted my teeth and forced my legs to carry me up the short flight of steps. Gavin kept a tight hold on me, which helped, but all I could think of was how slowly we were making progress. "Don't want to be the reason you die," I said between huffed breaths.

"No one is going to die," Gavin said, as a motor roared through the air. "Dinghy. Seems Arnie's making a run for it."

I called Arnie Dean some names I'd heard but never before used to describe another human being.

"Totally agree," Gavin said. "But we can't worry about him right now. We just need to get off this boat."

"Is there another dinghy or lifeboat?" I asked, as we reached the top of the steps.

"Doubtful." Gavin shifted his arm to my waist. "I'm afraid we're going to have to swim for it." When he cast me a sideways glance, I shivered at the concern in his eyes. "I think I remember you telling me about taking lessons when you were a kid?"

"Up through lifesaving." I concentrated on putting one foot in front of the other as we moved through the upper cabin.

"Good, you can save me, if necessary," he said with a grim smile.

"We should grab those." I pointed at a couple of life jackets hanging just inside the opening to the deck. "Even if we can't put them on . . ."

"Good thinking. Wait—lean against the doorframe for a second." Gavin snatched the life jackets off their hooks. "Hold out your arms," he said, before slipping one around me.

"Don't waste time with that. Put yours on," I said, as he stepped around to fasten the buckles.

"Nope. You need it more. Feeling light-headed is no way to go into the water." Gavin finished fastening the straps to my life jacket before slinging his over his shoulders. "Come on, time to get out of here."

He guided me to the railing at the bow. "Kick off your shoes."

I slid my feet out of my flats, immediately agreeing with this command. In lifesaving, we'd been taught that shoes and other heavy clothing, once wet, could create a deadly drag in the water.

Gavin tossed his running shoes off to one side. Can you step up?"

"Sure," I said. I wasn't sure, but I knew I had to manage, somehow. I fought back a wave of nausea and, clutching the top railing, placed my feet on the bottom rail and pulled my body upright.

Gavin moved in close behind me. "I'm going to toss you over," he said. "Try to stay relaxed."

"Oh, right," I said, before his hands clamped either side of my waist.

"Let go now," he commanded.

In one swift movement, he lifted me up and over the railing. Momentarily suspended in air, I instinctively tucked my head, as I'd been taught when diving, closed my mouth, and blew air out of my nose. *Don't want to inhale any water.* I hit the surface with a resounding splash.

The river was cold, but not so freezing that I feared hypothermia. I kept my mouth sealed and continued to exhale through my nose until the life jacket bobbed me up to the surface.

Taking a deep breath, I shook my wet hair from my eyes and looked around. Not far away, Gavin broke through the surface, also gulping for air. His life jacket, which he hadn't tightly secured, floated nearby.

In a few strong arm-over-arm strokes, Gavin swam to meet me.

"You should grab your life jacket," I managed to sputter out.

"Not necessary. I've had some pretty solid training for just this sort of operation." Gavin shoved his dripping curls back from his forehead. "Now—we need to swim as fast and far as we can. If the boat does blow, we don't want to be anywhere close. Ready?"

My life jacket had shifted and was pressed up against my chin, so I could barely tilt my head. "I'll do my best."

Gavin swung one of his arms up and pointed toward the glimmer of New Bern's lights. "That way. Follow me and keep focused on the lights. And watch for rocks," he said, before swimming away.

I followed, using a modified breaststroke, since my head was being held above the water. My cotton pants clung to my legs like mummy wrappings, but I'd perfected a strong enough frog kick when I was a young swimmer to propel my body forward. I kept my eyes on Gavin, following the movement of his arms, pale as knife blades against the dark river, cycling in and out of the water.

We were halfway to shore when a rumbling noise rattled behind us. I kicked harder, knowing I was falling behind Gavin's fast pace.

As a hiss like a great serpent filled the air, Gavin circled back and swam up to me. Grabbing the back straps of my life jacket, he began executing a version of a lifeguard's sidestroke, pulling me along while I faced Arnie's cabin cruiser, now thankfully at some distance from us.

A roar ripped through the air, followed by a fireball that bloomed from the boat's deck like a lotus blossom, its coral petals tipped with blazing white.

"Protect your eyes!" Gavin shouted, as debris, spewed from the exploding boat, rained down across the river.

Shielding my eyes with one hand, I stared in awe at the apocalyptic scene. As flaming bits from the boat hit the water, steam rose in ephemeral pillars. Sizzling sounds like rain hitting a hot grill hissed all around us.

Gavin continued swimming backward, dragging me along, until it became clear that we were out of the range of any flying debris. At that point, he released his grip and moved to my side. He treaded water as I bobbed in my life jacket, both of us still mesmerized by the burning wreck of the exploded boat.

"That could've been us," I said, as a shattered board from the cabin cruiser, carried by the river currents, sailed past.

"I think that was Arnie's plan." Gavin rested one hand on my shoulder, allowing my life jacket to help support him as he continued to circle his other arm through the water.

I glanced over at him. "You must be exhausted."

"Tired is better than dead," he said, sliding his hand up to cradle the side of my face. "How's your head?"

"Still throbbing, but as you've pointed out, at least we're alive. I think I can deal with any aftereffects, all things considered."

Sirens pierced the night air. We spun around in the water as a flotilla of small boats approached, several flashing red and blue lights.

"Stay where you are," someone called out through a megaphone. "We'll come to you."

Waiting for the rescue boat to approach, I reached up and covered Gavin's hand with my own. "One thing I'll say for you,

Gavin Howard—you sure know how to show a girl an exciting time."

Gavin guffawed, spurring me into gales of laughter as well. Which was why, at first, the emergency personnel who plucked us from the river were afraid we were suffering from hysteria.

Chapter
Twenty-Five

Despite Gavin's protests, we were both carted off to the hospital.

"I'm fine," he kept telling the emergency personnel, while he also insisted that I needed a full checkup.

"Look," one of the EMTs—a young woman less than half his height and body weight—finally said. "You're going to need an exam as well, whether you think you're fine or not. So why don't you just back down and let us do our jobs?"

Gavin grumbled but stopped resisting, simply grabbing my hand as I was loaded onto the ambulance and promising to find me in the hospital as soon as he was cleared by the doctors.

"I do need to talk to someone in law enforcement first," I heard him say before the ambulance doors closed. Of course—he wanted to provide them with the information that Arnie Dean was on the lam.

And still dangerous, I thought, as the lights of New Bern zipped across the darkened windows like streaks of lightning. "My head was hit pretty hard earlier," I told the EMT who was collecting my personal data and insurance information.

A Fatal Booking

He jotted that into his tablet and checked my pupils. "Hmm . . . maybe a concussion. Don't worry, we'll have them do a complete work-up," he said, before sitting back and urging me to rest.

At the hospital, I spent what felt like hours being ferried from curtained cubicle to labs and back to different cubicles before I was finally checked into an actual room. After dozing off for only an hour or two, I was awakened by someone bringing in a breakfast tray.

"He can come in," I told the attendant, after I noticed Gavin hovering in the doorway.

She cast me a smile as she set the tray on the movable side table. "Glad to hear it. He's been pestering the nurses' station for the last several hours."

Gavin strode into the room as she exited. "Finally," he said, leaning to brush my forehead with a kiss. "I've been waiting to see you since they gave me the all clear."

"You're fine?" I asked, pressing the button to raise the head of the bed so I could sit upright.

"A few scrapes and bruises, but nothing serious." Gavin sat down in the chair next to my bed. "I hear you have a slight concussion."

"Which is why they wanted to keep me under observation for a while. But I think they'll let me go home later today." I shifted the pillows behind my back. "Have you seen Ellen?"

"Not yet, but I understand she's doing well, all things considered. Detective Johnson's here, consulting with the New Bern police. She reassured me that Ellen will be fine. After some rest at home, of course, which is also what you're going to need."

"Good thing we don't have any special events planned at Chapters over the next few weeks. There are some overnight or two-day reservations coming up, but nothing too demanding."

Gavin gripped the hand I'd laid on top of the blanket. "Glad to hear it. I bet Alicia can handle those guests pretty much on her own."

"Oh, I'm sure I can help by then."

"Absolutely not." Gavin shook a finger at me. "I don't want to hear about you doing much of anything over the next couple of weeks. In fact, I think I'll stay in town just to make sure you don't."

I arched my eyebrows. "Simply to ensure I behave? Is that your only motivation?"

"Of course not." Gavin lifted our clasped fingers to kiss the back of my hand. "But I promise I'm going to keep an eye on you."

"Ah, excellent," said a voice from the hall. "You're together, which means I only have to share my information once."

Detective Amber Johnson strolled into the room, giving us a thorough examination. "Glad to see you both survived your ordeal without too much damage."

"Slight concussion is the worst of it. Arnie Dean decided to clock me upside my head with his revolver," I told her.

"One more thing we can charge him with. Definite assault and battery, especially as those wrists look like they took a bit of a beating too. Not to mention kidnapping." Detective Johnson leaned against the wooden door of the built-in wardrobe. "But you can rest easy—Arnie Dean was apprehended at the Raleigh airport a few hours ago. He had a false passport and a bundle of cash, as well as traveler's checks and credit cards under assumed names. Looks like he's been planning this escape for a while."

"I think he's lived that way for years," I said. "I expect he always anticipated the possibility of things going south, so he kept fake documents and funds at hand."

Detective Johnson straightened the lapel of her trim navy jacket. "Well, he wasn't quite fast enough. Partly due to your tip-off to the New Bern police," she said, addressing Gavin. "They were able to immediately notify the state police and FBI so they could be mobilized along with our local departments."

"What about Lora Kane?" I asked. "I know she was mixed up in Arnie's illegal activities, but she did try to warn Ellen in the end."

"She surrendered and is now singing like a canary." A smile quirked Amber Johnson's crimson-tinted lips. "As they say in those old detective films."

"I guess she's willing to turn state's witness against Dean at this point." Gavin released my hand and sat back in his chair, his intense gaze focused on the detective.

"Definitely. She's already told us about the workings of their stolen jewelry scheme, which they perpetrated with the assistance of Stacy Wilkin. Of course, Kane claims she had nothing to do with the murder. She says Dean stole the sodium cyanide from her jewelry studio without her knowledge. That was the tipping point for her, I think. Kane assumed he used that method to murder Ms. Wilkin to deflect suspicion off of him."

"And onto her," I said. "Quite a godfather Lora had there. No wonder she turned on him when she finally realized what was really going on."

"Did she provide a motive? I mean, any reason why Arnie Dean would want to kill Ms. Wilkin?" Gavin asked. "That seems counterintuitive, since she was helping him sell his ill-gotten gains. From what we've learned, he needed that money."

Amber Johnson shrugged. "Lora Kane claims that Stacy Wilkin was blackmailing Mr. Dean. According to Kane, Ms. Wilkin had gotten in too deep with some loan sharks and was pretty desperate for ready cash. I suppose she figured getting arrested for selling stolen jewelry was better than getting killed. Anyway, Lora Kane says that Ms. Wilkin thought she could force Mr. Dean, who appeared to be wealthy, to pay her off quite handsomely. In other words, she was offering to keep quiet about their illegal business arrangement in exchange for money."

"But Arnie actually didn't have that much cash." I glanced over at Gavin. "Except what he'd stashed for any future getaway, I mean." Turning my gaze back on Amber Johnson, I lifted my hands, wincing as I flexed my wrists. "Arnie was actually broke, and needed to steal again to replenish his coffers. He was searching for my great-aunt Isabella Harrington's jewelry—some valuable pieces he'd seen her wear at parties she threw back in the day."

"The disturbances in your attic," Detective Johnson said thoughtfully.

"Right. That was why he and Lora decided to hold the book club retreat at Chapters in the first place. Arnie thought the jewelry might be stashed somewhere at the B and B. But the joke was on him." I tapped the side of my nose with one finger. "Isabella sold it all years ago, donating the proceeds to charity. But she did it anonymously, so there weren't any news stories announcing her generosity. I guess that's why Arnie thought the jewelry might still be stashed at Chapters, or at least that Ellen or I might know where it was."

"A fitting end to his criminal career." Detective Johnson stepped away from the wardrobe. "All right, you're both up to speed. Of course, we'll need you to make more detailed statements soon, but I think we have enough information for now."

"Happy to help put Dean behind bars," Gavin said, his eyes narrowing. "Although, to be honest, I'd like to have had the chance to take one more swing at him before he was placed in custody."

"You can testify against him. That should suffice." Amber Johnson spread out her hands. "Good work, you two. But maybe, for your own sakes, you should avoid meddling in such matters in the future." She smiled. "Well, at least you, Charlotte. I know Mr. Howard's job requires him to place himself in danger from time to time."

"That might change." Gavin rose to his feet and crossed the small room to shake Detective Johnson's hand. "Thanks for all your help, as well as for, as always, taking Charlotte's concerns to heart. Not every cop would be willing to listen to an amateur detective's theories."

Amber Johnson's smile broadened. "Trust me, I've learned to consider any information Charlotte, and Ellen Montgomery, share with me seriously."

"Hopefully, neither of us will be forced to do any more sleuthing in the future," I said.

"That would be preferable," Detective Johnson said, as she headed for the door. "But if you do, make sure to keep me in the loop." She lifted her hand in a wave good-bye. "I think we make a pretty awesome team."

* * *

I was released from the hospital late Sunday evening, with orders to rest.

"No strenuous activity," the doctor told me in a warning tone. "And if you start experiencing more severe dizziness, worsening headaches, or any blackouts, head immediately for the nearest emergency room."

I meekly agreed, while Gavin, who had stayed at the hospital all day, assured the doctor that I would comply with her orders.

I spent the rest of the day in my bedroom at Chapters, Alicia supplying me with food and drink while Gavin made plans to stop by the station to provide a more detailed statement to the police.

"I also want to check on the boat," he told me as he gave me a kiss before leaving.

"Seeing Arnie's cabin cruiser go up in flames has you worried?" I asked with a smile.

Gavin brushed back my hair. "I'll admit it gave me pause. Thought I'd better examine all the valves on my boat."

"Especially any propane tanks," I said.

Rising to his feet, Gavin told me he'd probably sleep on the boat overnight. "But I'll be back tomorrow to check on you," he said. "And you know I can get a report from Alicia, so you'd better behave."

"Not a problem. You won't be around, so I don't really have a good reason not to," I said, earning another kiss.

About an hour after he left, Alicia bustled into my bedroom. "You have another visitor," she said, before standing back to allow Ellen to enter the room.

I gasped as Ellen approached. She had violet bruises discoloring both arms, a Band-Aid straddling the arch of her nose, and a bandage wrapping one wrist.

"It looks worse than it is." Ellen winced as she settled into the chair next to my bed.

I plumped the pillows behind me and sat up straighter. "You should be the one resting at home and me the one visiting."

"Honestly, it's mostly cosmetic," Ellen said, grimacing as she adjusted her position on the chair. "Nothing broken or even sprained."

"How did you manage that, with all those rocks and other objects in the water?"

"Training. I instinctively curled into a ball to protect the more vulnerable portions of my anatomy. And held my breath until I could surface, of course." Ellen fiddled with the tucked end of her wrist bandage. "Sometimes it helps to have encountered similar situations in the past."

"You've been tossed in a river before?" I rolled my eyes. "Of course you have. I should've known all your talk about desk work was nonsense."

Ellen shrugged, evoking another grimace. "I had to start somewhere. They don't make you a handler if you've never worked in the field."

"Anyway, did Detective Johnson fill you in on all the latest info?"

"She did." Ellen crossed her battered hands primly in her lap. "It confirmed our suspicions about Lora being involved, along with Stacy. I just wish we'd seen through Arnie's mask of innocence a little sooner."

"I think I was taken in by his age and jovial attitude." I shot Ellen a sympathetic glance. "Perhaps your former friendship obscured the truth from you?"

"It did. Even though we parted on bad terms, I'd never have imagined Arnie as a thief, much less a murderer. He was always a bit stuck on himself, and arrogant, but I don't remember seeing any signs indicating he had criminal tendencies." Ellen shook her head. "I suppose that's how he got away with it for so many years. No one saw that side of him."

"Except Lora and Stacy, later on." I rolled a tuft of my chenille coverlet between two fingers. "I understand how Stacy got caught up in the situation, since she apparently always had a rather fast-and-loose relationship with the law. But I don't get Lora's involvement. She was already a successful jewelry designer, with a growing reputation as a book illustrator. Why mess that up by working with thieves?"

"Money makes people do all sorts of stupid things," Ellen said dryly. "And you don't really know how successful Lora's various business interests are. We see things people post on social media, or hear them talk at parties or other events, and think everything in their lives is wonderful. But we don't actually know that. Who's to say Lora didn't have as many debts as Stacy Wilkin? Maybe she just hid things better."

"That's possible, I suppose." I pressed my back into the pillows behind me. "Also, you heard Arnie say he started out stealing jewelry for the thrill of it. Maybe that was part of Lora's motivation as well—the excitement of pulling off a high-stakes caper."

Ellen stretched out her legs. Since she was wearing a pair of brightly patterned palazzo pants, I couldn't tell if her legs were as bruised as her arms. But, judging by the pain that flashed across her face, I expected they were. "There's also the sense of satisfaction in getting away with something. I'd bet that fueled Arnie's criminal activities. I suspect he enjoyed knowing he'd fooled everyone. Even when he was younger, one of the joys in his life was reveling in his superiority over lesser mortals." She frowned. "There's a red flag I missed."

"It seems he lacks empathy. We've encountered other killers, but not any quite so cold-blooded. I must confess that I found it terrifying to stare into Arnie's eyes, realizing he simply did not care. He certainly didn't spare a thought for you when he knocked you into the river. The fact that you could drown didn't appear to have the slightest effect on him."

Ellen stared down at her feet. "He probably hoped I'd die."

"Fortunately, he didn't try to finish you off himself. Of course, I doubt he had any knowledge of your life after college, so he had no way of knowing that you possessed any special survival skills." Staring up at the whitewashed beadboard ceiling, I considered my next words carefully. "Do you think he was ever truly your friend? I know you felt you were quite close while you were in college, but it seems he's one of those individuals who only use people for what they can get out of them, without forming any real attachments." I dropped my gaze to glance at her thoughtful face.

"Don't worry, I've asked myself the same thing." Ellen offered me a wry smile. "I really can't be sure. I was very young when we met, as well as somewhat sheltered. I don't think I was the best judge of character back then."

I pulled the blanket up to my chest. "He did turn on you when you didn't give him what he desired."

"That he did." Ellen leaned in to pat my hand. "That's enough wallowing in the past. I think I'll head home so you can rest." She slowly rose to her feet and gingerly crossed the room. Holding onto the doorframe, she looked back at me and winked. "And, since I must admit feeling some aftereffects of our little adventure, so I can soak in a nice hot bath."

Chapter
Twenty-Six

A week later, I hosted a casual party for my friends who'd been entangled in the latest investigation involving Chapters.

Gavin had worried it was too soon for me to be throwing a party, but I assured him that I'd lean on Alicia and Julie when it came to preparing the food.

"According to Julie, Scott Kepler will be in town, so I thought you guys could help with the setup. If you're going to be around that long, I mean." I leaned back in one of the folding chaise longues he'd placed on the boat deck so we could watch the stars.

"I will." Gavin, relaxing in his chair, glanced over at me. "I have some leave I need to use before I start the new job, and where better to take it than here?"

"Tahiti, the Riviera, Saint John," I said, counting off those places on my fingers.

Gavin stretched out his tanned legs and wiggled his bare toes. "I'd only want to travel to those locales if you could come with me, and you can't right now."

"True." I cast him a smile. "And thanks."

"No thanks required. I want to save such trips for the future, when you can hopefully accompany me."

"I'll have to figure out a way to make that happen," I said, momentarily distracted by thoughts of traveling with Gavin to exotic locations. I cleared my throat. "When do you have to report to the new job again?"

"Not until mid-June. The training sessions I'm leading don't start until August, but I want to settle in long before that. First of all, I have to find an apartment. I have some feelers out, but the market's tight, so it may take a while."

"And I imagine you want some time to prepare for your classes too."

He cast me a raised-eyebrow look. "Yes, Ms. 'I've taught for years,' I do. The last thing I want to do is get up in front of a bunch of young agents with no clue as to what I'm going to say."

"I could help with that. I mean, I don't know anything about what you do, but I can structure a successful lesson plan."

"It'll be a little different than discussing the literary canon, but . . . okay. I certainly don't mind if you share some of your expertise."

A light breeze, carrying the spicy scent of the brackish water of the marina, wafted over us. The evening was warm but pleasant, bringing my thoughts back to the upcoming party. "The weather is supposed to be good Sunday afternoon, so I thought we could hold the party on the patio."

"Sounds like a plan," Gavin held out his hand to me. "Now—let's concentrate on the stars. I still need to teach you more about the constellations."

Taking his hand, I flashed him another smile before staring back up into the night sky. "So I can navigate during our future voyages?"

"Exactly," he said.

* * *

Sunday turned out to be a beautiful day—sunny, but not too hot or muggy. Gavin and Scott, under Alicia's expert direction, set up a folding banquet table, while Damian organized the bar.

"You shouldn't be working. You're supposed to be a guest," I told Damian, as he arranged some empty glasses on the bar top. "If I'd thought of it, I'd have hired someone else to bartend today. But I must confess I'm still not thinking as clearly as I'd like."

"It's not a problem. I don't mind serving drinks to friends." Damian looked me over, concern wrinkling his brow. "How are you doing, by the way? I know you had a concussion."

"Just a slight one."

"Still, I hope you're not trying to do too much too soon."

I glanced over at the two men lugging stacks of folding rattan chairs to the table. "Don't worry, Gavin is making sure I don't."

Damian arched his brows. "So you're a couple now, huh? That's pretty cool, especially considering he's Ellen's cousin."

I opened my mouth but shut it again without challenging that assumption. As far as my friends knew, Gavin was a free-lance researcher who was related in some way to Ellen, and I planned to keep up that facade. Even though he was no longer a field agent, I assumed it was better to err on the side of caution. At least until Gavin told me differently.

"Yes, all in the family," I replied. "What about you? Do you have any interesting news to share?"

Damian's smile lit up his face. "As a matter of fact, I do. Thought I'd wait until everyone was here to make the big announcement, though."

"Announcement about what?" Julie approached the bar, a wire basket filled with liquor bottles swinging from her hand.

"It's a surprise," Damian said. "But I will tell you, as soon as everyone is here."

Julie set the basket beside the bar. "I may have a little surprise as well. We should coordinate our announcements."

"Something you haven't shared with me yet?" I examined Julie's beaming face. "Looks like it's good news."

"Oh, it is, trust me." Julie tossed back her shining fall of dark hair. "But, like Damian, I want to wait until everyone arrives before I say anything more."

"It appears to be quite a day for announcements," I said, under my breath. Julie shot me a questioning look, but I simply smiled in return. "It seems Gavin and Scott have finally arranged everything to Alicia's satisfaction. Let's see about bringing out the food, shall we?"

Julie shook her head and laid a hand on my shoulder. "You go sit down. Alicia and I can juggle the bowls and trays and all that."

"I'm not some invalid," I muttered, as I wandered off toward the table.

Sitting down in a chair placed where I could see any new arrivals, I had to admit that it felt good to get off my feet for a while. After a few seconds, Gavin moved in behind me, wrapping his arms around my shoulders, until Alicia sailed by and tapped him on the arm.

"No time for that," she said. "You need to help carry out a couple of ice buckets. And you," she shouted out to Scott. "Make yourself useful. Help your girlfriend with the food trays, please."

Gavin leaned in to kiss my shoulder. "Duty calls, it seems." He stepped back. "My drill sergeant doesn't like malingerers."

"No, she does not. Better hop to it, mister."

He gave me a little salute before following Julie and Scott into the house.

"Oh, how lovely." Ophelia Sandburg said, as she and Bernadette strolled up the driveway and onto the patio. "Hello, Charlotte. What a glorious day. So nice of you to invite us over."

Bernadette narrowed her eyes as she examined me. "I hope you're feeling better. A head injury is nothing to fool with."

"I'm fine," I said.

"You shouldn't have gone to all this trouble. Rest is what you need," Bernadette said, her gruff tone softened by the genuine concern in her eyes.

"I've gotten plenty of that. Alicia has made sure of it." I motioned toward the back of the house, where Scott was descending the steps, carrying a serving tray, and Gavin had just appeared in the doorway, clutching two ice buckets. "As has Gavin. You remember Gavin, don't you?"

Ophelia clapped her hands together. "Of course I do. Ellen's charming cousin." She squinted, staring toward the house. "Is he visiting Ellen again?"

Bernadette, who'd snorted at the mention of *cousin*, tugged on her sister's full, daisy-print skirt. "Sit down, Fee. And for heaven's sake, stop gawking at all the young men."

"Young? Tell me more," Scott said, bending his lanky frame over the table. He set down the tray of fresh vegetables and dip before straightening to his full, impressive height. "I love such kind lies."

"You're young compared to me," Ophelia said, before sitting down next to her sister. "Just wait until you're in your seventies. You'll think someone forty is a mere child too."

"I'm actually forty-seven, but thanks anyway." Scott brushed his thick auburn hair back from his brow. "Of course, I can only hope to look as good as you two when I'm seventy-something."

"Goodness, such flattery," Ophelia said, her pale lashes fluttering.

Bernadette rolled her eyes. "Don't pay any attention to her, Scott. It just revs her up, and that's the last thing we need."

"Phooey." Ophelia sat back, plucking at one of the ruffles decorating the high neck of her lemon-yellow blouse. "You're no fun, Bernie."

"I've been told that before," Bernadette said dryly.

"Hello, all!" Sandy Nelson appeared around the corner of the house, followed by Pete. "I hope we aren't late. We had to do a little bookkeeping for the café this afternoon and lost track of the hours."

"Don't worry, you're right on time." Alicia set a tray containing bowls of tuna, chicken, and egg salad on the table. "We're just bringing out the food." She motioned toward the bar. "Check with Damian if you want a drink."

"No, sit down, sit down," Damian said, bounding over to the table. "I'll take everyone's orders from here."

"You need to sit down eventually too," I told him.

"I will, once everyone has what they want." Damian whipped out a small notepad and pen. "Okay, what can I get you all?"

He took drink orders as Julie, Scott, and Alicia brought out the remainder of the food.

Gavin, sitting next to me, leaned in to ask when I wanted to make my announcement.

"I think I'll wait until after Damian and Julie share whatever it is they want to tell everyone," I said.

Ophelia looked up from scooping some egg salad onto her plate, her light eyes sparkling with curiosity. "News? Someone has important news to share?"

"Apparently more than one person," Gavin said. "But I've been told they're waiting until everyone has arrived, and we're still missing Ellen."

"Here I am." Ellen opened the gate to her backyard and strolled over to the table. "Sorry, I had to feed Shandy and put him in his crate, and unfortunately, I'm still moving a little slower these days."

"How are those injuries healing up?" Bernadette's searching gaze swept over Ellen. "You got banged up pretty bad."

"There are only a few residual twinges," Ellen said, taking the empty seat next to Gavin. "Nothing too drastic."

I noticed she was wearing a filmy white cotton blouse over a multicolor top. Its long sleeves effectively hid any of the bruises on her arms, which had faded to a sickly chartreuse the last time

I'd seen them. "The main thing is that we both survived, and the perpetrators are now in custody."

"Details, details." Scott sat beside Julie at the other end of the table. "Julie's told me what she knows, but I think you two probably have a lot more to share."

I almost said, *Three, we three*, until Gavin squeezed my knee under the table. "All right, I'll provide what I know, and Ellen can chime in with anything I forget."

As I shared the details of the murder plot as well as the information on Arnie's past thefts, I could see Ophelia's eyes grow steadily wider.

"He was the cat burglar? That old man?" She pursed her lips, obviously upset that her fantasy about a handsome and charming young jewel thief had been shattered.

"He wasn't old at the time," Bernadette said.

"But he was always ruthless." Gavin leaned forward, his light-brown eyes focused on Ophelia's face. "Not someone you would've wanted to be close to, regardless of looks, charm, or youth."

"That he was," Ellen said, sorrow coloring her tone. "A man who truly cared only about himself."

Damian, arriving at the table with his own drink after serving everyone else, held up his wineglass. He tapped it lightly with a spoon. "Sorry to interrupt," he said, when our attention turned to him. "But I have some exciting news to share."

"Something to do with your career?" Pete shared a knowing glance with Sandy.

I bet they've already guessed, I thought. *They're tied in to the local food scene, after all. They've probably heard rumors.*

"That's right." Damian lifted his wineglass a little higher. "Congratulate me, because you're looking at the new, full-time sous chef at Près de la Mer."

"That new upscale restaurant on the Beaufort waterfront? Bravo!" Pete clapped his approval.

Everyone at the table followed suit, applauding and offering their congratulations.

Everyone except Alicia, who sat back in her chair, surprise and pride warring for control of her expression. "That's very nice," she said. "But we will miss you here."

Looking past Gavin and Ellen to stare at Alicia's stoic profile, I couldn't hide a grin.

Neither could Damian. "Thank you, Alicia, and may I say, I've learned a lot from you." He sketched a little bow. "My profound thanks."

Alicia made a great show of readjusting the napkin covering her lap. "It wasn't that much. I only taught you some basic recipes. Just down-home cooking."

"But excellent, all the same," Pete said, lifting his fork to salute Alicia. "And cooked from the heart, which is the real ingredient for success."

"Absolutely. And that's the most important thing I learned here." Damian sat down, still grinning from ear to ear.

Scott glanced at Julie, who nodded. He rose to his feet with his tumbler in his hand. "Since we're sharing happy news, I think it's time I made my own special announcement." Looking down at Julie for a second before gazing out over the group, he added, "Well, not just mine. This involves Julie as well."

"We're engaged!" Julie leapt to her feet, waving her left hand. Sunlight danced across the diamond-and-ruby ring on her finger.

After several minutes of being celebrated with joyful shouts, congratulations, and a few tears, Julie and Scott sat back down.

"Don't tell me there's anything else," Ophelia said, vigorously fanning her flushed cheeks with her napkin. "I might swoon."

"No, you won't," Bernadette said, before looking around the table. "But just to be clear, are there any other surprises? I'd like to be prepared, if so."

Gavin tapped my knee under the table.

"Well . . ." I said.

All eyes swiveled toward me.

"This is not quite the same thing. At all," I hastily added, when I noticed Ophelia looking from me to Gavin and back again. "I'm not getting married or anything like that. But I do have an announcement." I glanced down at Ellen and Alicia, with whom I'd already shared this news. "The thing is, you all know how much Chapters means to me."

"And to all of us," Sandy said.

"Yes, of course. So I want to assure you that nothing is going to change. Not really. It's simply that I feel it's time for me to return to teaching." I held up one hand as a rumble of voices erupted around the table. "But, as I've already discussed with Ellen, as trustee, and Alicia, who will be staying on here as long as she wishes, I don't intend to give up the B and B. I plan to teach part-time to start, while looking for someone who can manage Chapters."

"You're moving?" Ophelia asked, blinking back what looked like tears.

"No, no. Not at this time, anyway." I straightened in my chair and gazed around the table. Everyone present was a friend I cherished. *Even Alicia*, I thought with a smile. "I'll still live at Chapters and help out with special events. I just want to hire someone to come in and handle the day-to-day work. Alongside Alicia, of course."

Alicia lifted her chin and gazed out over the company. "And I'm getting part interest. A cut of the profits, along with my salary."

"I thought it was about time," I said, meeting Damian's approving gaze. "Anyway, I wanted you all to know this before word gets out in the community. I didn't want you to worry that I'd sell Chapters or anything like that. Honestly, I hope to keep it in the family. My nieces and nephews are young now, but they won't always be. I hope that someday, at least one of them will want to keep it going, with a manager, or even by themselves. So I want to hold on to it for them."

"Well, that's a relief." Julie flashed a bright smile. "What would our book club do without Chapters as a meeting place?"

"What would the community do without Chapters just being Chapters?" Pete said. "It's a landmark."

"I know, which is why, even if I ever do decide to move . . ." I sneaked a swift glance at Gavin, who rewarded me with a warm smile. "I'll never sell. I'll just install someone as manager, an employee who can handle the reservations and hostess duties and that sort of thing. Of course, I'll let Alicia actually be in charge. As long as she wants to be, of course."

Alicia flashed a wicked smile. "*Stay* in charge, you mean."

A statement with which, despite everyone's heartfelt laughter, no one disagreed.

Acknowledgments

I offer my sincere thanks and gratitude to:

My amazing agent, Frances Black of Literary Counsel.

My insightful and supportive editor, Faith Black Ross.

The entire team at Crooked Lane Books, especially: Matt Martz, Melissa Rechter, Madeline Rathle, Rebecca Nelson, and Rachel Keith.

Cover designer Ben Perini.

Fellow authors and friends—Richard Taylor Pearson, Lindsey Duga, T. C. Correy, Trish Esden, Keith Willis, Zac Bissonnette, and Tracy Gardner. Thanks for talking me through the rough spots!

Every blogger, podcaster, YouTuber, and reviewer who has mentioned, reviewed, and boosted my books.

All the bookstores and libraries who have acquired, stocked, and promoted my books.

My family and friends, including the online writers' community.

And, as always, the readers!